TRUE GRANDEUR

A Hollywood Novel

by

Cal R. Barnes

FIRST EDITION, SEPTEMBER 20th, 2017.

Magic Hour Press
Los Angeles, CA
MagicHourPress.com

Copyedit by Ren-Horng Wang.

ISBN: 978-0-9991610-1-2

1 3 5 7 9 10 8 6 4 2

Manufactured and printed in the United States of America.

TABLE OF CONTENTS

TO EVERYTHING ABOVE… EVERYTHING THAT IS
NOT OF THIS WORLD…
I ENVY YOU…

'True honor is to be found in the highest moral and
intellectual excellence, in the dignity of the human soul,
in its nearest approach to those qualities which we
reverence as the attributes of God.'
-Charles Sumner, The True Grandeur of Nations

'The misfortune of man has its source in his greatness.
For there is something infinite in him and he cannot
succeed in burying himself completely in the finite.'
-Thomas Carlyle

'Life should be shown not as it is, and not as it ought to be,
but as it appears in dreams...'
-Anton Chekhov, The Seagull

PROLOGUE
— THE LAST TRUE ARTIST —

Growing up, my father always told me, "Conrad, the time will come when you want to gain something from the world, and just know that you've been given more intellect and ability than any person could ever need to acquire it." Looking back, I can believe that the statement was true, for the Arlingtons have always been a very proud family, and a certain expectation of greatness is something I came to accept at a very young age. In fact, if there was ever a sole, singular thing that led me to California, that would undoubtedly be it — a need for some kind of greatness — and I've never claimed to be any better because of it.

The Arlington family has always been a youthful one, and my own physicality bared no exception. Combine the lean, stringy build from my father's side with the softer, lighter features from my mother's, and I basically held the resemblance of an adolescent boy damned to some kind of eternal youth. I'd heard it had its advantages though, and for most of my life I'd been trying to figure out what those were, for with any kind of greater beauty comes greater problems, and I haven't attempted to list them here, for this glorious and terrible pride which runs deep within me is a curious thing — something dark, wicked, and as fascinating as the morning sun — and I've given great care in my attempts to master it, for as undesirable as it may be it always comes from a place of truth, a place where the creative forces lie, and as an artist I'm likely destined to always be there, caught up in this place of great strength and weakness, and it's within these dualities that my life exists.

Everyone in my family was predominantly middle class — upper to lower — so anyone that felt that they had something important to say, whether it actually was or not, was absolutely going to say it. I never judged this too harshly, for family was family at the end of the day, and I was in some way eternally tied to these people. It was always the uneventfulness of it all that got me, that made me cringe, that kept me up into the early hours of the morning. I'd always considered myself the exception to the Arlington lot, not so much in personality but in scope, with a different attitude towards life, for I had done my fair share of trying to be different, and amongst the sifting, and the searching, and the countless summer evenings spent alone, real truth was the only thing that ever interested me. I didn't know what that was of course, but it had always been important to me that I stand for something. I had always been an extremely honest person — ever since I was young — I had never been one to hide in the shadows of my soul, and unfortunately, against my better of intentions, that always made me odd man out in the Arlington family.

Tired of the general restraints pressed upon me in my teenage years, I found myself alive in a new way as I made the choice to move to Los Angeles. I felt new, fresh, and vital with eyes wide open, for existence to me then was a strange thing, this idea of being a person, of observing and being observed, of romance and elegance, true love and social class — these things had always fascinated me — I was constantly fighting the push-pull battle of where I stood with the world, but at least here, in the heart of Hollywood, I had a chance. Here I could make something out of what was raw, and it was up to me to let that be enough to justify my actuality. It was a curious thing to be so young. With the presence of a few years one at least knows some things about the world — or so one hopes to know — the kind of things that lend direction to a life, for being aimlessness was a beautiful thing if it wasn't terrible, and that could change on any given day.

So there I was — all young and ready for the world — all bright and beaming as I sat in the driver's seat, making my grand entrance over the 101 into Hollywood and what would become the pinnacle of my moral acquisition. I was not completely naive, for I was fully aware that the small cluster of buildings that stood gleaming just off Vine Street was as much then my friend as it was my enemy, and it was up to me to decide which one of the two it would become. I was aware of the chances beforehand. I had weighed the odds, and knew the challenge of the task ahead. I had read the stories about the great writers and filmmakers and artists who found solace in the nooks of this town, whose haunts had lent the inspiration necessary to achieve greatness, then, in a single stroke of betrayal, brought the whole machine crashing down to its knees, laying waste to the best of them — laying waste to the greats — I had somewhat of an education and I was capable, but I was young, and the depth of hard-learning that spanned before me was as vast as some endless sea, but at the time I remained invincible.

I landed in a brassy apartment off Hollywood Boulevard and Wilcox Avenue, and it felt great to be in that apartment — to be surrounded by it — the cracks in the plaster wall, they spread across the room like splintering glass, and then split again with some sort of strange verity. I wondered how many great people had lived there before me, creating true art, writing great novels, and crafting great stories. I used that inspiration and began to familiarize myself with critically acclaimed scripts, classical plays, and literature, taking a liking to what some referred to as the 'Great American Novels,' although to me that was just a stamp of good writing, of good art, and of something relevant. Write something relevant and true about America, and if enough people liked it then I guess that was that. The job of the artist has always been to create what is true, and I saw no reason for that to ever change. I got a lot out of some of those novels, though, and through them I believe my soul came a long way.

There was a specific statement I never much liked when I first arrived in Hollywood, in fact, the Arlington in me downright detested it — 'paying your dues' — a bunch of people said that to me in that first year, but I always found that statement to be completely false and lacking in a very basic way. I remember a certain instance where a young actor came up to me after drama class. He was bright eyed, hopeful, and I knew he'd be gone in a month.

"Good scene, Conrad," he said. "Damn, you nearly made me cry up there. You had the whole class on edge."

"Thank you," I said, and I meant it. Despite my lesser qualities I was still very much human in that way, and I always appreciated a good compliment.

"How do you do it?" He asked eagerly. "Tap into emotion like that?"

"Fruits and vegetables," I said. "And being off book."

"All right, then," he replied, trying to keep it friendly. "Well keep paying your dues, and you'll be on the silver screen in no time."

I laughed out loud in his face.

"I know, it's funny," he continued. "But that's the way things are out here."

"I wasn't laughing at the statement," I said flatly. "I was laughing at you."

That shut him up. I didn't see him around much more after that — and I sure didn't get any more compliments — but I didn't need them. I had made it a point in life to stay light about things if at all possible, but this took up a great deal of my energy and efforts, and when I missed a beat I could be prone to moodiness of the darkest kind. I had a certain coldness streaking through my veins that I inherited from my mother's side that could make life a real drag sometimes, but one could argue that it equally served its purposes for survival. I was a hard worker by nature, and I'd get to wherever it was I was going whenever it was that I got there. I'd go as long and as hard as I needed to in order to make it, but put it in front of me, and I'd grab it, quick as that. I considered this to be a lesser aspect of innate talent — knowing when to grab — now of course there was raw talent, and raw talent could not be taught, it simply was. I had always believed true art to be the greatest possible expression of oneself, that is, inspiration laid out and then refined, but without raw talent that expression would never transcend with the higher things of the world, and I, Conrad Arlington, The Last True Artist had both these qualities — drive and talent — and I had a greater amount of both than I could ever need. Yes, I absolutely believed in my abilities and myself whole-heartedly… my father and the great Arlingtons before him made sure of that.

It wasn't long before I developed my first romance away from home. She was a singer — a southern bell — with natural beauty laid over a petite structure, followed by flowing blonde hair that fell perfect and stringy across her delicate features, and I fell for her immediately. I met her at some grandiose party on the thirty-first of October, and she had doe eyes — the kind of eyes I could just lose myself in — so when she tapped me on the shoulder, and I turned around, and she introduced herself, my body was completely taken by her, and I fell into those eyes like a child falls into the shallows of a tide pool, and I didn't come out for a while. It destroyed me, sitting at home in my apartment, not being with her. I thought about her constantly, of how she was making her way in Hollywood, of how she had a career and I didn't, of how she was out there, moving and shaking and stirring things up, and how I, Conrad Arlington, The Last True Artist, was a complete and wretched mess. I couldn't eat. I couldn't sleep. There was indeed nothing left of me, nothing but pure inspiration bottled up and ready to explode, inspiration without an outlet, and it was agony. Express! Express! Expression is what I needed! Day and night I found myself in torment by this girl — her blonde hair, her dark chocolaty eyes, her slim hips — God the agony! My franticness knew no end, for there was so much in there, and it would be let out or indeed it would destroy me from within, so I searched my apartment with the utmost urgency. I searched, and I searched, and then I finally found it — I found the one thing in the world that could make sense out of an existence like mine — and so begins the immortal charge of Conrad

Arlington, The Last True Artist, and his feeling will justify his existence in the end.

  With pen in hand I wrote like a madman, a madman that had found his reason to live, and I was captivated. My body wasted away around me, filling page after page, trying to capture what it was I felt on paper. It was truth — this I suspected — and my obsession was a necessary means to stability, for this girl was nothing more than inspiration for my art, and any attraction she had for me was held at bay by the stubborn insistence of my own artistic desires, and the longing to preserve that which was fueling such a guttural reaction in me. This drove me until it reached a point where it became more than unhealthy, and eventually, for the sake of my own sanity, I pushed her away. I pushed away the possibility of ever being with her, and it was terrible. I had never obsessed over a girl before, and I hoped to never again, but the process of de-etching her image from my mind was like going through the withdrawals of some devious substance, and my heart never hurt so much. It was a necessary hurt, however, for I had a purpose for being in this town, and the price of one young starlet for the art that poured from her wounds was a small sacrifice indeed for any true artist, but I could never do it again, no, I would never do it again, and the thought of never being with her is far too great to bear still, and I cannot withstand it, not ever again, and on that day when I stand face to face with the Bright One to account for what I have lost, I will not be ready for it, for I was nothing in her eyes, and in that nothingness she became everything.

  In hindsight, that first year in Hollywood was a lonely year, and despite the independence naturally distilled in my youth, I too succumbed to its pressures. To level my sanity I entertained myself with long walks down the Boulevard, imagining the glorious moment when my body would come in contact with that magical ether that exists within that small span of stars, that ether that gives way to inspiration, which then gives way to some kind of magical form. I studied those stars, looking down on those I did not know, for there was something beautifully sad about them — those stars — filled with the names of men and women the world once considered to be great artists, now mostly forgotten say for a name on some forlorn slab of stone. Yes, that is what they earned, a lifetime of artistic expression and this was their grand prize, a series of letters etched in marble for the world to walk over, and then look down upon from time to time if the mind was right. It was confounding to me, tumultuous as breathing itself, yet despite the absurdity of it all, and despite my quest for truth, I could not deny the degree to which I desired one, and I found myself actively seeking a way to contribute enough artistic expression to humanity that one day I too might have my name etched into that worn and tarnished Boulevard, immortalized by passerby's for generations to come. "Soon," I told myself as I planted my heel on La Brea Avenue and then turned east towards Vine, "soon." Then I walked passed all the names of the stars I never knew, and despite an endless sea of self-regard, I found something grand about them, and it was wonderful.

Time has a way of leaning towards liberation, and eventually I reached a point where I no longer cared. A year or so of fruitless auditions for stories with no soul can do a number on an artist, so I threw up my hands and stopped trying to control that which had no substance. In writing I had found a starting place for something relevant, and in the den of my lurid apartment I could see to it that my quota for expression was met. Oddly enough, that's when things changed. I began booking roles and bit parts, and my seemingly carefree attitude, which was a complete reversal from my usual sense of solemnity, was now my greatest strength. It was a complete turn around from the tortured artist — that is, of course, the way I preferred to view myself — but being tortured didn't pay the rent, so I pushed myself to be open, and then some kind of inner vitality flowed through me, that human vitality that says, "I don't give a damn, this is who I am," and the industry seemingly responded to it. I had access to funds I'd never had before, not a lot, but enough to move out of my swollen apartment into a place more suitable for a young man making his way in the Hollywood circle. I began frequenting new haunts during the weekdays, sipping on whiskey and entertaining thoughts of what it was to be a great man. Before, my spending money was reserved for the weekends, when I was more likely to meet a girl or make some friends — both of which were presumably scarce in my life — much scarcer than they should be for any bright young man at the age of twenty-two, for everybody needs somebody, and after a year of near solitude, I felt I was more than deserving of any pleasure that came my way in the approaching years, and I counted on it entirely.

I took up residence in a quaint village above Franklin Avenue, just due north of Hollywood between the 101 to the west and Los Feliz to the east, and here, friends, is where my tale truly begins, for many things have happened in the last few years — good things, bad things, things I wished I could forget, and things I wished I could relive forever — but none of these are now reality, so on those nights when I walk down the Boulevard, feeling the resonance of what the city once was, the lines between fantasy and reality have indeed begun to blur, for I have negated the fact that I am ever changing, I have ignored the truth of being shaped, pushed, pressed — of being constantly influenced — so as I speak of the events that occurred in the wake of what was my twenty-third year, it is wise to note that things are not what they are now, but what they appeared to be then — magical and truthful, full of personalities and experience.

CHAPTER 1
— GRACIE GARRISON —

Two years is enough time to start to know a place. It was fall now, and the bright, blown out colors of summer had begun to turn. The neighborhood I lived in was an artist's haven, a bohemian, eclectic community just a block shy of the Hollywood Hills. My complex was equally divided into two halves, with a rich, flowing garden path at its center that gave way to individual units lodged in its sides. It was home, my apartment, and with its hardwood floors and soft, Spanish style walls, it provided the perfect balance of energy and solitude I found necessary to do good work. It was essential to stay productive, and keeping the young towers of Hollywood in my backyard was of paramount importance, for there was an energy there, a certain presence, that when missed, I'd feel my motivation start to drop. As strong as this energy was it could at times be equally overwhelming, and I found it necessary to split the difference with the smooth and mellow vibrations emanating from the rolling hills of Los Feliz just due east to balance my tranquility. The result was rather European, and the bookstores, bars, and coffee shops located below off Franklin Avenue provided the perfect, afternoon escape when I found it necessary to clear my head.

This was the time when I finally found it, that is, I had achieved what I worked for some time to achieve — a bit of comfort — it's something all artists want, and driving back over the hill from the valley had become a completely different experience, for I was home now — I was a resident — and I was feeling at least for the moment, temporarily comfortable. I was a produced writer and a sometimes-working actor, and I liked knowing that I was well on my way to doing what I set into town to do. It felt great having more funds than I came out with, and I realized that Los Angeles was just as much a city of investment as it was a place to earn a living, and the more I invested in the city, the more I would get in return, and so it was the case, for before Los Angeles was a rough place, a dark place, filled with the cries of broken people, broken men and women lodged in between street corners on the Boulevard, and what poor wretches they were, wandering the street at night, finding solace in the shadows of the past. Only in Los Angeles could the rich and poor truly co-exist side by side, separated by a single boulevard or avenue, for there was very little middle ground here, and that which existed formed a line, a line that stood very tall, and very strong, and very formidable — a line between poverty and true grandeur.

But not me, for I now resided at the base of the hills, and I didn't have to worry about those things. I was focused on my work — my art — the only real thing capable of drowning out the noise I was prone to give into if I had nothing to occupy my time, for I was an impulsive person, emotional as they come, but overtime, I learned to give it structure. I developed my routine, with much of my work getting done early in the week and slowly tailoring off as the weekend approached. Then, when I had a free stretch, I'd take walks in the hills, or take a drive into Los Feliz to sit outside one of the many cafés that littered its landscape, reminiscing of summers past as I'd admire the color of the leaves, the change in season, feeling the effects of some fleeting energy that twirled all around from my perch. I'd watch the city move and change with the traffic like steady streams of life slowly moving into the sunset, and then the night would come — those balmy summer nights I wished would never end — the ones that lived and breathed deep into the twilight, filled with endless events, socials, and parties so fantastical by nature they made it impossible to cope with the sturdy darkness of September, when the days got shorter, the air got colder, and in some implausible way it managed to remain beautiful, like long strands of golden hair in a setting sun, and it was wonderful.

Usually, starting on Thursday, I would go out. The little success I achieved over the last year had opened doors to many things I was not previously aware of in the city, and I began visiting more trendy dives and secret haunts as my appetite for production continued. It was the previous summer that I fell in with a theatre company. I had a small play running at the time, and the group that shared the space was composed of a good handful of upcoming artists that possessed the same passion for expression as I did. They introduced me to a great deal of new experiences, that group of friends, and the way they lived, all young and true and undeniably hopeful, made for good company and a hearty dose of inspired creativity.

I felt I was beginning to find myself as a person, for the gift of time could be a beautiful thing, and having a position where I was able to pursue my passion in all hours in the day was of paramount importance. I worked doubly as hard — triply sometimes — in order to keep up with the pace I believed it took to become the best. I was young, but I wasn't that young, not in Los Angeles, and I believed that my talent combined with a vigorous work ethic could help turn years into months, months into weeks, for I hated waiting, and as much faith as I had in my abilities I was twice as impatient, believing that I had little control over my career in the film industry was not a healthy state of mind for a person like me to be in, so I opted instead to put all my efforts into that which I could control, and for me that started on the page. I wrote like a madman — a pressed man — one hundred, two hundred pages a week sometimes, shaping opportunities, creating stories. It was important I had a sense of ownership in life. Ownership was key. I finally had something to offer, something to bring to the table that was mine, and I cringed at the thought of good roles and opportunities slipping from my grasp because I was too thin, or too tall, or too gaunt, or too boyish, or too whatever other inconvenient factor it may be that was out of my control, and I rebelled against it entirely.

I pursued filmmaking, studying the great independent directors, writers, and actors of generations past. John Huston, John Cassavetes, and Billy Wilder were among my favorites. Their films inspired me, and I fell under the notion that something beautiful could be made for very little, and I quickly found that it was true. More and more young artists from around my neighborhood were starting their careers this way, learning how to write, then produce, and then in turn create opportunities for themselves that catapulted them into the cinematic, and I aspired to be one of them. There was one starlet in particular that lived close by who I thought was pretty great. She was working with investments on the East Coast and had her whole life spread out in front of her, then she met some filmmakers from the American Film Institute and decided to take it all the way. She could write, act, and produce, and all of her work was top notch. She was having a good deal of success and it was very inspiring. She was doing it. She was really making it.

This very mindset is what changed everything, for in Los Angeles existed a group of people that still believed in the American Dream, that believed in the fundamentals of independence and freedom from the tyranny of the powers that be, for it was the same there as it was anywhere else, and the way it manifested itself had a kind of staying affect that was universal among the city. It was a desire to create without limits — to say something without oppression — and the more I explored this way of thinking the more the underground of Los Angeles revealed itself to me. The theatres, the nooks, the thousands of individual groups that moved together to make something of their lives — they wanted to say what they wanted to say — and it was a beautiful thing to fall into. There was this idea of being independent, and I felt like I was a part of something higher, like some French Revolution was happening many years later in a different time and place, and I wanted more of it, in fact I wanted it all, and my desire to create true art flared up in me like the sun flares hot in July, and I was completely consumed by it.

As I tended to do, I threw myself in headfirst and decided it was time to make my own mark on this revolutionary movement. To the credit of my vigorous writing schedule, I had finally developed a few scripts I believed worthy for production. I loved old noirs, like Billy Wilder's *Sunset Boulevard* and Robert Towne's *Chinatown* — well, I suppose Roman Polanski directed *Chinatown*, but since I'm a writer and the script is considered one of the best of all time, I'll give this one to Towne — I loved how they captured Los Angeles in such a way that the city felt like a character all to its own. I had written a few fledgling noirs previously, but I was still inexperienced, and I quickly found that the scope of my projects were much too large for production on the minute scale I had access to. Nonetheless, I eventually wrote a noir I felt was contained enough to move forward with, so I did. I put out a casting call in the trades. There were many good roles to be filled, and I intended to scour the city until I found the perfect up and comer for every single part. Headshots flowed in by the hundreds, and I realized just how little control it was that young actors had, as I myself had to cut ninety percent of the submissions off the top due to sheer volume alone, and next to that there was no other reason. There was a great deal of helplessness about the whole process that I didn't like at all, and I'd never been one to leave things to chance when I could make things happen for myself. According to the Arlingtons, if one was to win at the game of life, they should do everything they say they are going to do, and they should do it better than anyone else — that was all — that was how one got what he wanted and that was how one became the best man, but when it came to dealing with people, I found them to be another thing that I did not entirely understand. They tended to be unpredictable and difficult most of the time — the bright ones, that is — the ones that I found myself attracted to, and given the extremity of my personality I often felt we would do each

other more harm than good, and so up went that damned
and impenetrable Arlington wall that served as my defense,
and none had ever breached it — man or woman — but
there have been specific moments in this grand expanse we
call time when the universe has decided to exercise its
authority, and even the bright beings of the world had little
control over who fate brought their way, and so it was for
me that Conrad Arlington, The Last True Artist, would
come to see true beauty where true beauty stood, true art
beyond what he ever imagined to be possible, and there was
nothing at all for him to do about it, nothing at all, and his
life would be changed forever.

***

It was a Thursday when I first laid eyes on her. I
recognized her immediately from her headshot, and my
mind dropped into my stomach as I gazed at her, sitting in
the wings, waiting to be called in for her reading. Her
structure was as delicate as a porcelain doll, and the way
her blonde hair fell in stringy golden curls over her tightly
framed shoulders made her look like a mermaid might if
one could be so perfectly girl. She wore a summer dress,
and never was a summer dress so grand, so pristinely suited
for a creature. It wrapped tightly around her slight waist,
then flowed freely down her slender legs in long, wavy
folds, creating a pixyish way about her that made her glow
all the more enduring.

"Gracie Garrison," I called out as naturally as I
could, reading her name off the call sheet.

She turned towards me, and what breath I had left
was stolen immediately, for her deep, blue eyes set against
her perfectly angular face rested sharply on mine, and like
shimmering pools of glass they reflected that which dared
to be beneath. Then she smiled the most fragile smile I had
ever seen as her faint lips spread tightly over little white
teeth that quivered slightly, as if she was aware of her
effect on men and didn't want to impose herself indirectly.

There was something beautifully sad about her — something broken, something fragile — and I immediately felt an urge to go to her, to hold her, to protect her, and yet, I found myself unable to move, not wanting to move, as if the slightest change of environment might offset her brittle structure, and she would disappear from the mortal world forever.

"Yes," she replied softly.

I mustered my courage and plunged in her direction, my heartbeat increasing with every closing step.

"I'm Conrad Arlington, it's good to meet you," I said, holding out my hand.

"It's lovely to meet you, Conrad," Gracie replied, then she took my hand in the slightest of ways, and our bodies connected for the first time. "I really enjoyed your writing."

"I appreciate it," I said evenly, for she had said the magic words, but I didn't want to let on. "Now I'll be reading with you. No pressure. We'll run it a few times, have some fun, and see what we come up with. I'm acting in it as well, so you'll have someone experienced to read with."

"Okay," she said softly.

"Are you ready?"

"Yes."

"Excellent. Right this way."

I motioned towards the audition room, and she drifted up and followed behind me. She wasn't like the others — I knew this immediately — for I had never seen such depth in a girl before, especially not an actress, not that early. It was as if I immediately knew who she was, and yet, I knew nothing about her at all, not a single thing. I opened the door for her and she walked inside. Then, suddenly and immediately, she began to tear up, her false confidence giving way to some mysterious fragility, and I couldn't have prepared myself for it.

"Are you all right?" I asked.

"Oh, it's nothing," she said between little blinks, holding back the little pools of tears that threatened to burst with the slightest cadence. "I just think… I think I am going to quit acting."

"But why?" I asked earnestly, finding it difficult to hide my objection.

"It's just that…. it's just that I had this terrible audition earlier today, and I prepared so hard for it. I'm just so sick of it all, I just don't know how much longer I can keep doing this to myself." She continued to whimper, and the pools under her eyelids managed to burst a little, forming slight tears that she didn't seem to mind at all, until her delicate fingers reached up and lightly brushed them away.

As shocked as I was it was absolutely captivating to witness, and before she even auditioned I knew in that moment that she was the girl for the part, for she was a real artist — a true artist — I knew this for a fact, but how a girl so beautiful could feel so low and down at any moment in her life is a phenomenon that I perhaps may never understand. I wouldn't tell her that of course, so we went ahead with the audition anyway. She sat down — all broken and beautiful and hopelessly lovely in front of the camera — and I read with her. It was an intense scene, the kind of scene where a man has to push his lover away in order to protect her, and she doesn't know why. It was an experience connecting with her. She was so open, available, and true that it became real, and in doing so the scene became real life, and real life became the scene, thus marking the beginning of our epic courtship, that first glimpse at some sort of endless possibility that exists between the heaven and the stars that most people just call love, but in that moment I was content with allowing it to be whatever it was, because it was real, and it was true, and from what I gathered it had happened to us both.

After a half hour or so of this, the audition was over. She was incredible, and the other producers agreed. I kept Gracie in the room longer than anyone else — I simply didn't want to let her go — as if she would be wisped away outside the theatre doors, never to be seen again. Nonetheless time had taken me, and the other actors were beginning to get slightly agitated that I had lost track of everything, so I walked her out, told her she did a remarkable job, and then with that same, thinly spread smile and eyes of a perfect blue, she thanked me and was gone from my presence as quickly as she came. For the rest of my life, she would never be forgotten.

***

The auditions were over and life resumed as usual. I had my callback list, and couldn't wait to get back to where I left off and keep up the fabulous amount of momentum I had going. It felt great — being a part of something, making something happen — I knew I was on the same track as the greats before me, writing, acting, and producing their way to the top. I felt like a real artist, an auteur, a filmmaker, and the thought of some beautiful idea becoming a piece of art which then became a tangible thing was a kind of surreal high I was quickly becoming addicted to, but then, just when all seemed calm, when all seemed verified, open, and true, the project received a major setback that I did not see coming, and I was forced to step aside and re-think things. Instead of wallowing in self-pity — which would have been easy considering the circumstances — I took once again to writing, figuring I would continue to control that which I could when I could control it, and then when I found the right people, individuals with equal amounts of drive, passion, and an endless appetite for art, I would be able to pick up where I left off without falling behind in my production ethic. I liked knowing that I was moving forward on my own accord, and I had no doubt matters would continue to improve as time went on.

That weekend I felt particularly good. I had been slaving away in my den all week and decided it was time to go out on the town. All of my friends were unusually absent that night, but I wouldn't let that stop me from allowing myself to unwind. It was an important aspect for me — this unwinding — a few years of trial and error at least taught me that much. If I didn't unwind it was possible for me to explode after a while, and self-destruction, a trait that I was particularly prone to, was something to be avoided at all costs. I jumped in my car and drove a mile down Franklin into Los Feliz. There was a little bar in Thai Town that was getting a lot of buzz at the time, and I thought it might not be a bad place to spread my wings a little and see whom I might meet. I found parking rather easily, which was rare for the hour in the neighborhood, and the thought of a nice, cold drink and the chance to talk to a pretty girl or two kept me company until I reached the entrance.

I waited in a short line for about five minutes — not bad for a Friday night — then I got the signal from the doorman and headed inside. It was interesting being back out by myself again, it gave me a whole different perspective, for I had not been out alone since roughly the same time last year, and I'd be lying if I said I felt completely comfortable. Going out in Los Angeles was always a strange experience. I suppose it might be that way in any other major metropolis, but I knew what I knew, and I knew for a fact there wasn't a whole lot of meeting going on — lots of people, but very little meeting — people went out to places in groups to be around people but not meet them. Everyone said it was all about making connections, but I saw very little connecting going on. I never got that. It seemed like a whole big waste of time to me, a whole big waste of time and perfectly good people.

The dark room was loud, and cramped, and filled with bodies. They lined the walls and drowned the floor like pickles in a mason jar. Still, I managed to make my way through the thick crowd of socialites and post up at the bar where a young bartender complete with beard and ponytail was posted to take my order.

"What can I get you?" He yelled, strong enough to be heard over the extremely loud music, which was some sort of eclectic mixture of something old and something sadly new.

"I'll take a pint of beer please. Something dark."

"That's our list of beers over there," he said, pointing at the wall. "We have a stout, it's quite good."

"I'll take one of those, thanks."

"That'll be seven dollars."

"That's fine." I shook my head, not liking the price.

After a few moments, the bartender came back with something dark that didn't taste half bad, so I gave him a ten note, told him to keep the rest, and manned my post. I found a decent-sized space to rest my elbow, which wasn't usually the case, the usual case was being stuck standing all tightly packed in the crowd, being bumped back and forth with beer spilling everywhere, making a complete mess of things, so this was definitely nice for a change. I took another sip and started looking around for any signs of life, observing the laughing, flirting, and mingling. I then thought I saw someone I knew, but after a better look I was mistaken, for it's not extremely common to see someone out and about — so many people in such a large city and all — but it does happen from time to time. Soon after I spotted a couple of cute girls in a corner, made some eyes, then in a blink a couple of young men swarmed them and stole the whole show. No problem, for the night was young for The Last True Artist, and there would be plenty of people to meet. I took a few more cool sips of beer, turned around, and lost my breath, for there she was — the girl with the gold, and the blue, and the eyes that went on forever — once again I was standing face to face with Gracie Garrison.

"Do you remember me?" Gracie asked with a bright smile and some kind of eternity.

Did I remember her? Of course I remembered her! I remembered her so much I couldn't even move. It took me a moment to get over the shock of seeing her, for there she was — all tiny, perfect, and pristine — all golden and beautiful. She shined like the sun on the surface of a dark world. Her hair was straightened from its usual curl, and it fell all blonde and lovely over a black cocktail dress that accented her tiny frame in all the right places. After a moment that seemed like forever, I managed to shift my gaze, and noticed that she was with two men, one of which I could only assume she was going with, but to me it didn't much matter at the moment, for her bright eyes rested only on me, and so I pulled myself together, determined to act as relaxed and as easy as possible — a difficult task in the wake of my rapidly increasing heart rate.

"Of course I remember you. You're Gracie," I said, and I felt like an idiot.

"That's right." She laughed, then turned to introduce me to her friends. "Maxwell, I want you to meet my friend Conrad. I auditioned for one of his films last week."

Maxwell Price, a hearty fellow with a big smile that flashed wide across his youthful, plump face, was just returning from the bar with a couple of cocktails. Right off the bat it was apparent that he had a great energy, and I wanted to like him immediately, although I was still unsure. His soulful, dark eyes sat joyfully beneath two heavy brows that seemed to dance up and down like a pair of brooding canopies under which he inspected my presence.

"Pleasure," I said, holding out my hand to greet him.

"Conrad." Maxwell responded as he took my hand between two fleshy palms. "It is a pleasure to meet you, my friend."

"Conrad's a terrific writer," Gracie gushed spiritedly. "His script is one of the best I've read."

"Oh, how wonderful. Congratulations."

I've always been quick to diffuse compliments, for I was eager to turn the attention back on Gracie whose presence undoubtedly required the most of it, and I wasn't the only man in the room aware of this fact. Her other friend — the one whom I had not met yet — leaned dark and brooding against the bar, back turned, apparently put off by the unexpected meeting.

"It's nothing, really," I said in haste. "Gracie really did a fantastic job with the material."

"Don't be so modest," Maxwell replied. "I'm sure it's wonderful."

"It's a lovely piece of fiction." Gracie extended her slender arm and took a grand sip of her cocktail.

"So how do you two know each other?" I asked, steering the conversation away from myself.

"Maxwell's my producing partner," Gracie said, taking the lead.

"Yes, we met at a gala."

"A gala?" I was impressed despite myself, for I had never been to a gala before. "Interesting. What kind?"

"Well a production gala of course."

"Again Conrad, your script is so lovely, I really do hope you find the means to make it," Gracie chimed in, effectively pointing the conversation, once again, back to myself.

"Thank you. I'm sure by now you've heard about the status of the project?"

Her bright smile instantly dropped into a remarkable expression of empathy. "Yes, I am sorry to hear that. May I ask what happened?" Her blue eyes peered — intense and curious — into mine.

"Yes, do tell?" Maxwell added quickly.

"Oh, you know how productions go. I'm afraid the reality is that I will be starting from scratch."

"No," said Maxwell, aghast.

"It's true," I replied. "A whole new production team and everything."

"I'm very sorry to hear that."

"That's no problem at all, Conrad, just no problem at all," Gracie interjected lightly — she was so whimsical about it all that I thought she might take flight right there in the bar — "You'll see, the right people will come along and they will help foster your lovely project right off the ground."

"That's right," Maxwell agreed. "That's absolutely right."

"Well, thank you," I said with as much dignity as I could. "I do appreciate the encouragement."

There was a slight lull, and I was once again aware of the energetically stagnant atmosphere grounded by the increasingly drunk personages who were pressing in around us. I took to my beer and found my tension ease with a few big gulps, for Gracie was indeed pondering me with those big, blue eyes, and I didn't want to risk returning the gesture for fear that I would give myself away. Still, I knew she was looking at me for a reason, and I couldn't help but wonder what it was.

"You know," Maxwell exclaimed musingly, his eyes rolling towards the ceiling as if he was entertaining some brilliant thought. "It just now occurred to me that Gracie really loves your work, perhaps we could discuss the possibility of doing a project together."

"That's a wonderful idea!" Gracie exclaimed. "What a perfectly, beautiful, wonderful idea! What do you think, Conrad?"

"I think that sounds great," I bumbled out sort of half-stupidly, hopelessly enamored by the thought of working side by side with such an artistically structured creature.

"Excellent. I'll read your script and we'll be in touch." Maxwell stated, extending his hand.

"Great." I took his hand, gave it a firm shake, and then watched as he turned and walked into the crowd.

"It was great to see you again, Conrad. Do write me soon won't you?" Gracie said in the loveliest of tones.

"Of course I will — I'll call you."

With that, she threw her carefree little arms around my neck and held me tightly, and I felt like the greatest man in the world.

"Goodnight. Speak soon," she said, and then she was gone... back into the crowd... back into the night... back to wherever her lovely little body would take her.

I stood for a moment at the edge of the social, staring at the spot where Gracie fluttered just moments before. Her image was burned into my memory like some bright flash from an exploding light bulb, and the afterglow that lingered in her transitory presence only increased and sustained it — it had a surreal effect on me — I peered into the bottom of the now empty glass, two little droplets remained there, and at the slightest touch they fell together in the most perfect way, creating a single orb that seemed to sit, satisfied, together at the bottom of the glass — and then my heart sank — for I realized that I had once again let her get away from me.

"Good night," I spoke into the shadowy air. "Good night, good night."

CHAPTER 2
— THE MEETING AND THE COCKTAIL —

It was cold now in the village. November had rolled around in just the right way, and the cool mists that settled over the hills made the decreasing daylight of the year-end, waning days appear even shorter. In response, I spent most of my time indoors, writing and re-writing my work, or setting up to read in the cafés around the neighborhood that served as little hideaways from the crisp temperatures just beyond their walls. At night, I'd throw on a nice winter coat, draw it tightly around my neck, and then take a stroll down to the street fronts to see what the evening would lend me. It was a wonderful place — that strip on Franklin Avenue — full of all that vicarious life of young people being young, trying to connect with something substantial before day's end. The quaint shops were packed side by side like little, adorned building blocks, which created nooks for the romantics and private crannies for the gaudy artists. There was a bar towards the east end, a cozy French spot that I was quite fond of, so if any particular excursion brought me little or no excitement, I was fine with stopping off and having a pint or two, rummaging through all the possible ways life might come along and sweep me up again. Despite my evening efforts to cut lose from my workspace and mingle with the world, my social life was undoubtedly lacking. Unlike many of my friends who could quickly court and start evening affairs with random women, I found myself resistant. I was probably the least sexually liberated of all my contemporaries, and usually preferred to spend my nights alone, in the solitude of my own bed, rather than wake up next to a complete stranger. I was a very monogamous person, and as often as I tried to shake that fact by testing the waters or pulling the strings attached to the beautiful creatures around me, the more often it betrayed me, for I was hopelessly difficult — much too difficult for most girls

— and if a girl didn't move me on the inside first there was no possible way she'd move me on the out, and there was no way I'd be ending the night with her either. It always came down to the experience, and how that experience fueled, or didn't fuel, my artistic expression. In light of my stubbornly innate resolution, I was uncommonly shy with women, and had a very difficult time expressing myself most of the time to girls I found attractive. On the other hand, if I deemed a girl unattractive, she had little value to me, and I could become so increasingly indifferent to her presence that it bordered on cruelty. This was instilled in me at a very young age by the Arlingtons false concept of perfection. It was not intentional, on the contrary it was quite involuntary, and if I ever caught myself in the act of mindlessly ignoring a girl, I'd do my best to stop and acknowledge her presence, as to avoid seeming overly aloof or pretentious, and to help her self-esteem stay intact. I had always valued and respected women a great deal, and I appreciated the time they took to dress up and look presentable, unlike most men I knew, including myself often of the time, but I admittedly had my faults, and unfortunately for myself they tended to be as extreme and dire as my personality... and so it was my life, that of an artist passing his winter mostly alone in his study, waiting for the moment in which the activity of being might call on him once again to venture out in the world.

Exactly two weeks later I received the call from Maxwell. I was sitting in my study one morning, going over notes and things, sipping on a French press consisting of the richest blend of coffees, and then, out of the blue, the phone rang. I answered.

"Conrad?"

"Yes."

"It's Maxwell — Maxwell Price from the bar."

I recognized his crooning voice immediately, although it boomed over the phone with a certain strength that I did not retain from before. His tone bumbled along in a manner that pushed the conversation forward, expressing right away that he meant business.

"Maxwell, why of course," I replied, surprised. "How have you been?"

"Mm. Yes. I've been great. Thank you — listen, Conrad. Gracie and I would like to request your presence for a meeting this weekend to discuss your work. Will you be available?"

"Yes, I should be, what day?"

"Friday, at eight o'clock — are you available?"

I was struck by the strangeness of the hour, as most industry meetings of any sort usually took place during the weekday afternoons, so the time of the meeting — on a Friday night no less — touched me as curious.

"Yes. That will work nicely," I replied, easily masking my suspicion.

"Excellent. I will send you a message with the details. We look forward to your company."

Before I could express my gratitude, he hung up, leaving me once again alone in my study with nothing but a dial tone pressed against my ear. I made a quick jot on my calendar and returned to my work, doing my best to evade the pressing curiosity of what might be in store for me.

***

Before long, the weekend came, and I started picking out my best clothes for what I could only assume would be a very formal meeting. It had been some time since I last dressed up, and I'd be lying if I said the thought of looking like a presentable gentleman in front of Gracie didn't increase my anticipation. I rummaged through my closet and managed to find a pair of black slacks and an old blazer I hadn't worn since my first year of college, and there was nothing at all remarkable about them — they simply wouldn't do — so I took a quick trip down to the Boulevard to purchase an inexpensive, but at least presentable suit.

After an hour or so I was back in my apartment, shaved, showered, and looking dapper. I threw the newly crisp suite jacket on and over my up and down frame, which still managed to hang off my wiry shoulders like it would off a coat hanger even though I purchased the slimmest size available, a thirty-six long. Regardless, I felt I cleaned up rather nicely, and as I looked in the mirror one last time, I reasoned myself nothing short of handsome and had no doubt Gracie would feel the same when she laid eyes on me.

Minutes later I was in my coupe and driving through the hills into Studio City — the district of Los Angeles that was to be the location of our meeting, and also, I could only assume, the place of their residence — Studio City was a fascinating place to me, built into the hills between Hollywood to the South and the San Fernando Valley to the North, it hung high overlooking Burbank, which was home to many of the major film studios, and sat directly in the East, hence its rather conventional name. In a way, Studio City served as a kind of central divider that twinkled of grandiose homes and lavish parties, exuding splendorous images of fame and fortune, black ties and cocktail dresses, cigars and flowing champagne — there was something very enchanting about it all.

I made good time. The whole trip took me only ten minutes, enough time to successfully navigate the hills and find parking, which I found rather easily given the hour. Then again, I was a very skilled driver, an innate talent expectantly mastered by any young man bearing the name of Arlington. I had a few minutes to spare, so I took a few breaths to calm my nerves, glancing around at my surroundings to take my mind off of everything, as I determined it essential to go into the meeting with a clear head. The neighborhood was beautiful, and each home was unique unto itself with its own eclectic way about it. I thought about the homeowners, wondering what kind of extravagant lifestyles each must live to be able to afford such places, and how I aspired to be one of them. Lost in the privy of my imagination, I glanced at the clock and realized I had let it get away from me, for it was now two-'til-eight, and time to get to my meeting.

I walked towards the address provided and saw light coming from the windows, and the way the curtains were drawn demonstrated that they were expecting company. I got closer, and saw that the place was extremely beautiful — very extravagant in a New York sort of way — and its loft-like appearance looked somewhat peculiar in the company of the more established mansions that surrounded it. I reached the door and heard the flutter of voices and the clinking of glasses from within, marking a social of sorts. I took a breath and knocked. The voices trailed off inside. There was murmuring, and before long, footsteps. The door opened, and a very pretty, petite, modelesque girl with silky, brown hair and deep, brown eyes stood before me. She wore a little cocktail dress that was perfectly contoured to her tight body, and she looked me up and down with a sort of self-entitled, smug smile that I would have found rather off-putting if she hadn't been so beautiful to begin with.

"Hello, there."

"Yes?" She answered gravely.

"I have a meeting with Gracie and Maxwell. Are they in?"

She didn't react, just looked at me rather blankly as a voice called from within — "Conrad, you're early!" I instantly recognized it to be Maxwell's voice. She gave me another vague look up and down, as if inspecting what it was about me that was so special that it had caught the attention of her friends, then retreated from the door to let me pass.

"Come in, Conrad, come in," I heard Maxwell continue.

I popped my head inside with a little nod and my body followed shortly after. The apartment was beautiful, with high-loft ceilings and an enormous, crystal chandelier that hung high and elegant from its golden chain, casting an illuminating light that sparkled in such a way as to preserve the mystery surrounding it. The furnishings were rich and European, and for a moment I imagined that I was in the lobby of some fabulous Parisian Hotel, waiting to be whisked away by the eminence and grandeur of the décor that filled it. I looked to my right and spotted Maxwell sitting in a chair next to a beautiful floor to ceiling window that took up the entire wall. He sipped a glass of scotch, and behind him the eastern valley twinkled and winked, as to affirm the pertinence of his position.

"Hi Maxwell," I said. "It's good to see you again." I stood awkwardly in the middle of the room, not sure what space was appropriate for the time being.

"Likewise, my friend," he replied, toasting his glass in my direction, oblivious to my discomfort.

Opposite him, at the far side of the room, Gracie dozed lazily on a black velvet couch. She was stretched out to her full length of five-foot-five, and the way her graceful arms dangled loosely behind her blonde head gave her a look of comfort that was so complete, it made me even more aware of how nervous I truly was.

"Hi Conrad." Gracie stretched her arms and pulled her lengthy torso up into a sitting position.

"Hello Gracie," I replied, feeling the pleasure of saying her name again, "how have you been?"

"I've been great, thanks for asking," she said with a yawn. "Have you met Evie?"

The girl from the door was posted up against the wall next to the couch, taking a condescending, leaning position that accentuated her frame to its full advantage, as to intentionally appear threatening in order to push my level of discomfort even further.

"Only at the door," I remarked easily. "I'm Conrad." I moved briskly across the room and took her hand, which she gave to me limply and without much effort.

"Evie," she replied, keeping her gaze out the window.

"Conrad's a writer, Eve, and a filmmaker, and he's quite good at both," Gracie proclaimed enthusiastically from the couch.

"Isn't that great," Evie mumbled.

I let go of her hand, and it fell limply back to her side like a wet string. She still couldn't look me in the eye, and I realized that she was investing a great deal of energy in trying to appear disinterested, and that gave me a boost of confidence. There was something about me that got to her, and at least for the time, that was all I needed.

"Oh don't mind Evie, Conrad. She's a model, and can be off-putting at times." Gracie stretched her arms once again behind her head with a yawn, and then let them fall, tangling them through her blonde hair on the way down, which made her ever the more captivating.

"Conrad, would you like a drink?" Maxwell chimed in.

"That sounds great, thanks."

"Evie, get Conrad a drink, will you?"

After a moment of hesitant distaste, Evie turned to me, not at all ecstatic about the menial request. "What would you like?"

"Scotch and soda, please. Thank you."

She paused for a moment as to purposely be smug about it, then turned on her heel and slithered away down the hall in such an inconvene way that I felt something sensual about the whole transaction that I couldn't yet place. I watched her until she rounded the corner into the kitchen.

"She only does that because she likes you," Gracie said dreamily. "It's just her way, don't give it any thought at all."

"Yes indeed," Maxwell agreed. "Have a seat, Conrad."

"Thank you." I took an eclectic, heart-shaped chair up staged in the room from Maxwell, and across from

Gracie, effectively creating a nice, social triangle. I noticed the black velvet cushions as I sat down. They both watched me with interest for a moment.

"Conrad, it's so good to see you," Gracie said with nearly as much enthusiasm as before, studying me as if she was laying eyes on me for the first time. "You look well. I like to see you this way."

I nodded a shy smile, unsure of what exactly to say.

"Yes, Conrad, it is great to see you," Maxwell followed. "So, tell me, what brings you so early tonight?"

"I'm sorry?"

"Tonight — why are you here so early?"

Maxwell looked at me with a big, genuine smile, signaling that my presence was no trouble for him. Gracie didn't seem to mind at all either, in fact she looked rather ecstatic, but we were not at all on the same page. I took a moment to respond.

"What do you mean?"

"Why, the party doesn't start until ten of course, and even then most people don't arrive until eleven," Maxwell stated.

"Eleven?"

"That's right."

"I'm sorry, I just thought — I thought we were scheduled to have a meeting tonight at eight o'clock to discuss my work."

Gracie and Maxwell shared an unknowing glance, and suddenly the air became thick with the tension of misunderstanding.

"Maxwell," I continued in bewilderment. "You just called me earlier this week."

But before he could respond, Evie returned down the hallway carrying my scotch and soda, and a double for her.

"Ah! Your drink," Maxwell exclaimed, getting up to grab it from Evie, who appeared to be even more disinterested then before. "Thank you my dear."

With a vague little nod of her head, she disappeared back down the hallway.

"Here you are," Maxwell said, bringing the drink over and handing it to me. "A lovely scotch and soda."

"Thanks." I took the drink, opting to set it in my lap until I received some sort of confession from one of them, or unraveled the elaborate hoax that was being played on me, but none came.

"So… you were saying something about a meeting," Maxwell began, rather confused.

"Yes, that is why I came here."

"Oh Connie, do relax won't you… have a drink, stay a while." Gracie got up from the couch and began fluttering around the room. "There will be plenty of time to talk about business later."

She called me Connie. No one had called me Connie since my mother in junior high, and I was having a hard time figuring out if I was smitten or just agitated by it all. Either way, Gracie was up on her feet, and she proved to be quite distracting in her evening dress, which made her dainty features appear quite supple with the way it clung to her — something told me she knew what she was doing.

"Yes, business later, of course," Maxwell added. "All in good time my friend. The night is young."

I looked down at my drink, then back to Gracie, and then down again. I was conflicted, something felt very strange about the night, and yet, very good at the same time. I liked being there, and I rationalized that whatever was so important to discuss could wait until the next day. After all, I had been working very hard, and what good was The Last True Artist without his inspiration? I took the first sip, making the choice to push any abnormal thoughts from my mind.

"Wow, that is quite good." I said, tasting the scotch. "Really good."

"That's a thirty year my friend."

"Oh, I'm so glad you decided to stay Connie! There are so many good times to be had!" Gracie fluttered back to the couch and took a sip of her half finished cocktail, which she must have turned to earlier to put her body to rest that evening.

"Many good times my friend," Maxwell added, taking a hearty gulp of his whiskey-soda.

"What's the occasion?" I asked, my curiosity was clearly starting to get the better of me.

"You'll see, Connie, you'll see. Be patient. The night is young," she turned towards Maxwell — "Maxie?"

"Yes, darling?"

"Do you know what we need right now?"

"What's that?"

"Music!"

"Music! Yes! That's a wonderful idea."

"Do you like music, Connie?"

"Yes, of course," I answered, taken by surprise. I was so involved in pondering the peculiar nature of their relationship that I completely lost track of the conversation.

Gracie glided across the room to an old record player that sat preserved against an old bookcase. "What kind of music do you like?"

"Well, I don't know. Anything I suppose."

"I have just the thing."

"Darling?" Maxwell spoke up. "Do you think we should wait until the other guests arrive? We don't want to run the risk of outdoing ourselves too early."

"Nonsense," Gracie laughed. "Connie is our guest — isn't that right, Connie?"

"I suppose I am," I answered with a sort of surprised smile, unsure of what to say.

"Alright then... the night is young," Maxwell mumbled into his scotch, satisfied that his opinion was at least made known.

Gracie put on her album of choice and then nimbly trotted back to the safety of the couch, once again stretching her lean body out and closing her eyes dreamily as if waiting to be swept away by the faint scratch of needle against nylon that popped and cracked over the speakers as the record began to spin. After a few moments, the number began, opening with a soulish voice over the crooning of French horns that was reminiscent of a different era. Judging by my knowledge of music alone — which was limited — I placed it somewhere in the twenties. Gracie's body began to swoon, the small of her back arched up in certain moments, and then receded again just as quickly, which made me imagine that she would like nothing more in the world than to be there — experiencing that time, experiencing that place — it was all very subtle. I looked over towards Maxwell, who sat contently in his chair with his eyes closed, whiskey-soda neatly in hand, soaking in the experience.

"Are you enjoying yourself, Conrad?" Gracie asked musingly, head bent back in absolute relaxation over the couch's arm.

"Yes," I answered, and I meant it, for I was just beginning to fall under its spell.

"I'm glad. I love to hear you say that."

"That's what we are all about my friend," Maxwell added. "Good times."

"I can tell."

They both smiled a bit at my response — satisfied — as if they were both very aware of the experience I was having, or the experience I was about to have.

"So, who lives here?" I asked, ready to satisfy some curiosity.

"This is Gracie's place," Maxwell answered.

"Oh, that's great — are you two...?" I asked, pointing to Gracie and then back to Maxwell.

Max looked at me curiously for a moment, and then picked up on my implication. "Oh, no, just partners my friend — business partners that is." He followed with a wink.

"Ah," I said, trying to mask the sudden leap that formulated in my stomach. "I see." Until then, I thought it possible that they might be dating, which I supposed —

given their apparent carefree lifestyle — was not too ridiculous to consider.

"Do you like it?" Gracie called out lazily from her lounge.

"Like what?"

"My apartment."

"Yes, it is beautiful. Do you live alone?"

"She lives here with Evie," Maxwell chimed.

"They're roommates?" I asked in a tone a little too implicating for its own good — I assumed that would be the scotch talking.

"Yes, I think that is the word for it," Maxwell said with a mischievous grin.

"She comes and goes," Gracie said with a wave of her arm.

Maxwell pointed to my now empty glass. "Another cocktail, my friend?"

"Please."

Maxwell took my glass and disappeared down the hallway. It was just Gracie and I alone in the room now, and she seemed completely content to lay back in silence, allowing me to observe her body as she drifted along with the music. I studied her, and I couldn't help but wonder what these two were getting at. There was something very misleading about the conversation until that point, and I felt like I was being pulled — step by step — into some sort of pre-planned involvement by two people that knew exactly what was in store. Before long, Maxwell returned with two drinks — one for the both of us — and then Gracie, to my disquiet, got up and retreated back into the hall, where I assumed she was getting herself ready.

For the next hour or so, Maxwell and I continued our exchange, speaking about all sorts of things from the nature of the industry to my life in Los Angeles to date, and how it was that I came to find myself there. Nearly the entire conversation was directed solely at me, and despite my insistence otherwise and constant attempts at redirection, I found out very little about either one of them.

Before I knew it, it was ten o'clock, and sure enough, guests began to arrive.

One by one they filtered in, and by eleven o'clock the party was in full swing. I was enamored with it all — taken by it — never in my life had I seen such beautiful people. Everybody in the room was either rich, famous, or both to some degree, and regardless of my attempts to appear disillusioned I spent most of my time off in a corner, watching the lives of privileged people play themselves out before me. Heiresses crossed paths with young starlets, clustering together in little groups as to act aloof to the advances of young, dapper men who vied for their attention. Socialites fluttered to and fro, moving freely between cliques of fashionistas and young models that stood all waif-like on the balcony, smoking cigarettes and sipping dry martinis to satiate their fledgling appetites. I even recognized a face or two amongst the crowd, and I wondered what it was that attracted them to the mysterious apartment, or what it was that made them choose this affair amongst an array of others that were surely available to them that evening.

Maxwell worked the room like a true professional, supporting my notion that he was indeed the main host of the party. Evie was spending her night on the balcony, smoking cigarettes and downing cocktails with the other models, giving a slight glance in my direction whenever she felt she could sneak one, still under the impression that I didn't notice. Gracie, on the other hand, was nowhere to be seen. From time to time, I thought I caught a glimpse of her slight figure flutter from one group to the next, only to realize that it was just another debutante or another socialite with a similar build and long, blonde hair.

Around one o'clock, I finally made it out onto the balcony. The cocktails had taken their affect, and the kinetic energy that crackled so intensely amongst the guests at the commencement of the party had momentarily leveled out, creating an intimacy that filtered into the majority of the surrounding conversation. I spotted a young man in the corner who stood by his lonesome, leaning against the railing and sipping a cocktail as he looked contently outward at the assortment of lights that twinkled cordially below. He appeared to be receptive enough, so I made my way over and took a place a few paces down the railing, mirroring my appreciation for the dazzling view.

"Nice night," he said after moment.

I nodded in agreement. "It is."

"My name's Benjamin — Benjamin Trask."

He extended his lean arm confidently, and I noticed that he was quite good looking — so much so I was surprised he didn't have one or more of the surrounding single women hanging off his arm.

"Conrad Arlington." I took his hand, and gave it a firm shake, seizing the opportunity to make a good impression.

"Nice to meet you."

"Likewise."

We both turned back towards the valley, opting to direct our conversation outwards as to keep things nonchalant. I rolled the ice around a bit in my scotch and soda, finding the 'clink, clink' of the cubes against the glass rather soothing.

"So, what brings you out tonight, Conrad?"

"Believe it or not I was already here."

"What for?" He seemed curios.

"A meeting, actually."

"A meeting?"

"That's right. With Gracie Garrison and Maxwell Price, they've shown interest in producing some of my work."

I felt a flush wash over my body when I mentioned Gracie's name. There was something about saying it out loud to another person that was exhilarating for me, as if at any moment I might be discovered or spotted for my interest like some sort of charmed school boy on a playground who watched his crush from a distance — and, if I wasn't mistaken, I thought I saw a subtle clench ripple through Benjamin's sinewy jaw muscles, signaling that he may indeed have felt the same internal longing to be near Gracie as I did, but before I had enough time to give it due thought, he pushed the conversation forward.

"Oh, are you a writer then?"

"Yes, amongst other things — yourself? Are you an actor?"

I instantly felt a twinge of regret for asking the most taboo question in Hollywood. There's something about asking an actor if he's an actor that is labeled terribly cliché by most industry people, and is considered by many to be the sure mark of an amateur. Although I've never quite understood this reasoning, it's always uncomfortable to gauge a receiving person's response, which was almost always a universal look of disdain, followed by a slight, awkward pause if the answer is "yes," and a quick, defensive shake of the head if the answer is "no." Benjamin, however, displayed none of this tendency, and was actually quite receptive, as if he'd been waiting to be asked the question all night.

"I am," he answered proudly.

"Have you been working?" I asked. "I won't ask what on."

"Yes, I've been working," he said easily. "It is going well, thank you."

I nodded my head, satisfied, and took a sip of my scotch. I had a great deal of respect for actors that were 'making it' — regardless of their connections — and the fact that he was working was all I needed to know. "Congratulations," I concluded.

"Well, how did it go then? — The meeting?"

"It was good — interesting."

"I bet it was," he said, releasing a knowing chuckle.

I wanted to pry further into the meaning behind his implication, but opted to stray from my impulse, at least momentarily, as to not appear too desperate for information too soon. After all, I still didn't know who Benjamin really was. I knew that he was at the party, which informed me that he was, at minimum, somebody important enough to be there. Besides, two models had strategically placed themselves in Benjamin's eye line, and I didn't like the thought of them eavesdropping on the details of our conversation.

"Do you come here often?" I asked.

"As often as I can. You could say it's the spot to be these days on the Holly-go-round"

"That's an interesting expression." I said after a moment, for his phrase took me off guard. "The Holly-go-round? What is that?"

Benjamin raised a brow and pierced me with tired, experienced, grey eyes, then a knowing smile spread across his face. "The Holly-go-round," he began, "come get on an endless ride where the only operator is yourself."

I didn't respond immediately, for I didn't quite know how I was feeling right then, but I reasoned I liked this explanation of his even less than the phrase before it. "Like I said, that's an interesting expression," I stated. "I guess I'm suppose to know what that means."

Benjamin let out a booming laugh — a bit stronger than I thought was called for.

"You'll figure it out," he said. "You just have to ride for a while, that's all — that is, if you can hold on."

"I'll hold on just fine, thanks," I said darkly, good and put off by then, for I didn't like people making assumptions about my abilities, and that smug, arrogant tone he was taking was starting to turn my stomach. We looked back out into the sea of light, drank for a while, and said nothing. It was clear by the way he smiled back sips of liquor that he was quite pleased with himself, and also, caught up in some kind of grand thought, as if reliving some pleasant memory, something deep, deep down there — sanctified — within the refuge of his mind.

"Do you know the host?" I had been looking for a way to work Gracie into the conversation, and it seemed to be the appropriate time.

"Who?" He asked, as if the title was foreign.

"Gracie Garrison."

Benjamin's drink stopped suddenly at his lips, as if he were searching for any possible alternative than to answer my direct inquiry. He didn't speak right away, but rather swept his eyes slowly side to side, unassumingly taking in the surrounding environment and the individuals occupying it. After a moment, he resumed the motion of his drink, and without skipping much of a beat at all, turned his attention back towards the valley, where he could allow his thoughts to mingle with the lights that filled it. He must have concluded that there was no way for him to push passed the acknowledgment of Gracie's name this time, for what happened next was rather strange indeed.

"Do you need another drink, Conrad?" He directed his attention away from me off the balcony, and leaned back in his shoes while he said it, like he was trying to convince himself that he was more comfortable somehow than he really was.

"No, I think I'm fine," I answered, curious as to why he was avoiding the question.

He turned back to me, and looked me square in the face. "I think you need another drink."

I could tell by the way his grey eyes locked firmly on mine that he couldn't be more serious. He held my gaze for another moment, and then, certain that he had my attention, he turned his face back towards the valley and once again spoke softly into the night air. "Wait a few minutes, then meet me at the bar in the back of the house."

He took another sip of his drink, finishing it, then broke from the railing and walked sharply past me into the still teeming crowd. I noticed several of the doting models eyes follow him as he did, but they quickly reverted back. One even looked in my direction to see if I had noticed, but I reciprocated the aversion and leaned back over the balcony like the conversation had simply come to a natural end, and I was not yet ready to leave my post. My heart began to beat rapidly. I was in the thick of it now, and I could hardly contain my eagerness to get back inside and find out what all this was about. Despite my growing anticipation, I forced myself to wait at least ten minutes, which I figured would diffuse all possible thoughts of suspicion. During that time my mind raced, filling with ideas of wonder surrounding this mystery, only to be emptied and punctured by thoughts of doubt, which then mended and filled up again just as quickly. I felt like some amateur detective, assigned to investigate the current happenings of some young starlet, and Gracie was to be my first case.

After fifteen minutes, I took one last look over the twinkling, starry vista, left my railing post, headed inside, and began to work my way through the room. The standing-room-only crowd had thinned significantly over the last hour, but that's not to say the party wasn't still in full swing. To the contrary, the bright chandelier had been dropped to its lowest setting, increasing the intimacy level significantly, and casting little flickers of light that rested on the heavy flirtations of budding romances and outlined the post-faux faces of necking couples that had taken their seclusion in one of the many, veiled corners. The more seasoned socialites still preferred to stand, holding their conversations in little cliques that scattered across the floor in such perfect, random fashion that their positioning appeared to be pre-determined in the most socially proofed of ways. I smiled at this thought, reasoning that it could not possibly be true, and instead, weaved my way through them, dodging the occasional, flailing cocktail glass from an unobservant starlet that may have had one too many.

I reached the entrance to the long, dark hall at the back of the room and began to make my way down it for the first time. The low, dim lights that hung embedded in the ceiling above cast just enough of a deep, orange glow for me to notice the Victorian style doors that sat closed on either side, and suddenly I came under the impression that I was going someplace very private. I felt like I was walking through a portal that was reserved for some kind of grand beauty or social elegance that few had ventured into, and few would ever come to see. As I reached the other side, I heard the voices resume again, and I was quite surprised as I emerged. The hallway opened into a comprehensive space that I would best identify as a personal art gallery, with high, polished, wooden walls that stood floor to ceiling, divided by a few scattered blocks of an off-white substance in which little spotlights illuminated the paintings and canvases that hung from their sides. Within the space, an impromptu social gathering was in mid-swing, with an eclectic mix of about thirty to forty well-seasoned socialites scattered cliquishly about the assortment of displays, sipping on Manhattans as they discussed the various eccentricities of each piece, offering their personal opinions only when they felt it appropriate to do so. The atmosphere was different in this room — it felt sober, less judgmental so to speak — as a result, I was instantly enamored with the knowledge that I was in some sort of 'inner circle,' and although it wasn't stated anywhere explicitly, I knew you either had to be an important enough, sober enough, or curious enough of an individual to venture down that diffident hallway in the first place, essentially completing the self-qualifying process that the rest deemed properly sufficient.

Benjamin was leaning against a bar in the back room, sipping on a dry martini which he must have found more suitable then the whiskey-soda he so thoughtfully took to before. I spotted him, and walked over. He greeted me with a genuine smile.

"You made it."

"I found it alright," I responded, suddenly keen to the notion that I might be being led on.

"Not many do," he stated lightly, then redirected — "I'm sorry about earlier, it's unwise to speak openly in such an exposed space, you never know who might be listening."

"And this is so much better?" I found the statement almost comical.

"Yes," Benjamin answered with all seriousness. "There's more light, the art provides a distraction — more nobility — and there's less models about. Never trust a model." He concluded his statement heartily. "I've been in this town long enough, Conrad, long enough to know when it's wise to keep my mouth shut, and earlier on the balcony, was one of those times."

I spotted Evie having a rendezvous with an extremely good looking couple at the other end of the room, so good looking in fact that I could only assume they were both models themselves, and I felt a slight shiver tingle up my spine.

"What are you drinking?" He asked, breaking my trance.

"Scotch and soda," I answered mechanically.

He called the bartender over, and within moments I had my drink. It was stiff, and it steeled my nerves as we gazed leisurely out at the crowd.

"What's this about?" I asked after a moment. "What is it about Gracie that makes you so uncomfortable?"

I noticed that same ripple move through his jaw muscle at the sound of her name. He looked around, not so subtle this time.

"The truth is Conrad, I don't know, but I've heard… rumors."

"Rumors?"

"Yes, but they are only rumors."

"Well, what are they?"

"I'm reluctant to say…"

"Please. Say it." I practically demanded the answer, not enjoying the mystery so much anymore, and the idea of talking about Gracie behind her back was beginning to make me uncomfortable. Benjamin looked both ways once more, then shifted forward in my direction with a pointed expression, making up his mind to speak.

"When you had your meeting earlier, did you actually… meet?"

"What do you mean?"

"Did you actually discuss your work at all — explore the potential of working together?"

I had to think about it for a moment, although I already knew the answer. "Well, no, I suppose not, we decided that it could wait another day."

"Right," he said, with a loose, knowing nod.

"What?" I didn't think it was funny.

"Conrad, don't you think it strange that you were called in for a meeting... at eight o'clock on a Friday night?"

I paused for a second, and it wasn't because he made a good point. "I'm sorry, I don't believe I ever said the meeting was at eight."

"Wasn't it?" He asked, pointedly.

"Well yes, but—"

"Did they avoid your questions when you asked them?"

"They did, but—"

"Did they dazzle you, play old music, get you drunk?"

"I don't know about that—"

"Did Gracie dance in front of you? Was she beautiful?"

I paused. "How could you know that?"

He looked me in the eye. His fine mouth lifted slightly in the corners as he realized he had hit his mark, and now he had my complete and undivided attention.

"Because that's exactly what they did when they asked to meet with me... this same time last year."

"You're lying," I said with an air of cynicism I found to be fully justified as it rolled disdainfully across my lips.

"It's true," he said frankly. "I was an upcoming actor the time — still am by industry standards — and they said they wanted to work with me, cast me in their productions, that sort of thing."

"Well, did you?"

"Of course not," he stated, rather appalled. "I thought the whole thing to be rather fraudulent. Besides, they had no financing so it was an easy decision."

"But why? I mean, what for?" I was completely dumbfounded. It all sounded completely ridiculous.

"I can only assume it was for the potential of money, other than that I don't know."

"Well that doesn't make any sense," I retorted. "This house, this party—"

"Expensive lifestyles call for expensive company my good man," he said coolly, slipping one hand in his pocket and bringing his drink to his lips with the other.

I stopped, and studied the young man in front of me inquisitively. I didn't like where this conversation was going. In fact, I was beginning to get extremely put off by it all. Who was he to know this and to say these things? I liked Gracie, I wanted to like her, and the idea of my image of her being skewed by some self-assured actor was quite unpleasant.

"What are you getting at?" I asked pointedly.

"This is where I stop, and the rumors begin…" He said it smoothly behind a drink. "Only if you want to hear them?"

We both looked around, suddenly becoming very aware of whose space it was that we were actually in. Not much had changed in the last twenty minutes or so, or at least nothing I could define as noticeable. The same socialites continued to socialize over the same images of oil on canvas, say for the few that strayed from one group to the next to satiate their inexhaustible need for intellectual stimulation. Cultured aristocrats continued to mingle with the same young starlets that had somehow managed to keep their tiny frames upright and into the night thus far, still sipping dangerously from distinct cocktail glasses that provided a most prominent accessory to their individual styles. The hosts, however, were nowhere to be seen, and I found my thoughts once again shifting from the room back to images of Gracie, and how much it was that I wanted to know everything about her.

Satisfied that we were in the clear, I nodded my head reluctantly, signaling to Benjamin that I was ready to hear the information, so he began. Between drinks of his cocktail that he would fill up several times during the conversation, he began spilling the rumors that he had heard about the pixyish girl, telling me the elaborate stories that created her mystery, going off on tangents of pure speculation, and then re-directing them with a quick bit of hearsay to bring it back, closer to home, thinking he was sweetening the pot in some way. Indeed, I heard many strange things about Gracie that night, how she was a complete tease, how she used men for their money, how she only dated aging celebrities — how she was still a virgin — and that was just the beginning. Benjamin hypothesized that she had made short work of young writers like me before, seducing them for their talents, enticing them to write her scripts in exchange for her charms — scripts that could make her a star — and then, whether they ran out of steam or she just got bored, she would toss them aside just as easily. One of the more absurd stories was based around some wild speculation that she was indeed from a different era, the fifties even, hence her obsession with late celebrities and old music. Still others thought she was simply stuck in a time loop, lucidly playing out the role of her dreams, grounded deeply by her unshakable faith in the prominence of French cinema, and whether she was conscious or unconscious of that fact, was an ongoing point of disputation.

"Who is she, really?" I asked after a moment, the way in which I read into the conversation could not have been more serious.

"That, my friend, is something I do not know," Benjamin stated honestly, "but I can tell you more about her if you like, all I know at least — where you holding up?"

"Excuse me?"

"What part of town are you living in? What neighborhood?"

"Oh. Los Feliz. Franklin area."

"That's a good neighborhood. It's quiet. Good for writing I imagine."

"Yes, it is."

He reached his hand into his back pocket, pulled out his wallet, and smoothly slipped out a piece of two-by-three cardstock. "Here's my card," he said, holding it out to me. "Give me a call next week and we'll talk more."

I took the card in my hands, studying it. It stated his name — Benjamin Trask — in black letters over plain white. The word 'Actor' and his union status were scribed just beneath, followed by his representation contact and personal phone number — clean and professional.

"Well, Conrad, it was pleasure to meet you," Benjamin continued, finishing his drink and setting the empty glass on the bar. "But I'm afraid it's time for me to call it a night."

"Yes," I said distractedly, managing to avert my eyes from the card as well as the peculiar thoughts the conversation had conjured up in my mind. "It was pleasure meeting you as well."

"Give me a call," he nodded in assurance.

We gave a basic handshake, and Benjamin headed for the exit, walking coolly and purposefully like the rest of them. I stood for a few more moments at the bar and finished my drink as I sorted through the copious amounts of ridiculous information I had just received. It was laughable really — the absurd things people thought and said about Gracie — and yet, it somehow shrouded her in mystery, creating a sort of secrecy around her life that gave her some kind of true grandeur, and I felt my resolve slowly deteriorating against the captivating nature of her alluring magic.

I walked through the gallery in such a dazed state I felt like I was in *The Twilight Zone*, caught in limbo someplace between fantasy and real life, waiting for the moment when I would receive the imposing stroke of my absolution, but none came. I was left to wander among them, among the magnificent couples that stood picturesque against the canvases and portraits that dotted the dreamscape of their intrinsic worlds, among the aristocracy of the upper class, the fortunate few who had been given the innate means to live above the constraints of society. Between the time it took to raise a cocktail glass to their entitled lips, and then drop again, I realized that this was true, that it was not imaginary, and that I had entered into a type of actuality far more real than I could have ever envisioned. I walked back down the narrow corridor of the surreal hallway, and when I reached the other side I found that the lights had dimmed considerably. Once again there was no sign of the hosts — of Gracie, Maxwell, Evie, or any of those that dwelled there. All that remained of the social were those who had fallen asleep, lounging in the corners or dozing pleasurably against one of the dignified structures of lavish furniture, dreaming of cocktails and fancy gowns, free to embark on their every desire.

Out on the balcony, I took one last look at the wondrous display of lights that flashed and winked in the valley, its yellow and gold hues pulsating a brilliant white and then down again like little breaths in the dark, rising and falling rhythmically to its slumber. For a moment I imagined that I was above them, that this life of waking and sleeping was only for the simple, and that I had somehow been enlightened to the realities of a higher society, drinking, socializing, and living splendidly into the night. The thought hung for a moment in the air above that starry valley, then I pushed it from my mind, finished my cocktail, and moved towards the exit. "Surely this was a dream," I thought. "It had to be."

CHAPTER 3
— THE KING AND QUEEN OF THE GALLERY —

It was nearly the afternoon by the time I woke up the next morning. I sat up in bed trying to recall the details of my trip home but found that they were blurry, making it difficult to determine exactly where the party stopped and my dreams began. "I shouldn't drink so much," I sighed to myself, running my hands through my hair and rubbing my eyes as I sleepily drew myself from my bed, trying to shake the tinge of uselessness I often felt after a night of excessive drinking. I took a shower, fixed a French press of good coffee, and sat down to write, reasoning that throwing myself back into a routine would help re-solidify my thought process and help put a label on the night, but no words came. After an hour or so my frustration became so complete that it was no use. I could never write when I was frustrated and today was no exception, so instead I grabbed my jacket and plummeted endlessly into the cool November.

It was a beautiful, crystal clear day. The sun reflected brightly off my dark jacket, creating a cozy, thermal effect that warmed my aching muscles from the outside in. I stopped by a used bookstore and picked up a copy of *This Side of Paradise* by F. Scott Fitzgerald, a book I had been wanting to read for quite some time — he wrote another one of my favorites as well, *Tender is the Night,* but it is too grand to talk about here — so with his first novel in hand, I settled into a little nook at one of my favorite cafés and got started. I had been a long-time fan of Mr. Fitzgerald ever since I read the *The Great Gatsby* when I was a teenager, preferring the flow of his prose and diction to the majority of his other contemporaries. I liked other writers. John Fante, Budd Schulberg, and Harold Robbins wrote great novels about Los Angeles. Harold Robbins in particular was a remarkably gifted storyteller. His Hollywood Novel, *The Dream Merchants,* was a very well written and engaging fictionalization of the early studio system, and proved to be quite reflective of some of the experiences and relationships I was having for myself in Tinseltown. Also, his novel, *The Carpetbaggers,* a fictional account of the Howard Hughes tale and the relationships that accentuated his life, was one of the most intense, savage, and brilliant novels I had ever read. Released to the public in 1961, it was considered to be an artifact of the sexual revolution at the time because of the detailed, explicit nature of some of the content. In my opinion it was tastefully done and pushed boundaries by making the human nature in people want to explode. It did for me, anyway, and God knows I needed it. Yes, it's quite funny I think, but I'd be lying if I said I wasn't praying to be influenced, because I most definitely was, even if it was just in my dreams for the time being. Other writers I enjoyed reading that wrote good Los Angeles fiction were Alison Lurie, Nathaniel West, Gavin Lambert, Norman Mailer, and Macdonald Harris.

Down on the Strip, I took to the pages of *This Side of Paradise* like a sheep takes to water, desperate to quench a thirst for inspiration that felt so withered and dry. I had to find a way to make sense of things, and despite twenty minutes or so of intellectual resistance, I eventually dropped into the story, following the character of Amory Blaine as he navigated the twists and turns of high society, dealing with highs and lows of growing up amidst aristocracy and the double standards of the upper class. Despite the difference in lifestyles, it wasn't long before I felt a connection to him, feeling that there was something about the soul of the character on the page that I could relate to, and unto which I could believe.

After fifty pages or so, I felt I had reset my motivation, so I closed the book and returned to my apartment to write. To my regret, however, I once again sat staring at the blank page, re-igniting that deep cauldron of frustration that returned vengefully from its slow simmer. I stared at the page for another hour or so, then again I grabbed up my jacket and took to the neighborhood to clear my head, hoping that through some divine touch or some cosmic intervention I would once again strike inspiration and regain the ability to continue my work. I returned to my desk, and again the same thing, and then again and again.

And so this trend continued, day in and day out, for the next couple of weeks or so. I'd sit at my desk, typing and pecking away, and no sooner would I form a few meager sentences then I'd just throw in the towel, believing that it was all pointless and that I would never amount to anything. All I could think about was her, Gracie Garrison, the girl unto which all the mystery in the world owed its observation. Her image hung in the air above my desk like some fractured fairytale on a string, and unto this, my mind was no exception. She filled the drafts of my room with such a stifling creativity that I deemed it toxic, and had to find something else upon which to rest my mind. The telephone became my crutch, and its glossy black finish smiled at me torturously from the corner of my desk, taunting me to pick it up and fabricate some kind of elaborate plan to go out with friends and drink myself back into artistic integrity. I would not fall to its charms, for I was above the weaknesses of simpletons and the fruitless impulses of irresponsible artists, and yet, I secretly hoped that it would somehow suddenly ring and take me to some far away place, far away from this worthless guilt and its monotony, but it never did, say for the occasional call from the agent or a random hail from a friend in some quest to burn the night away drinking about on the town — both just as equally destructive to my goals — then, on one lonely Wednesday afternoon, it rang like any other.

"Hello," I answered.

"Hi, Conrad!"

I instantly recognized Gracie's vibrantly light voice on the other end of the line. My heart turned to liquid, and the top of my head that hung lazily in my chair just moments before snapped up straight like a bowstring.

"Gracie. Hi. How have you been?" I asked, trying to sound as friendly and engaging as possible without giving too much away.

"To tell you the truth, I'm bored, Conrad, positively bored."

I imagined her lounging fair and long again across her black velvet couch, a plethora of midday cocktail glasses sitting empty against the veneer of the coffee table.

"Well, I'm sorry to hear that, Gracie." I managed to say it with true concern. "I wish there was something I could do."

"Oh, there's nothing to do. That's why I'm bored, don't you see? It's a terrible thing Connie, a positively awful, terrible, thing."

"Well… a girl like you should never be bored." It sounded stupid the way I said it, but I thought it witty all the same.

"I know, Connie. It's true."

"What about Maxwell? I'm sure he's around."

"Maxwell will have nothing to do with me, Connie, absolutely nothing at all. I'm afraid he's abandoned me."

"Abandoned?"

"Yes, he's left me all alone for the evening with no entertainment whatsoever. Isn't that horrible? It's a terrible thing being bored. Just terrible."

"But he'll be back?" I didn't like the idea of Gracie being left alone even for even a second, and it came across in my voice.

"Of course he'll be back, dear," Gracie stated rather matter of factly like I was crazy to even consider the thought. "But it doesn't change the fact that I'm all alone for the evening does it?"

"Well, maybe we could do something?" I threw it out there cautiously — I wasn't looking to scare her away.

"You know what…" Gracie considered it thoughtfully. "You're right, Connie, you're absolutely right. That's why I want you to come to my place this evening and swoop me up!"

My heart practically jumped out of my throat, and it was only by all the resolve and restraint in the world that I kept myself from asking her for clarification. Without sounding too excited, I steadied my hand on the phone and did my best to resist the natural tendency I had to speak from my throat at times like this.

"Yes, I think that could work tonight. I'll check my schedule." I didn't have a schedule — I was a writer, for Christ's sake — but the few years I had spent in Los Angeles told me that I at least had to have the appearance of being busy with girls like her, lest I lose her attraction altogether. I still don't know why that was important, but some things are what they are for no other reason than being what they are, and next to that there was no other reason.

"Oh do make yourself available, won't you?" Gracie interjected quickly.

"Ah, yes," I continued smoothly, doing my best to keep calm. "I did have something planned for tonight, but I suppose it is not so important — when shall I pick you up?"

Gracie was delighted. "Oh Connie, I knew you'd come through! I don't like driving you see, and you seem like such an excellent driver. You with your little coupe."

There was no doubt about it, the girl knew how to push all the right buttons.

"Now, you can pick me up at seven you hear, but don't be early, I'm never really ready early, in fact, you're better off coming late than early, so why don't you just be a little late — you know what, no, just be on time, how about that?"

"Sure. I'll pick you up at seven then," I said as logically as I could, for I always found it best to be as logical as possible when dealing with the sporadic emotions of women, and even then I wasn't necessarily good at it, in truth I was pretty terrible.

"Oh, and there's just one more thing, Connie."

"Yes?"

"You won't ask any questions. You have to promise me you won't ask any questions at all."

"I won't ask any questions," I stated, not seeing any problem with it.

"Promise me. You have to promise me, Conrad."

"I promise."

"I want you to say 'I promise I won't ask any questions,'" she continued insistently.

"I promise I won't ask any questions," I stated again, for I saw no real point to the repetition, and thus I had no problem with it, but I didn't deny that it was strange.

"Excellent!" She exclaimed excitedly. "When are you picking me up again?"

"Seven," I stated, and although she couldn't see it a big smile spread across my face, for I was barely able to contain my delight.

There was a slight pause.

"Seven-thirty," Gracie said, then she hung up.

That dial tone was the most beautiful sound I had ever heard. The emotion I was holding somewhere between my stomach and my throat exploded in a pent up ball of pure joy that I had never experienced before, and may never experience again. "She called me! She called me!" I said over and over again to myself as I danced around my apartment. "She wanted to spend time with someone, and she called me!" I was so overjoyed I didn't consider why or how or what the circumstances were, or any more of that nonsense I couldn't care less about. She called me, and at least for the moment, I was once again invincible.

The rest of the day was ruined artistically. I was so overjoyed I couldn't even sit still, or think, or do anything it takes to produce any kind of comprehensive workflow whatsoever, and I was okay with it because I knew I had earned it. I resolved to not waste any time, for it was a glorious moment, and one that deserved to be recognized. I threw on my best winter jacket, and walked down into the neighborhood to celebrate over an afternoon pint and indulge in my raging masculinity while entertaining heroic thoughts of greatness to welcome the coming evening — it was the best pint of beer I had ever had — the world was perfect in those few hours, and life was worth living for a while. I didn't even touch the book I brought.

The evening rolled around as it inevitably would, and I felt myself getting increasingly nervous, for with my excitement came a type of anxiety that could only be described as strangely pleasurable. My blood was cold in my skin. My hands and feet were clammy, and my breaths short. I really liked this girl, and the confidence I stood so strongly on before was shedding off my shoulders like layers on a summer afternoon. I sat myself down at my desk and gave myself a pep talk to try and calm down. If there ever was a time to be logical, this was it — logic was key — and I knew I had to stick to the elements of my personality that I believed had attracted her to me in the first place if I wanted to support even the slightest chance of being successful, so I began to write them out—

Confident — check.

Driven — check.

Artistically minded — check.

Personable — has potential.

Genuine — check.

Mysterious — of course, double check.

I wasn't sure what her physical type was, but I didn't think that mattered. I was so straight-up-and-down girls either liked it or they didn't, so the fact that she was calling me at all basically erased the whole thought from any sort of relevant consideration. When it was all said and done, the process of writing out my attributes proved to calm me considerably, and at the very least it helped re-establish a confidence that I found so lacking when I needed it most. I set down my pen, and looked up at the clock — it was nearly seven, and time for my date.

***

It was fifteen minutes past the hour by the time I climbed the starry hills into Studio City, and that same magical feeling was pressing. I parked my car, and as I walked to her door I pinched myself a couple of times to make sure it wasn't all some big dream and my devilish mind was playing tricks on me again — it wasn't — as the reality set in, all I could feel was a great sense of pride that I was the man she wanted walking up to her door that night, and I let the vitality of that thought radiate through me until it spread across my face in a big, warm smile. I knocked.

"Come in!" I heard from the other side.

I entered her beautiful living room, and it looked even more Parisian than before, with the large chandelier gleaming exquisitely across the rich interiors. Gracie was fluttering around the room in a hurry, fixing everything from her diamond earrings that swayed elegantly past her sweeping neckline, to the lampshade, which I thought to be more than fine. She was absolutely stunning in her evening attire, with her usual black cocktail dress over black tights that fit her body perfectly-wonderfully, with thin, long sleeves to keep the evening cold out.

"Hi Conrad," she said, looking up. "I'm afraid I'm still not ready yet as you can see." She laughed a little.

"No, not at all," I said at a loss. "You look amazing."

She hesitated for a second, but without breaking stride she brushed off the comment like it was some old garment, and she couldn't be bothered by it. "Thank you, Conrad — you like the dress?"

"Yes, it looks—"

"I just love black cocktail dresses. You can never go wrong with them."

"I'd have to agree."

"Oh Connie, now you got me all self-conscious." She did a little wave with her free hand as she continued about the place. "I just have to run back real quick. Do stay out here for a minute, won't you? Feel free to make yourself a drink."

"Of course, take your time." I tried to be as carefree as I could while saying it, for the art of acting aloof was a skill I found difficult, albeit necessary, because I knew that's what most girls liked, even if they weren't completely aware of it themselves.

"I'll be right out," Gracie said, and with that she disappeared down the same mysterious hallway I had walked down just weeks before, and I guessed one of the mysterious doors that stood tall and closed on the sides of those mysterious walls was the gateway to her mysterious bedroom. I imagined what her room must be like. I was sure it was large, and beautiful, and grandiose, and full of all sorts of amazing sights and smells, but before I became too swept up in the thought, I took a seat on the black velvet couch that served as Gracie's staple of the living room, opting to pass on the alcohol for the moment to see what the night would bring. I sat down on the cushion and was surprised by its firmness. I liked a firm couch, just like I liked a firm mattress, firmness was of necessary importance to any member of the Arlington family, as we all had intricate lower backs, and the natural resistance of a firm surface was essential to keep them inline. Again, the thought came and went as my hands came in contact with the fine, black veneer that ran its entirety. It was warm and inviting to the touch, and I imagined Gracie's long body laying across it, the way it extended slim and beautiful in every possible female direction, the way her intoxicating scent soaked through its every fiber, infusing it with such flawless effervescence that it was nothing short of sovereign, and I allowed myself to experience that sovereignty without any guilt at all — I needed nothing else.

"Hello."

Startled, I looked up and saw none other than Evie Clark standing all nonchalant near the liquor table, making herself a drink. Indeed, I was so taken with my thoughts I didn't even see her come in.

"Hello," I replied, unable to hide my surprise. "I'm sorry, you startled me."

"Why?" She asked in her usual, disinterested way.

"That's a good question," I laughed, trying to make light of it. "I guess I'm not sure."

She continued fixing her drink without a response, figuring it unnecessary to do so — either that or she had already used too much energy trying to appear disinterested, and I liked to think it was the latter.

"Going out?" I asked cordially.

For the first time she took her eyes from her drink and turned her head toward me, and I was stricken once again by how stunningly beautiful Evie truly was. Like Gracie, she had a near perfect facial structure with dainty features, but rather than bright and inviting in the way Gracie's were, hers were dark and dreamlike, and just as equally alluring. She turned her gaze back to her drink.

"Yes," she stated plainly.

There was a moment, but I was determined not to let her off that easily.

"Where?"

She looked over at me again, this time with eyes that flashed a bit fierce as if she couldn't believe I would inquire further. I took this as a sign of a natural female resistance, and I had no problems with seeing where it would lead. After all, the girl of my dreams was getting ready for me somewhere just down the hall, and by all accounts of the human condition, I really had nothing to lose.

"I'm going on a date," she said, looking back towards her drink.

"With whom?" I pressed, making sure to uphold my tone.

She finished mixing her drink and took a small sip, tasting it to see if it met her specifications. Satisfied, she gave a cute little nod of the head, then moved intently to the chair at the head of the room I sat in just nights before, facing me, as if she accepted the fact that I wasn't going to let up any time soon, and she at least wanted to make sure she was comfortable for it. Either way, whatever bit I had done until that point must have worked, because she looked at me in the most receptive way, like I had passed some sort of test of hers and now it was time to see if I could play ball.

"I'm going out with a friend." With a slight smile, she twiddled her cocktail straw in a nervous way — back and forth.

"That's nice." I paused. "Are you sure he's just a friend?"

"Yes," she answered, smiling into her drink. "I think so."

There was a bit of a pleasant silence. I liked the fact that we were talking, and I think she did as well. I didn't know how much she talked to people most of the time, but I didn't think it was all that much, and this was a probably a nice change of pace for her. Whether I was right or not in my presumption, I didn't feel the need to say anything after that, and I took that as a sign of good chemistry.

"So you're a writer?" She asked, breaking the silence.

"In my spare time, yes."

"That's neat."

"It is mostly."

Our conversation continued on a bit longer, and for some time we seemed to be lost in a moment together. It wasn't the words we exchanged that made it special, rather, it was the energy that naturally existed between us that made it so completely pleasant. Before we could get as caught up as we both would have liked, there was a noise at the end of the hall, which signaled that Gracie was ready to go. I, of course, couldn't have felt better about it, but there seemed to be a dark vacancy that washed over Evie's face in that instant, indicating that she didn't feel the same way at all. In fact, it looked more like the exact opposite.

"Well, that'll be Gracie," I said. "It was nice talking to you, Evie."

I stood up and took her limp hand just as I heard Gracie returning from the hallway. Evie smiled at me the saddest of smiles, and looked at me like I was something good that was about to disappear from her life forever, and would never be seen again.

"I hope you last," she said faintly.

I didn't know what to make of it. Her tone — which had been so sincerely sweet just moments before — was now so hollow and devoid of hope I simply didn't know what to do with it, so I didn't do anything at all. I just held her limp hand in mine, and looked into her deep, dark eyes that sustained my gaze eternal, and I knew that she was terrified.

"I see you two are getting on," Gracie stated flippantly, returning from the hall. "I just knew you two would be friends. I had an intuition about it when I first saw you together, and it turns out I was right." Gracie went straight for the liquor table and mixed herself a quick vodka tonic.

I took my eyes from Evie's worried face and let them fall on Gracie, and all concern for the present situation left me immediately, for she looked just as stunning, if not more stunning than before, except now she wore a black leather overcoat cinched tightly around her waist, giving her a very metropolitan look that screamed of nobility. Evie tipped back her head, lifted her chin, and returned to her default state of disinterest so quickly and discreetly that it was incredible it ever left her in the first place. I also thought I heard a disapproving "tut, tut" slip from her lips at the same time, solidifying her whole façade so seamlessly that I couldn't help but wonder just how deep the girl's fragility really was, and what it was that made her behave that way.

"Evie was just keeping me company," I said easily.

"That doesn't surprise me at all. Evie's always been a great conversationalist, isn't that right, Eve?"

"I can carry a conversation just fine, thank you," Evie retorted.

"Well don't get all desperate about it, I was trying to be nice," Gracie said. "Honestly, Eve, you're no fun sometimes."

"Fun is for the faint of heart, I'm afraid I haven't the time for it."

"That's your own fault. I rang Connie this afternoon and now we have a wonderful evening ahead of us. Isn't that right, Connie?"

"Ah, yes." I was uncertain of how to respond. I didn't like being the middle person in a conversation, least of all between two women. I'd take the up, or I'd take the down, but I wouldn't take the middle — the middle was for indecisive people, and I knew exactly what I wanted that night.

"You see, Eve," Gracie ended cheerfully. "Fun is just a phone call away."

"I guess I don't know anything about it, then."

"Oh, won't you come with us? I hate the idea of you spending the night alone. It saddens me. I want to have a good time, and I don't think I can unless I know you are as well."

I was completely surprised at Gracie's extended invitation to her standoffish friend, and aside from all the other qualities that made Gracie a true catch, I thought that she must be the kindest, sweetest girl I had ever met in my life, and I felt an entirely new wave of appreciation for her course through me.

"Thanks, but I've already made plans for the evening," stated Evie flatly.

"Evie was just telling me she is meeting up with a friend tonight," I added, trying to smooth things out.

"Oh, well that's great. You should meet up with us later then," Gracie said with enthusiasm.

"That would be great," I said.

"I'm not driving, so I'm afraid it's just not going to be possible tonight." Evie was strong in her remark.

I suddenly felt a great amount of distaste for Evie, for Gracie was trying so hard to be welcoming, and I couldn't understand why she was being so cold towards her invitation. It was a frigid attitude, borderline on horrible, and I was glad she wasn't coming. I wanted nothing more to do with her for the time being.

"Suit yourself then," Gracie said, unconcerned. "I offered, and I'm going out with a clear conscience." She paused. "But honestly, Evie, you're going to miss out on some lovely parties."

"I'm sure I'll be thoroughly disappointed."

"I'll say nothing more on the subject," Gracie concluded. "Will you at least give me your opinion on my outfit?"

"It looks great," I mumbled out in compliance.

"Thank you, Connie, I figured you would approve," she said to me in a way that I found to be altogether too emasculating, and it was clear she had practice. Then she turned to Evie, "but what I was really fishing for was a model's opinion."

"It will do, I suppose." Evie rolled her eyes upward, rather unimpressed.

"What's that suppose to mean?"

"I don't know." Evie held out her hand, examining her nails. "It just feels a little... inflated... that's all."

"Everything feels a little inflated to you, Eve, but that's just something you're going to have to live with, isn't it?" Gracie's reply wasn't defensive, and it wasn't mean spirited either, but there was a certain level of understanding and appreciation in it that could only come from a place of complete self-assuredness — a fierceness, even, in the tone and confidence — I was reminded of Vivien Leigh's portrayal of Scarlett O'Hara in *Gone with the Wind* in the way Gracie was masterfully steering the conversation, and I recognized that this was a much different performance than the one I experienced from the girl in the audition room.

Gracie took one more sip of her vodka tonic and set it down rather carelessly. "Come, Connie, let's leave the model alone for the night. We have far too many splendid things planned for the evening then to waste precious time getting caught up in inflation and what not."

Turning back towards Evie, I could tell that she was slightly hurt by Gracie's remark despite her apparent irreverence, but I didn't weigh it too heavily, reasoning that the way they went on for the last few minutes most likely encapsulated the entire, inherent nature of their relationship. After all, Evie wasn't the sweetest thing by any means, and for all intents and purposes I thought she had every bit of it coming.

"Good night, Evie," I stated with ease, opting to take the less serious route. "It was good talking to you, again."

Evie didn't answer, but smiled weakly up at me with her eyes before returning her gaze to the ground, and for a moment I saw that same trace of concern wash across her face, only this time it was much fainter. She was such a fragile creature, and I could only believe that she must have had her reasons for acting so cold — any human being would have had to.

"Good night, Eve," Gracie said, taking up my arm and leading me towards the door. "Have fun with your friend, and do try to be open won't you? Oh I know you will."

"Good night," I said, and then pulled the door closed behind me, leaving Evie all alone beneath the fading chandelier.

***

I raced with Gracie through the hills towards our first evening affair and felt a great sense of pride in having her next to me. It was one those simple pleasures, the way that she sat there all blonde and tiny and perfect in the passenger seat, it made me feel like I could do anything. It quickly became apparent that she loved my car even more than I thought, and she insisted we listen to music the whole way without saying a word to each other, as to 'preserve the mystery of the evening.' I was happy to comply, for indeed there was something surreal about the way the night was unfolding before us, and I became more and more aware of it the further we dropped into town, for even the bright, fluorescent sky that hung dimly over Los Angeles seemed to glow in my favor, and the neon billboards that stood high over La Brea Avenue offered their salutations as we passed them, indicating that whatever I was doing it was definitely good, and I should do my damndest to see that I continued to get more of it. That was the result-oriented side of my personality taking precedence, and as we neared our first destination for the evening — off La Brea, near Second Street — I resolved that I would do my best to simply exist in the coming moments of the night, suppressing my constant need to experience which seemed to religiously go hand in hand with my subconscious pursuit of truth. I parked the car, and looked over at Gracie, who looked back at me with the bluest eyes in the world, and I knew that whatever the universe had in store that night, it was destined to last forever, somewhere, up there, floating along with the ether of the earth. We looked at each other like that for a while, and then the door hinge clicked, and she became a glimmer outside the window.

The air was crisp and cool. It was just after nine o'clock as we took the short walk down Second Street to our first destination.

"We'll just stop in for a short while," she said. "There are a few more parties this evening that I am much more excited about attending."

"Right," I said, making a mental note. "Where are we going, again?"

"No questions, Connie."

I stretched an easy smile between light eyebrows. She must have got the reaction she needed.

"It's just a little gallery opening," she continued. "I didn't really want to go tonight, but my friend Bobby insisted — have you met Bobby?"

"No."

"You'll like him, Connie, he's great. I think you two will get along well with each other. In fact, I know you will."

"Great," I replied, charmed by Gracie's ceaseless self-assuredness. "Can't wait to meet him."

After another block, we reached the entrance to the gallery where ten or so artistic types stood outside smoking cigarettes. A big guard stood in front of the door, and after taking one look at Gracie he moved aside without a word, not bothering to identify either of us. I reasoned that it must have been the way Gracie held herself that managed to open the big, steel doors so quickly, a demeanor so inherently self-entitled that there was really nothing for anyone to do except get out of her way, and let her do whatever it was that she had set in her mind she wanted to do.

"Wait here Connie while I get us a drink."

Gracie disappeared into the crowd so quickly I didn't see which way she went, and I wouldn't have been able to follow her even if I had. I didn't know what she meant by "little gallery opening," but either we had the wrong address or she was delusional because I had never seen such a space before in my life! The place was amok with young Hollywood, and within several moments of standing at the edge of the crowd, I spotted the famous faces of several young movie stars, their presence heightened against the background of their less successful contemporaries. The rest of the gallery was packed to the walls with aristocracy and wreaked of old money like Renaissance England — it was the haut monde, the noblemen, the finest of the fine — sipping cocktails and conversing with the nighttime artists fortunate enough to have their abstract pieces illuminated under the bright lights that shone lamp-like from the plaster ceilings.

Suddenly, I felt something cold and cool thrust into one hand, and something warm and comforting in the other. I felt a tug, and realized I was being pulled through the crowd holding a glass of champagne. I looked down and forward, and saw Gracie's blonde head in front of me, moving through the crowd that parted in front of her brilliant presence like the Red Sea once did, and that's when it hit me — she was holding my hand. My stomach leaped a mile as my face lit up like a string of bright lights, and I felt her fingers, and the tone of her skin, and there was nothing more in the world I needed than more of her, and I think she felt the same way about me.

She continued pulling me through the dense crowd of socialites, and it wasn't until I was with a girl like Gracie that I witnessed the power of complete femininity in its most heightened form. Indeed, she turned the head of every single male she passed as we made our way deeper into the gallery, and I was free to quietly witness this phenomenon as I was pulled, cool and invisible, behind her. It was astonishing. Like clockwork, every eye, every sense was drawn straight to her presence. Even most of the women would look twice, and I imagined how difficult it must be for another female to share the same space as a creature as brilliant as she. I reasoned that out of all the starlets and all the heiresses in the gallery that night, Gracie was the most lovely, and although I felt a great sense of pride being the one attached to her, I couldn't help but wonder the affect such physical beauty has on one's psyche, and what it must be like to garner universal praise for such an uncontrollable, predetermined factor. "She can have any man she wants," I kept telling myself, "and right now she wants me." That thought never left my mind, not even for an instant, and it gave me a great deal of unshakable confidence — false confidence, perhaps — but still unshakable nonetheless, and as we continued to move past group after group of staring socialites masked by fake smiles of pure envy, I knew that as long as she held my hand, that I was king, and she was queen, and it was all the world could do to give us everything that existed, indeed, everything in the entire world, and I felt like God.

Between several fruitless attempts by brave young men vying for her attention, we stopped to socialize here and there or observe the various art pieces around the room. There was one painting Gracie was particularly fond of, which consisted of telephone poles up and down a catholic street that looked a lot like just about anywhere, and I would have bought it for her on the spot if I had even a trace amount of the means necessary to purchase it. Eventually we made it to the back of the gallery and entered a separate, closed space where several socialites gathered around an abstract film in which the projector flickered its image hauntingly against a plain white wall.

"Now Bobby should be back here somewhere, Connie, I really want you to meet him," Gracie said as we stopped for a moment to rendezvous.

"Who is he, anyway?"

"Questions," Gracie stated, quick and pragmatic.

I didn't smile this time. Instead, when I looked at her, my eyes narrowed a little, and she looked right back, and I knew that her rule was unbreakable. Then, once she had what she needed from me, her eyes softened, and her head turned back towards the party.

"Bobby Finch," Gracie continued. "I'm sure you've heard of him."

"No, I don't think I have."

"He's an art dealer, Connie. The best in LA."

"Gracie Garrison," rang a high-pitched, male voice from the back near the projector.

"Bobby!" Gracie ran into the arms of a bright, young man who stood thin and relaxed in a metropolitan suit near the back of the room. His curly, ginger, clean-cut hair was done up high above his head in a lofty fashion, and if anyone looked like they belonged there that night, it was Bobby Finch.

"Bobby, this is my friend Conrad."

"Oh yes, I've heard a lot about you."

"You have?" I was surprised at his recognition.

"Of course, I hear you're quite the talent."

"We talk," Gracie stated factually, interrupting, then she quickly grabbed Bobby's arm and pulled him away like she had something rather important to talk about, and I wasn't to be allowed in on it.

"Nice meeting you," I mumbled, for I didn't think much of it, and I didn't much care. I figured it probably had something to do with fashion lines or some other business, so I just stood there, nursing my drink, and ended up watching the fifteen minute film in its entirety, during which I realized two things — one, the gallery opening was for an experimental artist and novelist who was born in Austria, and two, Gracie disappeared from my side once again — I took a great deal of confidence in the fact that she was going to do whatever it was she wanted to do whenever it was she wanted to do it, so I gave it little thought, and sure enough, after twenty minutes or so she floated back around the corner, took up my hand, and we wafted back out into the gallery. I enjoyed the time I had with her as we made the rounds, and while other people were busy looking at her hanging on my arm, I was busy looking at everything else, for there were so many beautiful pieces of fine art on display, and I wanted to give each of them their due diligence, even if only for a moment.

Gracie introduced me to the celebrity host of the party, a trendy cast member of a certain syndicated TV show that gave him a very large and well-funded sandbox to play in. Then we continued on and found ourselves in a conversation with two middle-aged art dealers who both had pieces in the show and were as enamored with Gracie's presence as everyone else. I couldn't place why she chose to talk to them for so long — as I had a few drinks by that time and they were starting to take effect — but I found them to be quite boring.

Just as I was about to fall asleep standing up, Gracie whispered in my ear. "Come on, I want to show you something."

She pulled my arm and led me back through the crowd to the front of the gallery, taking me past the interior of the steel doors — past the bar — until we came to a flight of steps that led to an upper level. We neared the top and I saw that it was deserted.

"I don't see anyone," I said. "I don't think we're suppose to be up here."

Gracie didn't say anything, she just smiled knowingly and pulled me further down the deserted hall, until we came to an open entrance that led into a dark room.

"Sometimes you just have to trust," she said, and then she flipped on the light.

Gracie dove headfirst into the room, and I was left breathless at the entrance. Art of all kinds lined the walls — paintings, sculptures, pottery — everything. There was not a person in sight, and we had the whole space to ourselves. It was beautiful, but the most beautiful thing that stood out fair and bright amongst the great art was Gracie, and I couldn't take my eyes from her. I watched as she worked the room, as she examined the different pieces, the way she was drawn to them, the way they moved her — it was incredible — and I realized the lyrical make-up that composed the being in front of me was far more truthful than all the art in the world combined, and that the soulishness of her spirit was that of a higher verity — a higher art — and I was powerless against it. Indeed, I couldn't even move.

"Come here, Connie."

She spoke my name, and the spell was lifted. I then walked towards her in absolution to re-claim my mind. She stood in front of a large painting composed of three equal parts that spanned the entire wall, and on its canvases rested the image of the full moon that was suspended high over a lake of glass, which mirrored its image below.

"Isn't it beautiful?" She spoke, breathless, enamored by the sight.

I turned towards her — "Yes, it is" — then there was a moment.

She looked back at me quizzically, like she understood what I meant but was not yet ready to experience what was behind it. Then that look broke into the brightest of all smiles, and she laughed a little, then looked down and back up in the most girlish way, and in that moment I saw a person who had the world and everything in it, and I wondered how a simple turn of phrase could still bring so much light into her eyes, and what that light meant, and how to keep it.

"Connie Arlington," she said shyly, composing herself with a smile and a defensive shake of her blonde head. "Let's go."

I followed her back towards the hall, stopped at its entrance, and took one last look behind me at the painting that was the source of our first true connection, and I decided that I would keep the image in my mind forever no matter what the price — even if I had to die for it — then I turned off the light, and it was gone.

CHAPTER 4
— THE BALLAD OF CHESTER THE CHERRY —

"How did you like Bobby?" Gracie asked as we drove through town towards the next party.

"I don't know. You hardly let me speak a word to him."

"Not true," she said playfully, slapping my arm. "I won't be blamed for your lack of social ambition. If you want to talk to someone, you talk to them, that's how it works. You didn't talk to Bobby, so I don't believe you wanted to talk to him. That is my conclusion, and I'm sticking to it."

"Alright." I held back some laughter.

"What's so funny?"

"Nothing." I dismissed the situation before it got the better of me. "Where are we going, anyway?"

Gracie didn't answer. This time it was she who was narrowing her eyes at me.

"You're going to have to give me directions if you want me to get us there," I said off her look.

"Just take a right on Wilshire and drive for a while."

"How far?"

"I have a friend that lives in the Westside and she's invited us over for drinks."

"The Westside! I have to drive all the way to the Westside now?"

"Don't get all mad about it. I thought you liked driving?"

"I do, just not all the way to the Westside, and I probably would have had slightly less to drink if I knew beforehand."

"Then it wouldn't be a surprise, would it?" Gracie stated playfully. "Besides, you'd better get used to it because I have a few more parties we're expected to be at later and you are going to drive us there."

I looked over at her and gave her a hard stare, for as much as I didn't like being told what to do in general, when it came from her mouth it worked somehow, but I wasn't going out easy.

"Why does she live in the Westside anyway?" I sulked. "There's nothing there, just a bunch of agencies and business buildings and restaurants that no one goes to."

"Well, she's quite the brilliant director you see, and she makes all sorts of unique films. Oh, I can't wait for you to meet her! I really think you'll like each other."

"Okay, that still doesn't explain why she lives on the Westside."

"Oh, Connie," she said, speaking like I was some sort of hopeless case. "I'm sure you'll find out someday."

She looked dreamily back out the window as we drove down Wilshire through Beverly Hills, then down Santa Monica Boulevard and past the towers of Century City that shot black and deathlike into the night sky, softening ever so slightly in our misty wake. I smiled as we passed them, for I had been weighing her last comment for several miles now, and I couldn't help but appreciate how she always managed to retain a certain mystery about things. She seemed perfectly happy leaving everything open ended, and I never once felt that she had any desire to conclude things with anyone. Then again, perhaps that was how she preferred to live her life, alive and unrestrained, completely free and devoid of commitment.

We turned down a side street just before the 405 Freeway, into a little neighborhood south of Westwood near the park, and I was stricken with the sight — I didn't see the point to any of it — here was a section of Los Angeles that had no real identity in my eyes, perhaps it did in actuality, but I didn't see it that way. I just saw row after row of middle class houses, caught in limbo somewhere between the world and the ocean, and I didn't understand why anyone would ever want to live here. I had little time to put much more thought into it, however, because we turned down another side street on a rather steep hill that came to a dead end.

"Park here," Gracie said. "Her house is right over there."

It was nearly midnight by the time we finally reached the door of the little, quaint house, for we spent much more time at the gallery than either of us probably expected, so we had a bit of catching up to do. Gracie knocked.

"I just want to stop in and say hi," she said thoughtfully. "It shouldn't take more than half an hour."

"It's alright, I'm in no hurry." I meant it too, for I had already made up my mind that I was just along for the experience that evening, and I wouldn't let my own social anxiety or lack of patience get the best of me — two areas that I knew I needed to work on if I was ever to reach my full potential as a person.

A few moments later the door opened, and a quirky, middle-aged woman stood lazily and loopy at its entrance. Her curly, blonde hair tangled wildly in every direction, and for a moment I was reminded of Albert Einstein — a female version that is — in one hand she held a half-empty glass of chardonnay, and the other she used to support herself against the doorframe. She was clearly drunk, and I felt a rush of estranged excitement that came with not knowing what I was getting myself into.

"Alice!" Gracie exclaimed, throwing herself into her arms in her usual way.

"Hi Gracie," Alice exclaimed sloppily. "So nice of you to finally come by. I'm afraid you'll have to excuse me, for I believe I'm already drunk."

Despite Alice's intoxicated state, I liked her right away, and found her relaxed, self-deprecating sense of humor to be rather light, amusing, and interesting.

"Oh, I'm sorry we're late," Gracie said. "I'm afraid we got caught up at a gallery that was much more alive than I expected it to be."

"You young kids," said Alice. "Having all your fun, forgetting about poor Alice, stuck out here in the Westside." She took a hearty gulp of her drink.

"I am sorry, Alice, really, but we're here now, and this is my friend Conrad — I brought him all the way out here to meet you. Isn't that nice?"

Alice turned her dizzy eyes towards me, and pulled her chin in tight against her neck, leaning her head back in an attempt to get a good look at me.

"Is this your man?" She asked. "He's cute."

I didn't think much of it, and instead put out a hand. "I'm Conrad, nice to meet you."

"Oh drop the formalities, boy," she said playfully. "Come here and give me a hug."

She pulled me in tight, and buried her head in my chest. I didn't mind it. She was so aloof to it all I didn't even find it awkward. Gracie just smiled at the situation and looked at me helplessly.

"That's Alice," she said. "I think she likes you."

Alice let go without a word and stumbled backward into her house. "Come in, have a drink. I got a bottle of champagne I've been wanting to crack open for a while now."

I followed Gracie through the little door and once again found myself in a highly new environment, except this one was the strangest by far. It was a little enclave, packed floor to ceiling with art of all kinds — paintings, sculptures, books, literature, films, records, framed pictures, posters — years and years worth of art packed into a box on the edge of the Westside. It was marvelous! But what I was most stricken by was the enormous three-dimensional figure that stood abstract and alone in the corner. It looked like a giant tomato.

"I'm sorry, the place is a little bit of a mess," Alice stated, grabbing random books off the ground and tossing them into a pile. "I just moved in last week and I haven't had time to organize."

"Is that a tomato?" I asked, cutting straight to the question that was burning in my mind.

"Does that look like a tomato to you?" She put two disgruntled hands on her hips.

"Well, yes. It does."

"Well, it's not, boy. It's a cherry. It's a giant cherry. Can't you see that?"

"Oh go on, Alice," Gracie stated, rather indignant. "You know everybody thinks it's a tomato when they first see it."

"Yes, but it doesn't make it any more right now does it?" She stated, continuing her fruitless cleaning spree.

"It doesn't matter if it's right or not, it is what it is, and to give Connie a hard time about it just because he thinks it's a tomato, well, that's just narrow, Alice. He was only trying to be nice. Right, Connie?"

"Uh. That's right."

"Well, I'm sorry then," Alice said, stopping once again to catch her breath. "I just don't want his feelings getting hurt that's all. He's very sensitive."

"A sensitive cherry." I stated without much cadence. "Who would have thought."

"Yes." Alice shot me a look across the room. "A sensitive cherry. *Not* a tomato."

"Well, I'm glad we got that all cleared up," said Gracie half-cheerfully. "Alice, didn't you say you had a bottle of champagne you've been meaning to get to?"

On the word 'champagne' Alice's entire form snapped to attention, like some bright idea flashed into her head, and there was no more room up there to entertain any lesser thought. I then realized that Gracie was quite adept at handling her — like she was with most people — and I assumed they must have some sort of deeper history.

"That's right! The champagne! Oh, the champagne!" Alice exclaimed, dropping the random books she was carrying. "Would you like a glass of champagne, Chester?"

"Chester? Who's Chester?" I asked, confused.

"The cherry, Conrad," Gracie answered. "Be polite."

"Don't you two say another word," Alice exclaimed. "I'll be right out with glasses, and oh, the champagne! The endless, endless, champagne!"

She disappeared into the kitchen, leaving me and Gracie alone with Chester the giant cherry that loomed over both of us in a kind of strange, ominous way, that could have made me slightly uncomfortable if I allowed it to, but ultimately it wasn't real, and Gracie's presence was more than enough to keep me occupied.

Gracie leaned over very close. "Alice is an alcoholic, Conrad," she said rather matter-of-factly. "I don't know if you could tell."

"Not at all." I lied.

"You're probably wondering why I spend time with her, aren't you?" At the same time she asked, a flush of sadness washed over her face that I couldn't help but reciprocate.

"I don't question it, but I could be curious if you want me to be."

"Well, then I better tell you."

"Only if you want to," I assured her, but deep down I secretly wanted to know, because I found the whole thing fascinating, and I welcomed discovering Gracie's connection to it. Then I saw in her transparent eyes that she had made up her mind to tell me, and I felt a small jump of victory at this little bit of trust in me — whatever it was — that I was still waiting to see.

"Well," she started, then abruptly and forcefully redirected. "I like European cinema, this much you know about me, yes?"

"Yes."

"Okay, good. I wasn't sure." Her tone once again softened to a subtle sympathy. "Well, Alice Button — that's her full name, Alice Button — is a film director," she started again. "You did know that, didn't you?"

"Yes, you told me in the car."

I could tell Gracie was using these little avoidances to transition herself into disclosing whatever it was that she wanted to tell me, and I didn't mind it at all, for it was one of the most enduring things I had ever seen in a girl, and I would have been content to sit like that all night if she called for it.

"Yes, that's right, well, I met Alice a little over four years ago on the French Riviera at Cannes. I was there with a friend on vacation, and she had a film in the festival that year."

She glanced at me to see if I was following. I nodded my understanding.

"It was a beautiful in France that year, and the lights on the Riviera twinkled deep into the twilight every evening, so that it felt like summer every night — it was really spring of course — but that year was particularly warm, and it felt like summer all the same."

"Go on."

"Well, one night I was having a drink in the French tent after one of the many galas — I also happened to be standing alone and no one was bothering me, which was a very rare thing on the Riviera — and that's when I saw her. I recognized her from her picture you see. She was one of the Americans in the festival that year, and I had heard that her film was quite good. I was absolutely into film at the time — still am of course — but not like I used to be, and I've always had a thing for brilliant people, and I just knew she was brilliant, so I just had to go talk to her."

"So you did," I added.

"Yes, now let me tell the story, Conrad," she stated quickly. "Well, I went up to her and introduced myself, and we instantly hit it off. I was an up and coming actress — or aspiring actress, I don't know, I don't want to get to ahead of myself — and she was a budding filmmaker. We made plans to work together the following year, and it was so wonderful for the both of us. We complemented each other very well, and her brilliance combined with some of my social graces proved us to be a very lovely pair, and we soon became the talk of the town — 'this upcoming filmmaker with her new starlet' — it felt like Paris, Connie, Paris in the twenties. Have you ever been to Paris?

"No, I haven't," I answered honestly.

"Oh, how I want to go to Paris! I admit I've never been. Maybe we can go sometime. Would you take me?"

"I'd like to, of course."

"Oh that would be so wonderful, and you're a writer, and it would just be so like the twenties — you and I — it would be like the Jazz Age. Well, I don't know, I don't want to get too ahead of myself now. I tend to do that sometimes, but I'm getting better at it — where was I?"

We heard a 'pop!' followed by a slight screech from down the hall — Alice must have finally figured out how to get the champagne open.

"It's alright," I said, eager to draw her attention back to the story at hand, for my curiosity was now completely piqued, and I wanted to know as much about her in this wonderful place as I could. "You were talking about the Rivera, and how you met Alice."

"Oh, that's right," Gracie said formally, centering herself. "So, Alice and I hit if off of course, and we spent the remainder of our time on the Riviera that year drinking and socializing and thwarting the efforts of self-entitled producers that couldn't take their eyes off us, and that's how I met her."

"That sounds like an amazing time."

"Oh it was Connie, it really was, but you see, that's when it happened."

"When what happened?" I asked, but before Gracie could finish, Alice turned the corner from the kitchen with a tattered bottle of champagne and four glasses — a quarter of the bottle was already gone.

"Sorry it took me so long," she said warily. " I couldn't get the damn thing off."

"All you do is pull." Gracie stated practically.

"Don't you think I know that?" Alice snapped. "I just don't like the 'pop' sound, that's all. It scares me."

"Well, it looks like you got it," I said, trying to be encouraging.

"Oh, William," Alice said, looking directly at me and falling a bit over herself. "You are quite the charmer, but you need to learn to relax."

"What? Who's William?"

"We've met before." Alice stated, looking directly at me.

"No, I don't think so. I just met you tonight — who's William?"

"He's no one, Conrad," Gracie said bluntly, then, turning to Alice — "Alice, let's have some drinks shall we?"

"Drinks!" Alice exclaimed in triumph. "Yes, that is why we are here tonight — to drink!"

Alice proceeded to set up four glasses — one for me, one for Gracie, one for her, and one for Chester the cherry, which she sat down softly on the floor in front of his bulbous, eight foot frame — the whole display lacked about as much finesse as humanly possible.

"There you go, Chester," she said, filling his glass to overflowing with champagne. "Now sit there and be a good boy, we have guests to entertain."

She topped off his glass a bit more, so that it went spilling everywhere down the side and pooled in sparkling puddles on the hardwood floor. I watched this absurd display of lackluster social poise in complete fascination, splitting my attention between her and Gracie, who was absolutely stunning in that black dress, so much so that I figured her nothing short of iconic. She looked like a true-life representation of a young Audrey Hepburn — save for the blonde hair of course — and I pictured her like I did in those scenes from *Breakfast at Tiffany's,* where Audrey is at her best when she does nothing at all. Then I became aware that I was staring, but I still couldn't take my eyes off her.

"You're in love with Gracie aren't you?"

I turned abruptly to face Alice, who still knelt estranged on the floor at the feet of the giant cherry next to the pooling champagne, only this time she stared at me with big, malicious eyes as if she was trying to pierce me dead. It was completely and utterly absurd to witness, and I had no idea how to respond to the bluntness of the comment that came so suddenly and out of context.

"Alice," Gracie stated, seemingly unaffected. "Why don't you join me over here on the couch?"

Alice managed to pull herself up from the ground, then slowly made her way towards the couch, stood there for a moment, then eventually agreed to sit and join Gracie, pressing herself into the corner far opposite her. The whole process was particularly painful to watch — wretched even — and not once did she take her eyes from me.

"Why don't you tell us about how you met Chester," Gracie suggested after a moment.

That seemed to snap her out of it, and her face changed back to its previous state of relaxed excitement so quickly that I wondered if she retained any connection at all to the events that had just passed. Either way, I felt I was in for a long one, and I began to drink champagne immediately, so did Gracie, who must have shared my feelings.

"I didn't meet Chester," Alice goaded, rising to her feet. "I made him!"

"Well, tell us how you made him," Gracie replied with patience.

"Of course, I didn't make him in the literal sense of the word, but I made him who he was — who he is today — I made him famous!" She took up what was left of the champagne and began to drink straight from the bottle, then she looked at me with those big eyes again — "You are completely in love with Gracie. I can see it in your face."

I stared at the woman like she was insane for talking, for I had met my share of bad drunks in my life, but this one just called it like it was. Although I didn't care that she was pointing her drunken remarks at me — after all, I figured Gracie had at least picked up on my interest by then, and I was fine with it — but the sheer inappropriateness of it all was making me agitated.

"Chester is a movie star, Conrad," Gracie stated, playing along.

"That's right! That's absolutely right. He's my little movie star!" Alice exclaimed, reveling in her own imaginary triumph.

I wasn't having it, and I didn't care how sorry the sight was in front of me, or how much Gracie wanted me to play pretend. I was about fed up with it all and wanted some kind of explanation of some sort, at least enough to justify the fact that I drove all the way with my date to the godforsaken Westside in order to sit in some strange living room with a giant cherry and a mad woman that took pleasure in putting me on the spot.

"How?" I asked innocently.

Alice stopped and stared at me, a certain rage brewing below the surface. "How? How?!"

"Yes, how is Chester a movie star?"

At that, Alice burst into a hysterical fit of laughter that was borderline on terrifying. "You don't know anything about cinema, do you boy!" She cackled.

"Suppose I don't," I said calmly. "Why don't you enlighten me?"

I felt Gracie staring a hole through the side of my head, but I didn't care, I wanted to hear it from her, for there was nothing more I detested in the world than a completely ignorant person. I wasn't mad, but I wanted to make my stance known. We Arlingtons can be quite stubborn when we want to get our point across, and I also wanted to show Gracie that I was a man that wouldn't tolerate outlandish or crude behavior — even from drunk friends — I held myself to the same standard, and even though I had lost my head on the bottle more times than I could remember, I fully expected someone to come along and put me in my place if I were ever as out of line as she was.

"What, you've never seen Chester in a film before? Surely you must be joking?" Alice looked at me like a foolish child who knew nothing about anyone or anything, and I was amazed at her ability to control her personality, however, I still had no intention of giving up any ground.

"I'm not," I stated plainly, taking care to retain my cool.

"Ha!" She cackled again like a decrepit hag, and although she was pleasant enough physically for an older woman, that cackle made her appear fifteen years older. Then I thought of the story of Hansel and Gretel, in which I was Hansel, Gracie was Gretel, and Alice was the witch that aimed to ruin us, right there in the gaudy confides of her Westside cottage, but I would not go out like that — no, not tonight — for tonight I was Conrad Arlington, The Last True Artist, Savior from Los Angeles, and I would put this hack where she belonged.

"You're telling me you've never seen *A Night on Cherry Lane?*" She asked.

"Oh, don't listen to him Alice, of course he's seen it, haven't you Conrad?" Gracie couldn't stand it any longer, and for the first time I saw her emotions break through her powerful front in a reckless display of color. She looked at me with demanding, pleading eyes, and I knew exactly what I should do — I should shut my mouth, cut my losses, and drop the whole damned thing — but I didn't. Instead I looked Gracie right in the eye, and said —

"I'm afraid I haven't."

I instantly regretted the decision, for all light left Gracie's angelic face in that moment, and for the first time since I was with her I felt alone, and it was terrible. Nonetheless, I was going to finish the war I started with this madwoman. The way I saw it, if it wasn't for her insanity none of this would have ever started in the first place, and I would have never been forced to take such drastic action that led to the terrible guilt I was now feeling.

"Never?" Alice prodded, still speaking to me like she would to an infant.

"Conrad," Gracie stated.

I paid Gracie no attention, staring right back at Alice. "Never."

"Not even heard of it? I know you've at least heard of it, William."

"My name's not William."

"Conrad, stop!" Gracie was half demanding, half pleading with me to step down. Her blue eyes brimming with a watery gloss.

"I'll be patient. I'm a patient woman," Alice said.

"Lady, you can be as patient as you want to be, but I'm afraid I haven't heard a damned thing about your little film, probably because it's not worth hearing about in the least, if it even exists at all."

There was nothing but silence, and for a moment I thought Alice was going to up and burst into tears, but to my surprise she didn't, in fact the exact opposite happened.

"Ha!" She croaked with more raw force than ever. "I knew you were an amateur the moment I laid eyes on you!"

She became powerful in that moment, so much so that I wondered if I had really made the right decision in challenging her, but then it hit me — she truly believed these things she was saying — even if they were false, and I was a fool to allow it to come to this. I had compromised my integrity in Gracie's eyes, and I knew it, but the cat was out of the bag now. I had done it, I had pushed to far, and in that moment all laughter died, all good faith was extinguished from the room, the estranged became the stranger in her own home, and all stood deathly still on the Westside, awaiting the coming wrath in the dark.

"Chester was the lead in the film that made me who I am, you child! He is synonymous with my success! There is no Alice Button without Chester! He is my muse! My confidant! And I am his forever! Don't you see! You are nothing! You are a love-struck fool! And you will burn like the rest of them! You are a vagrant! A fame-seeking whore! And you will die cold and alone! And my name will live on forever! Forever on the Boulevard! I am the artist! I am the last auteur of world cinema, and Chester and I will never die, but we will live on forever!"

Suddenly, right in the midst of her raving, rage-like hysteria, Alice burst into tears — not just any tears — but deep tears of pure remorse, wretched sobs of pure displeasure, and it was horrible. She dropped the champagne bottle with a crash to the floor, and pulled herself across the room, supporting all her weight by the back of the couch, until she stood face to face with the big red figment of her own creation. She reeled her head back and looked up into the big, smiling eyes of Chester the cherry, and for a moment, smiled back, but that smile soon gave way to melancholy, and in one large burst of insane passion and with a loud shout she threw herself fully into the breadth of Chester's meaty body, giving her entire being to it completely as she crashed haggardly through its hollow structure, and landed with a grief-stricken crash on the floor, bursting once again into deep, sorrowful sobs that seemed to siphon any trace amount of joy from the air. It was a truly terrible sight — seeing a woman like that at such a low point — I wanted to comfort her, to make it all better, to tell her that Chester was real and that this would be all over in the morning, but that was lie, what was done was done, and there was nothing left to do but sit back and watch the aftermath of my own childishness play itself out.

I looked over at Gracie who sat stolid on the couch, her face drawn forward with all focus. Indeed, she wouldn't even look at me, and I felt if I were to touch her she would explode like lighting confined in a bottle. I wanted to apologize — I wanted to say a thousand things — but I felt the worst had happened that possibly could, and there was nothing at all to do about it now. We sat like that for what seemed like a great long while.

"I'm sorry," I eventually said, and I meant it.

With that, Gracie stood up in a determined flash, took a breath, and walked over to Alice who lay in shambles on the floor, next to scraps of Chester the cherry's tattered body and puddles of spilt champagne. With a little effort and encouragement Gracie helped Alice off the floor, and took her sobbing and weeping to her bedroom to put her down for the night. Once again I was left in the room, this time with no one to keep me company. I looked around at all the crowded art everywhere — the books, the paintings, the sculptures that filled every nook and cranny — and I wondered what it was that pressed a person to live like this, to hoard endless memories of years gone by, and then, through my strangled puzzlement my eyes landed once again on Chester's mangled torso. It was a dreadful sight, and despite having a gaping hole right through its midsection where Alice fell through, it still managed to stay standing somehow — all eight feet of it — still up on its big, fat feet and even more ominous and terrible than ever before, with those giant black pupils gazing down on me inside of big friendly ovals that seemed to sentence every inch of my irreconcilable judgment, and that broken, Cheshire cat smile that now lay in pieces on the floorboards, smiling back at me with cavernous emptiness reminding me of what a fool I'd been to ever think I could get the best of a big, giant cherry. I hated it. It was all to like me to let it come to this, and it was pathetic. The fact that I let something as ridiculous as a drunken woman and her bulbous muse potentially put a rift in my relationship with Gracie was positively maddening. I wanted to light what was left of that despicable cherry on fire, and let the source of my current demise go up in flames with the rest of that wretched place. I wanted to see it all burn!

Then suddenly, I stopped, and I felt a great deal of pity and remorse begin to grow deep within the pit of my stomach. My heart rate subsided, and my anger gave away to reason, and my rage to thankfulness, for I was alive and still young, and I had my youth, and whatever had happened to poor Alice Button that turned her into whoever she was had not yet happened to me, and I hoped it never would. Then suddenly I felt sick again, sick to my stomach, and I realized how cruel the world could be to some people

— good, nice people, people that didn't deserve pain at all — and then tears flooded my eyes, then subsided again before they broke, and in the pool of my utmost remorse, I wondered if I would ever be a good person.

CHAPTER 5
— THE GHOSTS OF SUNSET BOULEVARD —

Gracie and I entered the car and then just sat for a moment — neither of us really knew what to say, but we knew we had to say something.

"Gracie…" I began to apologize.

"It's not your fault, Conrad," she interrupted.

"I think it is."

"No, it's not. This isn't the first time it's happened, I should have told you sooner. Her career might be over now, but she is still a good person, and she is still my friend. Are you okay with that?"

Gracie spoke very deliberately. I could tell that it was very difficult for her, and I felt a great deal of guilt that she even had to ask me such a question. It was then that I knew that Gracie was a completely true person, and I wanted to tell her how brave she was — how good she was — I wanted to tell her that she had a beautiful spirit, and a beautiful mind, and so many other beautiful qualities that made her an absolutely magnificent human being, but I didn't — I did not yet have the right to.

"Of course." I said strongly, and I let that be the end of it.

Suddenly, unable to hold on any longer, Gracie burst into tears. "Oh Conrad, I should have told you." She buried her face into my shoulder. "It's all my fault. I'm horrible, absolutely horrible!"

I patted her shoulder. "Gracie, it's okay."

"Don't hate her. Please don't hate her. She's a good person," Gracie pleaded. "She's been hurt, but she's still good, she's still good. Oh, please don't hate her, Conrad, please."

Gracie was in a fit of emotional tears. I felt awful. I didn't know what to do. She was so sensitive, so fragile, and I had done enough damage already, but she needed to be comforted — that was what she wanted — so I did the only logical thing a man in that situation can do.

"Gracie," I said strong and stern, grabbing her by the shoulders, then I proceeded to speak very clearly, point by point. "I don't hate her — I know she is a good person — it's going to be alright."

She froze up for a moment and just stared at me. There was so much sincerity and trust in her eyes I could hardly stand it.

"Really?" She asked. "Do you mean it?"

"Yes," I said, looking as deep into those crystal eyes as I possibly could. "Yes."

There was a moment, then I saw it sink in.

"Good. Then let's not talk any more about it, alright?"

I agreed in silence. Then Gracie straightened herself up in the passenger seat.

"I don't know about you, but I'm all dressed up. I'm not at all sufficiently drunk, and I think there's still some fun to be had this evening."

I smiled. "Where to, Madam?"

"Just drive," she commanded lightly, rolling back her eyes with a faint smile.

We drove, and it felt great to leave that house behind — the whole decadent Westside for that matter — and I became increasingly happier with each mile we distanced ourselves from it. There was still a lot of magic in the air that night, and I was delighted to hear that Gracie still wanted to try and make something of the evening, and I felt — at least for the moment — that I had dodged a bullet of some kind, either way, I considered myself to be extremely lucky, and made it a point to watch my mouth from then on. I took the north route up through Westwood, past the UCLA campus, until I hit Sunset Boulevard on which I turned east. It wasn't the fastest route back to Hollywood, but I figured the long, windy turns through the hills would help take our minds off everything and give us a fresh perspective, which I figured we'd both appreciate.

In truth I was right, and through the dark I could see Gracie's posture grow more and more content with the current state of things, and I felt like a man that had his car, and his girl, and there wasn't much more in the world for me to do but drive, taking the dips and turns through the nighttime mist.

After what felt like a while, we took the final S-bend turn out of the Sunset Canyons and flattened off in Beverly Hills, where Sunset Boulevard goes straight for a few miles and runs perfectly between the picturesque mansions of the make-believe city. I always had mixed feelings about Beverly Hills, not intentionally so like some people seemed to have, but there was something inherently false about it that I could never put my finger on. I also realized that was a clichéd way to feel, and I didn't pride myself on it, but I figured if enough people felt a certain way about a place, then there must be at least something about it that feeling that was true. That said, I did love to drive through it, and there was something about all that fame, and all that glamour, and all that privilege that suspended a feeling of importance, and yes, the money, how could one forget the money. The air was so rich with money that it seemed to flow right out of the hills and spill right onto Sunset Boulevard, and then continued its trickling down through West Hollywood until it reached mid-town and then eventually dissolved just past the 10 freeway. It was nothing worth thinking about, however — not for two virtuosos like us — so I opened the window and let the cool, crisp air whisk the thought away.

It was deep into the night by the time we reached the bright lights of the Sunset Strip, and the bars and clubs were in full swing. No sooner had we reached its entrance then I hit a wall of traffic that crawled on and on, and to the untrained traveler it probably looked more like rush hour on a Friday evening than one o'clock on a Wednesday night. There was plenty to look at, however, as there always was, and neither Gracie nor I found any reason to complain, rather, we both seemed to be enjoying the pleasant silence of each other's company — young and alive and glorious — there was no point mucking all that up with words. After a while, the traffic evened out and I once again realized that I had never really bothered to ask her where it was we were going. It wasn't until Gracie told me to turn left off the Boulevard that I finally made the discovery, for word had been getting around about a fairly exclusive night spot that had just opened in the area, and I knew the second we veered off to the left that it was exactly where we were headed. I learned to expect these kinds of things from Gracie, and I didn't bother to question it, because it wasn't worth questioning. If it was expensive, and it was exclusive, then Gracie knew about it first, and if we were going it meant it was worth going to.

"Don't you want to valet?" I asked.

"I want to walk tonight," she stated plainly, and after that came no more words.

We parked in the hills just above the Strip and walked a few blocks through the neighborhood in silence. The air was still and cold, and I saw Gracie wrap her arms around her little, shivering body from the corner of my eye, and it was all I could do to keep myself from grabbing her and pulling her tight to me. I wanted her close to me. I wanted to keep her warm, but I knew that I was still on trial as I walked next to her, and that I was closer to her now than few men had ever been, and I did not yet have the courage to attempt it. We neared the Strip, its bright lights and rushing cars flickering just beyond the darkness, and suddenly I felt something slight and warm against the palm of my hand, and realized Gracie's fingers had found a way to find mine. She rested them there, as if wrestling with whether or not it was safe for her to commit, and taking the initiative I ran my fingers through hers and intertwined them with mine, and together we emerged out onto the Boulevard.

We walked east a block or so and came to a little hole in the wall. A big guard stood in front of the door in a black business suit, and I figured this wasn't the kind of place you could just walk into unless you were someone worth knowing or knew someone worth knowing inside. He apparently saw us coming because he smiled wide when he saw Gracie, and I figured it probably wasn't his standard way of greeting people.

"Gracie Garrison, long time no see," he said as we drew near. "How are you, honey?"

"I'm good, Bill. Yourself?"

"I'm fine, baby. I see you got a friend tonight."

"This is Conrad. Bill — Conrad," Gracie said, quickly introducing us.

"Hi," I said bluntly.

I didn't like the way he was talking to her. In fact I didn't like the way a lot of guards talked to women — especially this one — and the addition of his big, hulking, presence only added to my discomfort. He nodded without a word, for he was far more interested in Gracie, so much so that I was little more than nonexistent, and I felt a burning desire to make him pay for his disrespect, but I needed at least another hundred pounds to do any real damage, so I spared myself a beating and held my tongue.

"Listen, Bill, I know it's late, but we got held up earlier and we really just want to run in quickly and say hello."

"You don't have to explain yourself to me, honey," he said with a cheeky smile, then, looking at me, "I'm sure you got your reasons."

I couldn't tell whether that was a compliment or a threat as he unlatched the velvet rope.

"It's good inside I hope?" Gracie asked in passing.

"Oh it's mellow, but not bad for a Wednesday night."

We entered the lounge, and whatever he meant by mellow, I'm not sure, but the place was jam-packed. This was young Hollywood's playground, the new world, the beginning and the end of old money, and I knew that the overpriced cocktails and glorified booth seating only lead to one thing. Then, suddenly, I felt a wave of hopelessness for the human race — a bunch of animals, a bunch of fools in the dark — and I knew that this was where true art came to die, and I felt like less of an artist for being there. I scowled from the edge of the crowd, and wanted more than anything to turn and walk out the same way I came, but then I felt Gracie's hand squeeze mine, and as long as I was with her I knew that I could do anything, so I squeezed back, and together we plunged into the pulsing sea of lost souls.

It was dark, and loud, and the crowd was so thick I couldn't even see two feet in front of me. From all sides, beautiful, reckless bodies of fallen aristocracy banged against me, searching for meaning in the dark. Like ghosts they were — those heiresses of the Boulevard — poor, neglected souls with no true love, no moral fiber, and like hollow vessels they floated around me, looking to fill their empty catacombs with love reserved for another, craving that which I would not give. I did not hate them, for it was not by any fault of their own that they were nothing to me, for everything in their lives consisted of only paper, and everything that was once good was now sullen ash, and then like hungry ghouls they drifted past, their hot breaths lingering on the conscious surfaces of my neck, and yet they were nothing, nothing at all, just beautiful faces in the dark.

I managed to hold onto Gracie's guiding hand the whole way through until we emerged on the other side into a little private enclave that was reserved for a specific class of people.

"Do you want a drink?" Gracie yelled.

"What?" I yelled back.

"Do — you — want — a — drink?" She spelled it out for me.

"Please!"

She had a bartender make us two vodka tonics from the center table, and then we proceeded to drink. I intended to drink as much as was necessary to dull myself down to a level where I could at least attempt to enjoy the time. We both downed our first glass in about a minute, and then proceeded with our second as Gracie attempted to introduce me to a few of her friends over the surging noise. From what I could make out in the dark, two of them were tall, boyishly handsome, well-dressed gentlemen and the other a cute little model that reminded me a bit of Evie, at least from what I could tell, and even in the dim light I could see the silhouette of a gorgeous body. It was a rather empty introduction overall, for I couldn't hear their names, and I figured they couldn't hear mine, so I just reciprocated the pre-determined nodding of the head, and the fake smile which I took to be standard for a place like this, and coincided to have a good time.

Thirty minutes in and about five much needed cocktails later, things started to pick up. The place started to feel less dull, and my inhibitions — which so often got the best of me early on — began to come down a bit. I knew that Gracie wanted to be here for some reason or other, and even though I didn't know what it was, I decided that was good enough for me, and I would continue to take advantage of the free alcohol that was so readily being pushed in my direction. I stood by myself on the edge of the social, which was my usual way, and then a young man that claimed he was a director came up to me. We talked for a few minutes, pretending to understand what each other were saying, but that eventually died out and he meandered aimlessly back into the crowd to engage the next unfortunate chap that found himself standing alone. As the party swirled around me, I could only think of Gracie, and I felt content. I had realized by now there was no controlling the girl. She was going to do what she wanted to do when she wanted to do it — just like at the gallery — and I had confidence that if she wanted to find me she would, and I allowed that thought to have the space it needed to breathe.

Sure enough, after about five more minutes I saw her pretty blonde head appear behind a group of people and she came my way. She walked right up to me. She didn't say anything — I couldn't have heard her if even if she did — it was that time of night, the music was surreal, and the alcohol had finally caught up with the both of us, daring us to take the risks we'd never take. I looked right back at her, our eyes darting back and forth off each other, feeling each other's impulses, exploring each other's energy. Her body screamed to be touched, and in a burst of courage I extended a trying hand, then allowed it to fall softly, grazing her slender hip, and I felt a rush leap up my entire body, landing in my heart, which began to beat faster, and then faster still. Gracie's crystal eyes swooned back, and then her eyelids closed around them, and her body began to sway, and before I knew it we were dancing with each other, and time slowed all around us, and existence held its breath, and the pleasure of feeling her against me created its own eternity, an eternity that was completely ours, and it was overbearing. I decided right then and there that I could die in that moment and never think twice about it, but that sweet scent that fell off her in waves kept me grounded in mortality, down here, somewhere with the living.

Then suddenly I became aware. I could feel them looking at us, those creatures of the night, both man and woman, wanting to take what we had and make it their own. I felt them closing in around us. I grew intensely cold, and Gracie stopped, and she looked up at me with eyes like doves, wanting to understand, but she couldn't, for this was her world, a world of reproductions, imitations, and counterfeit romances, and I would have no part in it, not anymore. I held her at bay by her hips, and felt her warmth reaching towards me, the only lovely thing in a deathly room, and I wanted to pull her into me, I wanted to believe it was everything that I thought it was, but I could not — I could not lie to myself — and I would not play this game anymore. Then I did it, with all suffering I did it, and I pushed her away from me. Her eyes melted against my steel resolve, and I felt the art inside of me scream its victory as it pierced my fleshy heart, and once again I could feel all emotion. I could feel the lifeblood rushing through my veins. I could feel my mind processing, and my breathing became true, for I was not false, no, I was not a false person. I was Conrad Arlington, The Last True Artist, and I did not have to have her. I did not have to have this creature from the garden, this creature from another world, and I would not be controlled. Then I felt the great light leave me, and the darkness press in all around, and I knew that this was real, that this was reality, and I would not use her as a shield. I would not use her as a sword. I would not forge my artistic battles in the drudges of a fabricated actuality, no, I would face the blackest dusk, the deepest regions of dark — the ghosts, the ghouls, the fallen ones — the creatures that hide at night and beg not to be uncovered, and I would conquer every single one of them, for there was a truth in me — a truth that burned beautiful and bright — and I would not be deceived.

And then a dream took me, and I watched from five feet away as a young girl's heart broke, as little pools of glass that filled trusting eyes spilled out, and ran tortured down murky cheeks where they dropped in all suffering to the floor, and then I saw death, and dying, and the haunting of one's soul that comes from missed opportunities, the emptiness that comes from not knowing love at a young age, and the bleakness of a life lived alone, from being too consumed by true art to see true art where it stood, there, in the form of a girl, beautiful, and broken, who was reaching out for a solid surface on which to finally rest, and then I saw pain, and suffering, and strife, and all the loneliness of fractured loves in the world flash before my eyes, and I knew right then that I could not do that to this girl. I could not do that to such a blameless creature, sent from heaven to the earth, to be preserved as white as snow is to eternity, for I was the stranger in her world, and my passage would be judged forever.

My front melted, and I held out my arms, and the distance between us shortened until the contours of her slender body fell into the hard lines of mine, and her face rested against my chest, and we fit together perfectly like one piece of a puzzle to another, then slowly, in the presence of the great wide open our bodies began to make amends, there, in the midst of all uncertainty, amidst the multitudes of the ghosts, and the goblins, and ghouls, we followed our reconciliation to its end, to the beautiful dawning of its epic closure.

Gracie nodded, and I knew that it was time to go. She grabbed my hand tightly, this time like a vice, and we plunged back into the deep sea of reckless bodies. Our resolve was solid, and it radiated off us with so much brilliance that the ghosts did not bother us, but parted before us with the utmost consent. There was no more fear to feed on, no insecurity to call their own, for there were certain things in existence that should not be tampered with — the makings of true love was one of them — and even the villainous knew the consequences.

We reached the other side and left the darkness behind, stepping out into the shining lights of Sunset Boulevard, and I felt the moisture of the night on my face, and the smell of clean air as it filled my nostrils, washing away the sweaty stench of lonely, aimless bodies. I looked at Gracie and smiled, and she smiled back, and in that moment we both felt lucky to be standing next to each other. She rested her head on my shoulder, and we stood there for a while, taking it in, making peace with the silence and the traffic and the lights, and I felt like a man, content with his girl, right there, right on the edge of the Boulevard, and I could have stayed like that forever.

CHAPTER 6
— THE ROMANTIC CONSIDERS —

I felt Gracie shiver next to me, which I took as my signal that it was time to go — to take this lovely thing home and get her warm — so I gave her hand a squeeze, she lifted her head from my shoulder, and we turned to walk back towards my car. Now, I wish I could have said it was then that the universe had been at peace with us, content with the understanding we showed each other in those moments, with our silence, with our happiness, and then reasoned to reward us accordingly for being good, young things of the world, but as we reached the end of the block, the night revealed that it had no such intention.

There was a loud honking of a horn. We turned and a terrific black limousine pulled over to the shoulder next to us. The window rolled down revealing three of Gracie's friends from inside — the two boyishly handsome gentlemen who looked somewhat alike, and the one girl whom I thought looked a bit like Evie through the darkness earlier, but now that I could see clearly she really looked nothing like her in actuality — very beautiful — but much different. Clearly well liquored, they all smiled stupidly, and they reeked of raw privilege, so much so that I could practically feel the irresponsibility of an endless trust fund emanating off them. Still, they were a very attractive trio — I had to give them that — and the fact that they still looked charming without the shroud of covering darkness testified to their nobility as being genetically gifted. This wasn't all that surprising, after all, they were Gracie's friends, but it mattered very little to me in the moment, for I was tired, and annoyed, and before they could open their mouths to speak I already had a bad feeling about what could happen if we stuck around long enough to allow it.

"Gracie!" One of the boys yelled through the window — he was the first to open his mouth — "Where did you go?"

We kept walking, and the limo rolled slowly along beside us, keeping pace.

"Oh Harry, we wanted to stay, we really did, but we were so tired you see."

"Nonsense," the other boy said. "We're going to another party. You're coming with us."

"Of course I already know about it. You're going to Bobby's."

"So?"

"So, if I wanted to go we would be going, and I told you we're tired."

"Oh, come on. You know it's never a party without Gracie Garrison around. You can even bring your friend here."

"Conrad." I said bluntly.

"It's alright," said Harry lightly. "I'm Harry, in case you don't remember."

"I wouldn't expect him to," mocked the other boy.

Harry brushed him off. "This idiot here is my brother, Alex, and that's our cousin Gwendolyn over there. She just got in from New York. Quite the catch she is. She doesn't talk much, even though she moved out her to pursue, ahem," he cleared his throat, "the film business."

I didn't doubt it, for she was beautiful — more actress than model — with dark hair and dark eyes like Evie, except slightly shorter and little more filled out in all the right places that the camera seemed to love. She gave Harry a shy slap and then stole a glance in my direction, and I felt Gracie's arm tighten slightly around mine as she did.

"You can't just show up to Harry's birthday party and then proceed to go home early, you'll drive him crazy," said Alex. "You know how deeply he's in love with you, that's all he ever talks about."

"That's right," continued Harry. "And nothing else. It will drive me positively mad."

This time it was my arm that tightened around Gracie's, and I didn't even have to look at her to tell her how I felt about my competition — she knew.

"Come on, get in already, or we'll be here all night," said Alex.

"Hold on," Gracie said, then turned to face me. "Let's go."

"Whatever you want." I said as neutrally as possible. I didn't want to force her to choose, and I didn't want to influence her either. She didn't owe me anything, at least not yet, but she knew where I stood, and I wasn't going to budge either way.

"Oh Connie, come on. Tonight's been one emotional high after another. Let's have a good time while we still can. It will be fun, I promise."

"I thought we were having fun."

"We are."

"Well, I'm tired, and I have my car, so I can't go either way, but if you want to go, then go."

"Do you mean it?"

I wanted her to choose me, but I smiled anyway. "Of course."

I didn't know why she wanted to go so badly. It was like she was holding onto some distant idea of a night that was not meant to be, and was grasping at everything in her means to see that it still managed to happen. If there was one thing about life and girls I already knew, it was that forcing a situation rarely worked — if it didn't happen naturally it wouldn't happen at all — and unlike the others I knew that this night of all nights was not my last night on earth, for there was always tomorrow to look forward to, but Gracie didn't seem to get that at all.

"Won't you meet us there? Please," she begged.

"Gracie, there will be other nights."

"But I want to go tonight!"

"Then go."

"I want to go tonight, and I want you to be there."

"Why?"

"Because I want you to, that's why. You promised you wouldn't ask questions."

Indeed, it was a low blow, but she had me cornered, and as much as I didn't want to admit it, she was right — in theory at least.

"You're right."

"What's that?"

"I said you're right."

"Thank you," she said snobbishly, then turned and walked towards the limousine with the entitlement of a French queen.

This sudden change in her behavior struck a particular chord in me, one that I was not at all okay with, and as much as I detested myself for it, I felt an overwhelming desire to correct this girl — some deep seeded resentment of a self-destructive origin beckoning me to punish her for this unacceptable behavior. Maybe it was the Arlington in me, or maybe it was just my pride, but as I watched her perfect body sway tightly back and forth as she moved away from me, enticing me, daring me to do anything otherwise, I knew that there stood a girl that got everything in the world she ever wanted —whenever she wanted — but she would not have me so easily.

"I'm not going." I stated it flatly.

Gracie stopped cold, turned on her heel, and faced me with more wrath than I had ever witnessed in such a slight person.

"Look here man, what's the problem?" Harry called out from the vehicle.

I paid him no attention. Either did Gracie.

"What?" Gracie asked, slow and cold.

"I'm not going and that's the end of it."

"Conrad," she said with a surprising lightness. "Get your car, dear, I'll see you at the party." She turned and continued towards the limousine.

"I won't be there," I said again, using as much disinterest as I could muster.

She didn't say anything for a moment. She just turned and stewed at me like a small, stubborn child that received the wrong toy for Christmas, and was then either going to pout their way to a new one or raise hell altogether. There was something very enduring about all of it, and despite my agitation with the childish display I couldn't help but lift a smile, one that started slow and landed perfectly amused before it broke, and it did nothing at all to help the situation.

"What are you smiling at, Conrad?" She asked, the lightness of her veil threatening to burst into flames.

"You."

"What?"

"You — I'm smiling at you." There was a pause. The way I said it was so awfully pointed I was surprised it came from my mouth, but she had me going, dammit, and there was little I could do to stop it now. "Now, I'm tired, and I'm going home. So, you can either come with me now, or ask one of your darling gentlemen to take you home later."

The sharp language snapped like a whip and landed hard against the icy wall of Gracie's cold, impenetrable front, and once again I was inundated with instant regret, one of self-hatred and deep loathing, for I saw Gracie's eyes once again turn to glass, and her thin mouth quiver against stringy blonde ringlets that came cascading down all around, and I felt like the cruelest person in the universe, but I had to stand, I had to show her what I was, and I knew those eyes, and I knew that blonde hair, and I knew that as long as they existed so would the deep tumultuousness of my eternal digression, and I could either deal with that fact, or I couldn't, and I resolved right there that I would.

"Goodbye, Conrad." Gracie stated, restraining the tears in her eyes, and then she bent her ivory neck, threw back her head, and entered the limousine.

I put my hands in my pockets and stood hard and strong, straining against all strain not to be affected. I wanted to run to her, I wanted to pull her out of that wretched, godforsaken vehicle and hold her tightly to me and tell her I was sorry. I wanted to kiss her! But my pride would not let me move, and like an anvil it bore its ugly head down on me, and forced me to watch as she took her place on another man's lap, and I felt helpless against it.

"See you later, mate," Harry said. "I hope you stop by."

I just stared at her through the open side door, laughing, smiling, continuing to weave the same intrinsic pattern of her glamorous life as though she had never met me in the first place, as though I was nothing but a breath to her, just another poor schmuck standing on the Boulevard desperate for a glance of true recognition. Then, against what was her steady fashion, I saw the pretense of her body switch. She looked over at me, and in that final moment she gave herself away, and I saw in those eyes that it wasn't true, that I had gotten to her, that I had left a mark on an area where no marks had been left for some time, that I had struck some carnal fiber in her being that said I was perhaps a man worth having, that I was good, clean, and bright — a beacon of feeling in the emptiness of the night — and that she was indeed drifting away from me.

Then that open door closed, and the brightness of life was shut out by the monotony of tinted glass, and I felt the great sickness return as the car pulled away from the curb and joined the river of faceless souls that flowed on forever. Oh, how I hated it! That wretched Boulevard! The way it shined shameless in the face of human suffering! The way it scoffed blatantly at the pursuit of truth! It was false, an eternal funnel of lies and decadence! It was filthy! Sick! Corrupt! The way it trailed on forever, weaving its way into the night like a black snake waiting to strike anything and everything that was good. I wanted to kill it, to slice off its head, to be done with it. I wanted to wipe its immoral existence from the face of creation! I wanted to smear its brazen corpse down the vile streets of its own construction, until all its evil was extinguished and there was nothing left but good on its ruined foundation! That was my plea as I stood face to face with the cars, with the traffic, with the lights, but I was beaten. My mind was battered and I had lost. I had let go of the truth that I so longed for. I had let go of this bright creature from the heavens. I had let the terrible dark ones whisk her away from me, and I would never be forgiven! No, I would never forgive myself! Never! My life was forfeit! All art was dead! All good conquered! Oh, that wretched Boulevard! Such a terrible place it was then! It was my tormentor, and I had become its victim.

No! I would not stand for it! I would not fail! I was not a coward! I was not false! I was Conrad Arlington! The Last True Artist, defender of true art, true love, and guardian of heavenly things! I would not lose, I would not let this irreverent establishment of concrete, and steel, and flesh become my enemy! I would not be deceived by any falsehood! I would open my eyes to it! I would choose to see the good! To see the truth! Art! Art! Come back to me! Gracie come back to me! Now is the time! Go forth, young man! Go and get her! Go and get your girl!

I turned and I sprinted down the Boulevard like a fugitive running for his life, then, realizing I didn't have the address, I turned and sprinted back towards my only possible source — that godforsaken nightclub — I moved past the guard with deliberation, and with perfect focus I plunged back into the sea of ghosts, where their empty bodies still crowded and floated together vacantly in a hopeless quest for artificial fulfillment, but I would have none of it. My resolve was set. I moved with all purpose until I emerged on the other side of the crowd, where the lone director I had met earlier now sat with a girl who looked like she had no idea where she was or what she was doing. He didn't seem to mind, however, and the sight of them slumped over on each other was dismal at best.

"Hey!" I yelled.

There was no response, and it was then I realized that they were both asleep from intoxication, shrouded by the darkness. So I slapped him awake.

"Wha — what's going on," he said, opening his eyes and moving them a little.

"Do you remember me?" I asked pointedly.

He noticed the girl on his arm — who wasn't half bad looking — and a kind of sick grin spread across his face.

"I need to find out where they went," I continued. "Harry and the group. You're friends with them, aren't you?"

"Hey, leave me alone will ya'? Can't you see I'm with a girl."

"Does she know that?"

"Well, o' course she does. She's here ain't she?" He grabbed her drunken corpse and pulled her tightly to him.

She groaned a slobbery groan. The poor girl looked like she couldn't be much older than eighteen, if that. It was despicable, but I wasn't interested in his business. I just wanted to hear what I needed to know and get out of there as quickly as possible.

"I'm suppose to go to the next party, but I don't have the address. Would you kindly give it to me." It wasn't a question, but I did my best to shroud the demand in smart word choice.

"Buzz off." He started rising to his feet, the poor girl clinging to his waist as if he was actually worth clinging to.

"Hey!" I said sharply, holding out a strong arm, which caught him mid-rise and sent him crashing back down to his seat where he looked at me in a drunken mix of fear and stupidity. "There's no need for any of this. You talked to me earlier tonight, and you know who I am. Harry invited me to the party, and I asked you nicely, so kindly give me the address."

Desperate to salvage what remained of his drunken night, he quickly complied and gave me the information I asked for, and as I turned to leave I was surprised at my own deliberation. I was by no means a physical person by any standard sense of the word, but I could be ridiculously passionate when I wanted something, and that passion would turn to aggression if my body perceived it necessary to do so, and in this case, it did. I felt good, and strong, and ready to take on anything else the unforeseeable night had in store for me. So intense was this feeling of insurmountable invincibility that it carried me through the sea of ghosts with little to no recognition of them, and before my awareness returned to me, I was already back in my coupe, racing down Sunset Boulevard, in pursuit of the girl who once again got away from me.

***

Once clear of the Strip, the traffic opened up past Fairfax leaving nothing but blank pavement and glowing street lights in my path as I raced back towards Hollywood, the place that I had come to know so well in the last few years, and the place where the truest of ambitions could live fully, turn, and then die just as easily if that same truth was lost, and so it was that I existed, right where it all began, with the addition of the other, and faced with a series of choices in which I would have to choose but one possible course of action. What that action would become, I did not yet know, for I was driving off impulse — I was a pressed man, a driven man — and from some great refusal of failure I prayed that at least an ounce of goodness would come from it, and enough patience and understanding could be generated that I could be who I needed to be when I needed to be him, and then, from that same source of honest worth, from that same soulish sense of self that was constantly searching for real integrity, I might become who I was striving so desperately to be — a true person.

I turned north onto Highland off Sunset and followed it to a little enclave of new, expensive, high-rise apartments just east across the street from Hollywood and Highland. This was the new Hollywood — the new money — the land of the wealthy transplants and the oil barons and the trust fund children and the heiresses who were gone, ghosting down the Boulevard in the darkness, indeed, there was little personality here, only glass, and steel, and construction, and shards of broken souls attempting to create something of a whole — there was no history here, and if there could be, it was yet to be made.

I eventually found a tight parking spot into which I could fit my coupe, and I zoomed in with expert precision. I then stepped out and admired my handy work, letting the downright expertise of it all fill my confidence. That was another gift I prided myself to having — I could drive, in fact I could drive with best of them — and I really only had my father's side of the family to thank for that.

Getting what I needed from it I turned to walk on, and I dealt with the reality of what it was that I was indeed doing, and what it would look like, and what it would ultimately mean. The truth of the matter was, I was chasing after a girl. I, Conrad Arlington, The Last True Artist, was chasing after a girl — that meant something — I had never known love before, not true love, not honest love, and before me I had the great task of finding out what that was. And then there was Gracie, sweet and eternal Gracie, all crystal and glass, the pristine golden girl, the mysterious bundle of traits, talents, and personality more rare than diamonds, the girl that men chased after forever, and then when forever came, chased after some more. Yes, I had to deal with that as well — what that would look like to her, and what that also would ultimately mean to us both.

"This girl," I mumbled as I exited the elevator onto the tenth floor of the high-rise. "Either we'll make history or she'll be the death of me."

I came to the apartment number that the director gave me, then knocked loudly and rang multiple times to make sure I was heard over the music that was blaring from inside, and I knew that whatever was waiting for me beyond those walls, it was either friendly, hostile, or a little bit of both, and I couldn't have been more eager to find out.

Someone blindly opened the door from inside, giving the impression that it had magically swung open by itself, and as I gazed lucidly at the new environment that expanded before me, it would have been quite possible to believe that it did. The apartment was beautiful — standard, but beautiful — good enough to call a temporary home for most members of high society, but it wasn't the magnificent splendor of its halls that made it so alluring. No, it wasn't the splendor at all. It was the women, and the women alone that had my attention. Never in my life had I seen such women, sucked, and pumped, and tucked, and nipped to an ideal of scientific perfection that was almost inhuman in shape and form — yes, that's what they were — scientific, that's exactly it. They were not beautiful. No, I would not venture to call them beautiful, for that was not the right word. They were not like Gracie. They were not natural, or bright, or wonderful, or elegant, or true, or even good for that matter, but rather pure creatures of carnal desire, sexual goddesses in storybook form, come back from ancient times to taunt and tantalize and seduce and steal from the foolish men of the world, and what I feared the most was that somewhere, buried beneath all that truth, and love, and reconciliation that I claimed to build my life upon, I might be one of those men, that I might be one of those fools that had the ability to lose everything to one of these creatures, and as I walked into that room I knew it was true. The moment I crossed the threshold into that den of ambiguity, amongst the stares, and the desires, and the lascivious thoughts, I knew that I was every bit as fallen as every one of those men, and I had to be extremely careful, for I was there to find Gracie, nothing more.

"Conrad!"

I turned and saw Harry pushing his way through the dense crowd of lucid flesh. He seemed to be all right, however, at least compared to the majority of his well-liquored company — actually, he looked better than all right, he looked practically brand new — he finally reached me, and stuck out his hand, which I took.

"Harry," he said.

"I know." That was three times I had met him now, I hoped there wouldn't be a fourth.

"Listen, I'm glad you're here."

"Why's that?"

"Look, I think we got off to a bad start. You probably think I'm a regular prick for whisking your girl away — it is bad form, I know — I wouldn't worry too much about it though, we're old friends. I've known Gracie for a long time, and if she's interested anyone tonight it would have to be you because she hasn't been the same since she left the club."

He seemed rather eager to apologize, and I could tell by his voice that he was sincere.

"Don't worry about it — where is she?"

"She's fine. She's in the back with Alex. She's been chain smoking since she got here. Oh, and don't even get me started about the ride over. She was absolutely maniacal, colder than I've ever seen her."

I had to admit I was not expecting this. Although I wasn't exactly proud of it, I felt a slight bit of satisfaction knowing that she was outside torturing herself for leaving me, especially after all we had been through together that night, and all I had done with her, and said to her, and made known to her. I wondered what she thought of me. She probably thought I was off somewhere doing something grand without her, living some kind of vicarious life and doing all sorts of vicarious things without her by my side — maybe even seeing another girl — and although I would never consider such a thing within the context of a legitimate relationship, we were not yet together. That was the truth. Then once again that Great Arlington Pride rose up within me, and amidst all the tiredness, and the emotion, and the passion of the night, I felt myself succumbing to its devious, self-destructive charm, and against my own true desires, I gave myself to it completely.

"Serves her right," I said bluntly, "leaving me like that. I shouldn't even be here." It felt good saying it, but rather vile at the same time, and the stench of it hung in the air like a soiled towel on a clothesline that had not been properly washed.

"That's the spirit mate," said Harry, patting my back cheerfully. "There's too many beautiful women in the world to ever go with just one. It's good to see you're a reasonable man. Look around, there's plenty to be had."

That was probably the first thing Harry had said all night that I couldn't completely disagree with. The gathering was an outright feast of human flesh, nothing more, and nothing less — bone, body, blood — human beings blown out of proportion piling on top of each other like chickens for the slaughter. If there was ever such a thing as absolute iniquity, this was it, and I was stricken with the horrid images of Sodom and Gomorrah that were pounded into me as a child. "Abstain! Abstain! Abstain!" The priest or the pastor or whoever would say. "Abstain or be destroyed like the Sodomites!" I hated all that eternal damnation garbage. It never did an ounce of good for me. Still, it was very visceral, and it took a bit of effort to vanquish the terrible images of earthquakes, and burning cities, and miserable salt pillars in favor of a good time. Tonight, I was going to follow what was true, that was all, and if I did not yet know what that was, I would just have to venture out and find it, and so, reasoning myself a justified man — a man of flesh, and blood, and true feeling — I let my hungry eyes dance freely across the array of life, in search of some forbidden pleasure to be had.

"Does she want to see me?" I asked.

"Sure does. I'd put pretty much anything on that."

And then my eyes rested on Gwendolyn — that ridiculous creature from New York. Picturesque in sexuality, cousin to Harry and Alex, and out to pursue 'the film business' — she was dancing with another girl, and judging by the way they related to each other I could only assume 'film business' meant one thing. However, I resolved that tonight I would pass no judgment, indeed, I really had no right to, and so I allowed physicality to step in and fill my heart with lust, all in hopes to spite a creature far more heavenly and beautiful than I deserved in life itself, and once again I played the role of the arrogant fool.

"Tell her I'm here," I said, throwing back my head. "Tell her I'm having a grand ol' time, and if she wants to see me she can come out here and see for herself."

"Ah, I see what you're doing. The ol' jealousy card, eh?" Harry said, nudging my arm.

"Whoever said anything about jealousy?"

"Well that's what you're doing, ain't ya? Trying to make her jealous and all. Works on most girls, sure, works like a charm, but I'm telling you mate, a girl like Gracie, she's different. That jealously stuff won't work on her. I've tried it before. If you really like her, just tell her how you feel, that will up your chances mate, you'll see."

"I won't see anything," I said with rising strength, unable to hide my hostility.

"Look here man, there's no need for that. I'm only trying to help."

I was full in it now. I was committed, and I didn't need a lecture from some 'chum,' especially not the one I blamed for me being here in the first place.

"Harry, it seems to me that if you tried to make her jealous, and she didn't get jealous, it's because there was nothing to get jealous about in the first place." It came out in such a self-righteous way that I felt like the afterbirth of some overly involved aristocrat.

Harry just looked at me for a moment. "I'll tell her for you mate."

"Thank you."

Harry sulked away from me back into the lucid sea of flesh, and I felt completely horrible, and completely devious, and completely amazing at the same time, for I was the creator of my own destiny, and whatever choices I made was because I wanted to make them, so I grabbed a cocktail, and headed in the direction of Gwendolyn and her audience of languid immortals.

Gwendolyn! Oh, Gwendolyn of New York!
She saw me coming from clear across the room. In fact, she
had been keeping one eye on me ever since I entered that
apartment, and so I approached her. It was true what her
cousins said about her — she didn't say much, but what she
lacked in verbal cues she more than made up for in raw
physicality. This was a creature that was built for non-
verbal communication. She never even had to open her
mouth as far as I was concerned. Her nature was purely
carnal, and only in my darkest of depravities would I allow
my mind to consider a woman like this. I was but two feet
away from her, standing there, staring her down like a
predator stares down its prey, and she stood frozen —
caught — like a deer in the headlights, her eyes dark and
lusty, and I could tell that there was no spirit behind them,
only drifts and echoes. Her full lips gave way to a sensual
smile, and she turned to one of her immortal
contemporaries and kissed her on the mouth in the deepest
of ways, and I felt my body involuntarily lurch like a
vehicle suddenly thrown out of transmission, then she
turned back towards me with all desire, and I knew that I
was doomed.

Then once again a dark vision took me, and I
watched a beautiful girls heart break as two blue mirrors
spilled liquid glass onto the floor, and that glass turned to
red satin and rose up in ribbons that wrapped themselves
around my neck, and I couldn't breath. I couldn't move. I
could only watch as perfection was spilt before my eyes,
and then I became that perfection, and all the novices of the
world howled in laughter all around me as true art died, and
I was its central cause. Conrad Arlington, The Last True
Artist, the one sent to protect the heavenly things of the
world had finally failed, and all goodness and purity and
truth had failed with him, and Gracie, perfect Gracie was
the victim of this outside failure. Her last hope at earthly
completion was lost, and then I became her, and I saw
through her bright eyes, and I felt my pure and blameless
body being conquered by the sicknesses of corrupt and

willful men, and I watched as the carnal creatures of the
night danced all around, singing jealous praises to the tune
of my eminence passing, and then I saw Conrad's face
staring back at me, and I saw how beautiful and good and
true he wanted to be, how terribly bad he wanted to protect
me, to be a good man, and I reached out for him, and I
screamed his name, but he could not hear me, for he had
failed. Then I saw the sharp knife raise high above me, and
in a silver flash it came streaking down in all terror, and
then there was silence, and dust, and nothing in the place
where true love had fallen. Then from a distant place I
heard Conrad's screams crack the silence as I lay dying,
screams of pure agony, the most wretched screams I had
ever heard in all my years on this earth, screams worse then
death, and then I didn't want to live anymore — I wanted to
die — and so I did. Life left me, and my spirit floated cold
and alone and afraid in the eternal absence of light, forever.
Then my bright eyes opened, and I knew that it was only a
dream… it was only a dream…

When reality came back to me I stood face to face
with the true Gracie. She looked at me in the softest of
ways, her blue eyes set a brilliant gloss against the
illustriousness of my façade, and I crumbled before her like
nothingness lost in eternity's span. My own eyes turned to
glass and I felt the whole spectrum of human emotion rush
through me all at once — love, hate, joy, grief, hope,
sadness, anger, tranquility, life, death — and I saw in her
angelic face the ability to impress upon her any one of
those magnificent qualities that I so chose, and so was the
moment of The Great Consideration for The Last True
Artist, the great inner turmoil, and what he was to do
became the pressing question.

Time seemed to slow as I continued to look at her,
falling in and out of her stare, considering her porcelain
skin, her finely whittled mouth, her perfectly spun hair all
golden blonde and cascading down like forever cascades
through a day, and I knew then that I had her, that she was
mine, and that I had the power to hurt her, to hold her, to

shame her, or to love her. Indeed, I wanted to love this
girl. I wanted to love her more than any singular thing that
was ever created since the dawn of time, but then, in all its
dark ferocity, the Great Arlington Pride rose up within me,
and it pulled my eyes from the heavenly one, and once
again rested them horribly on the creature from the night —
Gwendolyn, that ridiculous creature from New York —
sleek and cunning, dark and prowling through the crowd.
Her carnal desire began to draw me in, and then came the
great lust, and the desire to punish, and to hurt, and to
scold, and I felt the distance begin to grow, taking from me
the only true thing in my life, and then I felt the young girls
heart begin to break, and I felt those little pools of glass that
glowed so perfectly brilliant begin to brim with a salty
gloom as the forces of life and death battled inside of me,
waging war over my last sense of truth. Then, with one last
bit of strength coupled with the allied forces of all that was
good, clean, and bright, a clear voice rang through the
darkness —

"Conrad!"

At once all truth returned to me, and the darkness
of the night splintered apart in thin shards that disappeared
altogether, and the glorious brightness of a perfect being
blinded my senses as I took down the wall disclosing her,
and in all my shame, and my pain, and my regret, and my
foolishness, and in all the miles of my wretched remorse, I
found the ability to look into the everlasting eyes that
seemed to know me forever, and with one last stroke of true
resolve I reached out a courageous right hand, cupped her
tiny waist, and pulled her tightly to me. I felt her body give
itself to me, and mine to hers, and once again we held each
other, complete and alone, there, in the center of the storm.

***

We made it out of the party with such little effort it
was surprising. Gracie said a warm goodbye to Harry and
the gang while I gave a rather polite nod that was met with

the faintest hint of half-hearted enthusiasm. I didn't really expect much else from them. After all, I got what I came for and in doing so I took away what was considered to be the best thing about Harry's birthday, which was Gracie herself. Judging by all the craned necks of single men and the low scowls of resentful women who were still cognizant enough to notice us move boldly and swiftly to the exit, it was apparent that everyone had reached one of two possible levels of agreement about me — either I was a damn nuisance that was insistent on causing a commotion and ruining a good time by taking the most lovely thing from the room, or I was so positively and unprecedentedly cool there was nothing at all to do but silently applaud me as I swept up the only girl worth having and effortlessly made my grand exit — for the sake of my own ego, I liked to think it was the latter, and I didn't necessarily think I was completely wrong.

By the time Gracie and I reached my coupe we were both exhausted. It had been an extremely emotional night for both of us, and after all the twists and turns, highs and lows, cocktails and conversations, I was surprised either one of us still managed to keep our eyes open. I enjoyed that silence, and as I dropped into the contours of my cool, leather seat I was half expecting Gracie to burst out with some exclamation of how there was another party we were expected to be at or some late social we still needed to go to in Glendale or Pasadena or some other distant place that would take forever to drive to, but it never came — it was time to go home. I started the engine and began our short drive back to Studio City, the glittering lights of the Hollywood Hills winking solemn goodbyes as we took to the winding turns up and over the Cahuenga Pass.

"Gracie," I stated softly, preparing to enter into a reflective discussion on the evening. "I want to talk to you."

I pulled my gaze from the road and looked over at her, but she was gone, fast asleep, her tiny body curled up tastefully in the passenger seat like a kitten that had played itself out, her elegant, porcelain face held graceful against the door, revealing quiet, peaceful coverings over sapphire eyes that rested so brilliantly beneath. It was a completely true and beautiful sight. So magnificent was her posture that it justified the entire night, and I imagined if I was a painter I would have found my masterpiece in that moment, but being gifted with the pen before the brush I was content to simply look at her, experiencing the moment fully and etching the feeling deep, deep into my memory to be called upon when I needed to remember that life was good, and once again a great satisfaction with the world washed over me, a complete contentedness with its simple pleasures, and I let this all effect me as I drove over the pass, onward, deeper, into the starry night.

CHAPTER 7
— THE END OF AN EVENING —

It was well past four in the morning by the time we reached her door. Gracie's body awoke the very moment I parked the car and shut off the engine, as if by magic she internally sensed her bed drawing nearer and had an automatic response to it. She groggily unlocked the door and we walked inside. It was dark for a moment, and I once again found it strange being in a completely empty room that was so full of life not long ago. Then there was a 'click,' and the grandeur of the French space was filled with the illumination of that marvelous chandelier, and all the distant feelings fled with the darkness. There was no mistake about it, I didn't want to leave, in fact, I was so excited by being in Gracie's home at this hour that it was all I could do to hold my breath. However, I also didn't want to impose, and after all we had been through that night it felt a bit strange standing in the middle of her living room, and I was having difficulty discerning if Gracie was waiting for me to make some kind of advance, or to leave her alone in peace. Deciding that either decision would be brash, I proceeded to test the waters a bit.

"It was a good night, wasn't it?" I asked as Gracie floated about the space, taking off her earrings and flipping on the stray lamps that had not yet been lit as she passed them.

"Yes, it was fun. Did you have a good time, Conrad?" She posed the question rather flat, almost routine-like, and I tried to catch her eye, but she would not return it.

"I did."

"Oh, I'm so tired. Are you tired? You must be."

"I am a bit," I answered as Gracie continued to roam the room, doing everything she could to avoid my gaze. "Gracie, would you like me to go?"

"Do you want to go?"

"Not necessarily."

"Then stay. The night is still young. Don't you think so?"

I wasn't sure what she was leading at, or what she wanted from me for that matter, for she just mentioned how she was tired just moments before, but girls rarely said what they were thinking, and I was there, in her apartment, and there was really only one answer worth giving — "I suppose it could be."

"Then why would you go?" She asked, prompting me, and the cool shiver that shot through my spine informed me of her direction, but it was strange — there was something strange about everything that was happening — something very different, and I wanted to get a handle on it before we moved forward.

"Gracie... I want to talk to you." I took a seat on the couch — that same black velvet couch that Gracie lounged on every day of her life, and the scent of it was intoxicating.

She rushed over to the liquor table and began hastily making herself a drink. Her hands were trembling just enough that I could tell she was having some difficulty putting it together.

"Why on earth would you want to talk right now, Conrad?"

"Because I want to, that's why. Because we've had a long night, and I think we should discuss it. Would you come sit down on the couch for a moment please?"

"Words, words, words, that's all anybody ever has for me is words," she said, taking a large gulp of her concoction that contained mostly vodka. "I don't want to hear any more words as long as I live."

"I think that might be difficult. You're an actress, you're going to have to deal with them sooner or later," I chuckled, trying to make light of the situation.

"That's work, Conrad. I don't want to work right now. I want to have fun, so how about you be quiet, and I'll be quiet, and we'll let our bodies do the talking. Then, if our mouths feel like they have something important to say, we'll let them speak accordingly. Okay?"

The mystery was made known, and if I was any other man alive I would have shut my mouth right then and let her have her way, but it was the way she said it, dammit, that hit a chord in me. It was that girlish sense of entitlement that she lorded over everybody that she was now lording over me, and I felt like nothing more than a plaything to her — a poor, naive, stupid young man dumb enough to drive her around, take her to her fancy parties, compliment her, chase her, and then make her feel good about herself at the end of the night. There was no substance there, just dust and echoes as empty as those of the ghosts on Sunset Boulevard, for I liked this girl — I liked her more than any girl I had ever met in my entire life — and perhaps I was the fool for it, perhaps after all the glitz, and all the glamour, and all the cocktails, and all the socialites, and all the debutantes, and all the aristocrats, and all the privilege, and all the adventure, and all the emotion, and all the suspense, and all the writing, and acting, and true art, and true love, and true grandeur, and all the true things of this world I considered true, perhaps I was indeed the fool, but I did not yet know, and I would not go a step further until I knew — exactly — what I was.

"No," I said.

"What was that, Conrad?"

"I said, 'no.' We're not doing anything until you come sit here and talk to me."

Gracie looked at me curiously, as if wondering who it was that was feebly attempting to deny her, and those eyes — oh those eyes — they burned forever a bright blue as hot as the hottest fire, and her mouth opened slightly in the most inviting way, and with the pure rawness of that look she might have made me the first man in her lifetime that ever denied even her slightest advance. Then it was like something switched, and without a word she glided over to me gracefully and sat down on the couch opposite me. She didn't move, she didn't speak, she didn't even blink, she just stared directly at me with her enormous blue eyes, and I felt completely exposed by them.

"G-Gracie," I stuttered, trying to speak.

I already knew she had an affect on me, but it was never so apparent as it was right then. I got all tied up, and all my confidence was stripped away like a sheep is stripped of its wool. I looked to her for support, for some kind of sign that I was doing a good thing and that she wanted me to continue, but none came, just unwavering eyes like mirrors, reflecting back at me the very thing that I asked for — her attention — and I could have not prepared myself for it, no, never at all, for indeed, I had never felt such fear.

"Gracie," I continued. "I want to talk about what's going on — between us, I mean."

"Shh," she spoke softly. "No more words, Conrad. You'll find that now isn't the time for them."

Her eyes did not pull from me but burrowed ever deeper into my soul, and I could feel the moment at hand. I had it! It was right in front of me. This was my chance. She was looking at me, studying me, waiting for me to connect, waiting for me to do something dear and beautiful and true. Oh the simplicity of it. Her marvelous face, her beautiful eyes, if only I could look at them. If only I could look deep into them and shut my mouth right there and kiss her! But every time I tried my mind would dance away, and my eyes would float to the walls, or the ceiling, or the floor, or some other despicable place not meant for eyes with such true intention. She tried with all her might to pull me to her, but my wretched pride wouldn't have it, and I could feel the inner turmoil of my nature waging war against the self-destructive tendencies that were my other half. My head jerked back and forth, fighting to avoid her gaze, for my body knew what that gaze meant, what it was, and to look into its loveliness would be to forfeit all purpose, all cause, all art in the world, and it would spare none of these — it was all consuming.

"Conrad." She spoke softly in the most understanding way, placing a delicate hand on my shoulder near my chest.

My body continued to struggle, my mouth tightened, my eyes glazed over in frustration. I didn't know why this was coursing through me — why now? Why here? What was this darkness inside of me? Wasn't this what I always wanted?

"Conrad." She spoke again. "Look at me."

I fought the strain with my last breath. My body wanted to give itself over, but I would not be nothing to her — I refused to be nothing.

Then one more time her soft voice spoke. "Look at me."

And that was that.

"No! Gracie," I blurted out, still unable to meet her gaze. "I like you. I think you're amazing and — and I want to know what this is?"

"This is life, Conrad," she began softly, moving closer. "You promised you wouldn't ask any questions. Those were the rules. You've been good so far, and they won't help you now."

I could feel her warm breath against my mouth and the critical thoughts of my mind began to give way to a tantalizing mix of excitement and tranquility. "Surely this is it," I thought. "Surely this is the truth — two creatures, one of art and the other of beauty, giving each other their precious youth — this is what I always wanted. I had dreamt about it my entire life, to experience the body of such a glorious being, there could be nothing like it, nothing on earth." Then, suddenly, as her lips neared my face, I saw past the flesh and the blood to the very art inside of us. I thought of her, and I thought of what we could be if we discovered truth together, and I knew that if I touched those lips now I would give up control forever. I would be a slave to my body, and all objectivity would be lost in some unstoppable passion — and I wanted this passion, more than anything in the world I wanted it — but I wanted truth more, the truth that comes from knowing, and so with a final burst of strength I pulled the necessary will from the depths of my stomach and placed it at the tip of my mouth.

"No," I commanded. "I don't give a damn about the rules. I need to know what I am to you. I need to know if you feel the same way."

It was then that I looked at her, full on, directly into those blue pools that glistened innocently just like the first time we connected so many months ago.

"What do you want me to say?" She asked.

"Say you like me. Say you feel the same way. I know you do." I was practically pleading with her. Then for the first time Gracie pulled her eyes from me, and it was now I who was doing the searching. "Say anything, I don't care, just say what's true."

She pulled back, regaining some composure. "Conrad... I can't be whoever it is you want me to be. I'm not ready for it."

"I don't want you to be anything, don't you see? I like you for who you are. I'm just trying to make this real."

"It's not real," she snapped. "I'm not real."

"What do you mean you're not real? You're sitting right here."

We both were getting emotional rather quickly, our faces illuminated by the faint white orbs of light that scattered and moved about the room, and once again I lost something beautiful.

"I mean you can't possibly like me. You don't know anything about me. You like an idea of me and that's it."

"Then what is this? What has this whole night been about? Why did you call me?"

"I called you because I wanted to have fun, Conrad, nothing more, and this isn't fun." Emotion flooded her eyes in little pools that threatened to spill over at any moment. Then, as if realizing it was a bit brash, she calmed herself and let her eyes cool. She then turned to face me, and her blue stare consumed me forevermore, and I longed to know who she really was.

"Relationships don't work, Conrad," Gracie stated in absolution. "Trust me on this, they don't, so I think it's best that you and I leave it at that."

"How can you say that to me right now?" I asked, my eyes glistening with a glossy sincerity, for that had hurt — I'd never forget how much that had hurt — it was probably the single most solitary gut wrenching feeling I had ever felt in my entire life, and my whole body recoiled from it. Then she spoke again, and the truth in the softness of her voice would haunt the soul of The Last True Artist for the rest of his life.

"Because I fall in love easily, Conrad," Gracie stated with all vulnerability, and I could see in her eyes that she was truly afraid. "I lose myself in those I love, and it won't do to have my heart broken again."

"It needn't be so," I stated, feeling frustrated at the situation, for there was a lack of faith there that I never expected, and I simply couldn't have prepared myself for it. "You mustn't worry about these things, Gracie. You mustn't try and control them. Don't you know I'm true?"

"Oh, I know you are!" She exclaimed, and little crystal tears ran perfectly down her porcelain skin.

"Then believe."

"I-I can't," she stuttered as her little golden head fell towards the floor.

"But why?" Indeed, I was almost pleading now, for there was no more fear in me — not a single ounce of it — for I had cast it out to stay next to her, and I had no idea such a formidable emotion could exist in a creature so bright, or how to stand against it. "Don't you know you're dear to me? You're the brightest, most special, beautiful girl I have ever met... and... and I feel that I could love you forever..."

Gracie's eyes rose from the floor to meet mine, and upon me they held steady and bright, and I never felt more helpless.

"I don't know for sure of course," I continued. "But I'm willing to try... because you are dear to me Gracie. You are so very, very dear."

Silence took the room, and in that moment time stopped, just stopped completely like a clock would if it lost its tick, and all the darkness of the night was held captive by the golden girl, dancing between an endless glow, eternity, and her violet stare... and there never before existed a truth so beautifully broken.

"When I love, Conrad." She began slowly, her eyes never wavering from mine. "I love so hard that there is no more of me... and I can no longer bear it." There was a pause, and in the depths of her crystal eyes, I saw the beginning of what would kill me. Then she opened her perfect mouth, and formed the words that would pierce my heart, and I felt all truth inside of me scream against the coming moment. "I'll never fall in love again," she stated in absolution, and I knew then that I was done.

The pain was too much, so I looked away, and I felt the Great Arlington Pride begin to rise within in me to aid my survival, and it was immensely powerful. There was a long moment of recovery where both of us said nothing. I couldn't look at her now. My tired eyes stung with tears through a hazy strain as they clung to the opposite wall, and I felt that same sense of hopelessness, that same sense of love lost shooting through my mind as it began to barricade a wall to keep the damage at bay. I had no patience, absolutely no patience at all, and once again I was on the verge of destroying something that had the potential to be so good if I could only give it time to grow, for in Gracie's eyes I knew that she wanted to believe. Perhaps if I was patient with her, and kind to her, I could build up enough trust that she would find the courage to follow me into the depths of something greater, the place where only the lovely things of the world could exist, but no, for the sake of some ridiculous abstract purpose of truth — a truth which even I didn't fully understand — I took a breath, and without thinking, I laid down the gift of endless possibility

— the possibility that comes inherently with faith, truth, and being a good person — and I ended its actuality completely.

"So that's it then." I said, and my voice became frigid and cold.

"What do you mean that's it?" Gracie asked, her beautiful voice suddenly alive with a desperate panic.

"I mean that's it," I rose to my feet, and my pride pushed my mind to run and evade that awful sense of rejection that my body both despised and craved in some sick contrast.

Gracie grabbed me by the arm and pulled me forcefully down to the couch with a marvelous display of physical strength. She didn't speak, but instead brought me in so close that our noses almost touched. Her eyes darted back and forth on mine in the most alive way, like she was searching for what it was that made me who I am, and I was remind of her unreal nature, her sovereignty, for she was perfect, worthy of all worship man had ever given her, or would ever give, and I was mesmerized. I was nothing next to her, indeed I was ash, an epic display of weakness and problems, yet as Ophelia pondered death Gracie pondered me, and I wondered in that moment everything there was to wonder about her, who she was, where she came from, what she was capable of becoming, and then, looking deeper into those bright circlets of glass that served as earthly eyes, I discovered something I had never seen before, deep down, past all the blue, and the gold, and the white, I saw something incomplete, and it was terrifying. Before me sat a girl that had never known true love. All the truth in the world was at her fingertips, but she had never experienced the greatest truth of all. As she continued to study me I saw her porcelain skin tighten as she realized the state of her personal betrayal, her golden hair flowing down as witness to the secret that sat reflected on the surface of my own eyes, and then there were only pools, and glass, and then a little blink as white covered blue, and the moment solidified itself all around us, and then she got up, and the moment was gone.

"Gracie," I said softly.

"It's alright Conrad," Gracie stated, doing her best to compose herself as she moved towards the hallway.

"Gracie." I called.

"Not to worry, I'm just going to run to my room real quick."

"Would you like me to come with you?"

"It's not necessary."

"Would you like me to go?"

"No, please."

"I'm going." I stated.

"Stay," she demanded, then added in complete softness — "please."

She stood at the entrance to the hallway, looking back at me in the most fragile, curious, and enduring way imaginable.

"Okay," I said.

She gave a soft smile, the kind a maiden might give to her sailor as he disappeared into the unknown sunset, and then with a slight turn of her golden head she was gone, removed, ever deeper, into the endless hall.

I felt the chill of her absence like a warm jacket being stripped from my bones in the dead of winter. I sat down on the edge of the couch to steady my senses, once again taken with the full scent of Gracie that only served as a shadow of her true actuality. "It was done," I thought. "The truth was out, and there was no going back." I realized that I had just become aware of how to truly complete her — that I had the attributes necessary to make her a whole person — and with that came a great amount of power. Gracie was also aware of this, and I felt a great deal of responsibility towards her, for she was trusting me with so much, and I wondered what it was she was doing in her room, what it was she thought about me — great things I imagined — and I felt an incredible warmth wash over me for being so close to her, but as I sat alone in the quiet of the room, darker thoughts took me, selfish thoughts of a melancholic nature, and so began the voice of my internal monologue...

"I finally had it! I had found what I was looking for! It was truth! Pure truth! Raw! Visceral! I needed nothing else! I could create for a thousand years solely off this feeling. It was everlasting, an eternal spring of pure condition that I could draw from forever. How beautiful it was, and how tragic! The intensity of her gaze that kept going and going like some deep mine stripped of all its resources. Indeed, she was perfect — she was the most perfect being ever created since the beginning of mankind — and I, Conrad Arlington, The Last True Artist, had been refined by her. She was nothing to me anymore, only emptiness and death, weighing down my shoulders, burdening my soul with her slight frame, her beauty, her blonde hair, her glass eyes. God! She was everything that was girl, nothing more. She was perfectly female, and I was the user. Her love was only a commodity, and it was my duty as an artist to consume her."

"No," I yelled audibly, straining my eyes and neck. "No!"

"Yes," the voice said, marking the entrance of an internal dialogue. "You have taken what you need from her. You know her heart. Now go and have her."

"What truth is there in that?" I questioned.

"Physical truth," answered the voice. "You need her physicality. Take it. She wants you to take it. She's waiting for you."

"What good does it do me? What purpose does that give?"

"It gives you everything!" The voice snapped
"Why?"

"Because you want to possess her."

"You're sick to say that."

"Call it whatever you want, but it's your mind."

"I want to love her," I reasoned back. "She doesn't know what love is."

"Then show her," the voice said strongly. "Take her body in your arms and show her."

I looked across the room to the entrance of the dark hallway — it never looked so inviting.

"No," I said, averting my gaze. "She's confused."

"It's the only thing she knows," the voice reasoned.

I found it difficult to argue that. There was a moment.

"Do you want to be close to her?"

"Yes," I said

"Then have her body, and you will be."

"I want more than her body — I want her mind. I want her heart."

"You have to go through her body to get it."

"There's more to her then that!"

I could feel myself giving into myself, and I felt my mind and spirit caving in, and then I felt something like a weight forming in the bottom of my stomach, and I realized that the voice was not my mind, but my body, and it was overbearing.

"She doesn't believe in herself. She offered you her body. You must take it now, or you may lose her forever."

"Is there no other way?"

"No. You have her now. There will not be another chance."

The voice was sly and cunning, and my flesh was figuratively screaming to comply. I felt exhausted, depleted, and Gracie's face was the only good thing I had in my life, not even the greatest art or the truest expression of myself could compare to her, and the thought of being without her was too much to bear.

"It's the only way, and you know it," said the voice. "Have her now, or this night will haunt you forever." Then the voice was gone.

I took a breath and looked back towards the dark hallway, its entrance just barely visible under the low-lit ambiance of the great chandelier, and my choice was made known. I stood from the couch, immediately experiencing the absence of soft black velvet against my body and the comfort that came with it. I felt open, exposed as I moved, like every step I took was being watched by some unlimited presence that resided somewhere in the room, and I was reminded of that same obsolete feeling that came with being under those big, ominous eyes of Chester the Cherry, and how that felt, and I resented it. Eager to get away, I quickly approached the entrance of the hallway and stopped, once again face to face with the deep, dark corridor that appeared to never end. Then I wondered for a moment about its endlessness, and if the gallery at the end of the hall that seemed so magical just weeks before wasn't all part of some grandiose illusion in the epic scope of some strange dream that I was caught in, and I wondered if I would ever come out of it.

I took my first step into the hall and was immediately enclosed by the darkness. It was comforting to be out of the light, and the tension residing just below my neck in my shoulders loosened and my breaths deepened with every step I took. I walked past the first set of overarching, Victorian doorways that stood embedded against the sides, and I got that same intrinsic feeling I got when passing them the last time, wondering what mysteries lie in waiting behind their magnificent frames. Then my mind thought of Gracie's bedroom, and how truly perfect it must be, and how one of these forbidding doors must surely be the portal into her private world, where the true tears, and the memories, and all the mysteries of her life were made known to the air, and how few, if any, had ever borne witness to them. Then I suddenly became aware of my heartbeat, which increased with every passing moment, taking me deeper and deeper into the hallway. I stopped and looked back at the living room, its faint light still gleaming from a distance, and it felt further removed than it had ever felt before, and I grew nervous, and excited, and I became very aware of my body, and I remembered the internal conversation I had that made me come this far, and I knew what I must do. I continued forward in suspension, caught up in some kind of surreal place where time seemed to slow all around me — the moment of The Great Consideration was near — I could feel it, for the whole night had been leading towards it, and my body pulled me forward, and my mind did not resist. There was truth there, some kind of rawness, something intimate that I had never experienced before in such a specific way, and I realized that I had passed the point of no return, the choice had been made, and now the world would have its way with me.

I neared the end of the hallway, and on my left a great door stood ajar, and a faint light cast a luminous slice across the floor that trickled up the opposite wall and peaked near the ceiling, creating a kind of otherworldly barrier that was both beautiful and terrifying at the same time. I felt that this light held within its glow the power over life and death, with the capacity to choose whom would enter and whom would be cast out, for surely its contents were more precious then the richest stones, and only those who were worthy would be allowed access. I stood there for a moment, realizing what this meant, and then with a breath of courage I stepped into its glow. Immediately its brightness filled my vision, and as my eyes adjusted I looked through the crack and saw the most brilliant expanse I had ever seen, and I knew immediately what I was looking at — this was Gracie's room — and it was filled with more goodness and truth then I had ever seen.

Slowly, I pushed the door open and light flooded out. A small lamp was illuminated on the nightstand, and the whole room seemed to glow and shimmer like the air itself was filled with some kind of magical ether from a place far greater than the mortal world. I breathed and experienced its purity. It was in the whole room! The whole room smelled like her! I opened my eyes and saw nothing but white everywhere. Wispy, linen curtains hung down from the ceiling, and a large mirror stood against the wall, reflecting the ambiance into an epic display of perfect radiance that danced across the various paintings that had been deemed both beautiful and true enough to be placed upon the glorious walls. Towards the right was a rich wooden chest with a lovely display of perfumes, and I could smell their scents mixing and mingling as they wafted across the room in a warm draft that came from an invisible source that could only be preeminent in nature. My heart rate slowed to a perfectly natural state, and I felt the artistic storehouses in my body being filled fully with each breath, and I felt like I could die right then, a completely full person, and the life of The Last True Artist would be complete.

Then my eyes looked towards the center, and I saw the being responsible for all the beauty in the room, and my heart stopped. Gracie was laying face down across the foot of her bed, her porcelain face resting softly in a nest of golden blonde that tangled wonderfully across the white linens, and she looked like an angel. All grandeur was emanating off her tiny body, and an aura of perfection glowed inches above the little black cocktail dress that she never found her way out of. There was no question, this was the most beautiful sight I had ever seen in my life, and I didn't want to move in fear that I might cause a ripple of falseness in the completely pure environment that was necessary to sustain her. I leaned against the doorway and watched her sleep for a moment. "She was so glorious," I thought. "Indeed she was a glorious girl."

My curiosity continued to grow, and I found myself moving towards her across the room, the perfection of the space deepening with each step until I was standing above her at the foot of the bed. I looked down at her for a moment, wondering if she knew I was there, if perhaps she felt the sovereignty of the space broken by my false presence, and then my eyes moved across her face and I admired the contours of her mouth and nose that moved lightly with each breath. She was so peaceful, so calm, far away from the pressures, and the threats, and the corruption of the world, and I wished that I could preserve her forever. Then, suddenly, by pure physical impulse, I reached out and placed my hand on the small of her back, considering the warmth of her inviting flesh, and I felt my body react accordingly. I began to shake slightly, for I was losing control, and I knew that it was only a matter of time before I lost myself completely.

"Gracie?" I asked softly to her sleeping form, but she did not wake, she did not speak, and then the darkness of the great voice returned, and I found myself once again locked in an internal dialogue of flesh and blood.

"She feels good doesn't she?" The voice suggested.

"Yes," I said, unable to lie. "She does."

"Do you want her?"

"Yes."

"Then take her."

I breathed heavily as I looked down at Gracie's perfect body, and I knew that I was standing above the most desirable creature ever created to walk the earth, and I never felt so much power. I moved my hand up her back to her hair and let its golden ringlets dance gracefully through my fingertips. My mind began to cloud over as her scent took me, and I knew that it would all be over in a moment. There was no fighting it — it was an impossibility — even for Conrad Arlington, The Last True Artist, there could be no victory, and I was foolish to try and stand against it. All lust, all desire, and all sensuality would have its way, then I would finally have her, and our union would be complete. I would conquer her just like she wanted me to do, just like all of the other fakes, and the fools, and the nobodies she ever knew, and so I would become one of them, just another nothing in her physical world, devoid of true love and all substance. Then my hand moved back down to her waist, and I knew the moment had come.

"Do it," said the voice.

I reached around her hips and her stomach quivered at my touch. I could feel the warmth of her blood rush through her body as her heart rate increased and her breath began to draw quick and heavy upon the linens. Bliss took me, and I could see my conscience-waving farewell from the harbors of my mind as I drifted further and further away from it. Yes, this was it, the moment of The Great Consideration, and I would fail. There was no such thing as true love, only decadence, only physicality, all romance was truly dead, and any idea of it broke hard against the rocky shores of sexual passion, in which none could survive. My hand began to move further downward, her stomach rising and falling harder and harder with each sensual inch, our physical connection deepening as my heart rate increased with hers until they beat together rhythmically to the tempo of our bodies. I bent down to kiss her face and I could see her tiny mouth quivering lightly through her dreams, for her eyes did not open, but rested peacefully below closed lashes that fluttered lightly upon her skin, and I could tell that wherever she was she was far away from here — far away from me — and I was indeed nothing to her, nothing but emptiness on the outskirts of her mind, and I would pass through her just like the rest of them, and then I would be gone from her life forever.

Suddenly my conscience returned to me, and all at once I became sick. A deep darkness flooded my senses and I suddenly felt completely exposed, unwelcome, like an intruder that was pulled abruptly from his hiding place, and the shadows would no longer avail him. With all my will I took my hand from her body and I felt my flesh scream in an unexpected defeat. I stumbled backwards in a haste of self-hatred and nearly fell over, crashing hard into the frame of the entryway in which I found my only support. I was completely dizzy, and drew in deep, gasping breaths that were greedily consumed by my beating heart as my vision found it's way back to me. My legs gave out and I slid weakly down the doorpost until my back touched the ground, and with steadying breaths I looked back at Gracie's sleeping form, all elegant and seemingly unaffected by my false attempts at completion, and I never felt such guilt. There was no truth there, none at all, and I felt like a reduced man — a weak, feeble, reduced man — for Conrad Arlington, The Last True Artist, had risked everything for the sake of being false, but he would not do it, no, he would not take her, not like this. Even though she made it easy for him. Even though she wanted him to do it — even though she lay there, dreaming for him to do it — he would not be reduced to this. He would not be fake. He would be real. He would be true, and if he was the last man alive to believe in what truth was, in art, in love, in romance, then he would do it, he would be that man, and the heavens would commend his existence in the end.

With a shoulder against the door frame I slid up the wall, and I felt the darkness recede from my mind as truth once again filled my heart. With eyes of appreciation I looked back at the most amazing girl I had ever met in my life, and then a warm smile spread across my face in all thankfulness, and the tears that pooled my eyes trickled down. I felt that I had saved her somehow — even if it was from myself — I had saved her, and I knew the love that I had showed her that night would stay with her forever as she lay sleeping, and she would never forget me. Then suddenly, once more, I felt drawn forward, and again I was standing over her, but it was different now. There was no lust present, and if there was it was overshadowed by the truth I felt bursting through my veins, and so I considered her for what she was — a guiding light, a perfect being, and I was the one chosen to stand there next to her.

My shadow fell lightly upon her face as I bent down to kiss her forehead. Her tight brow softened as my lips touched her skin, and I could feel her breathing deepen as she drifted ever deeper into that beautiful place that existed between the magical spaces of her mind — a place where the most extraordinary things could happen, a place where dreams came true — and I only wished I could be there. Then with a last dose of courage I laid down on the bed next to her, wrapped her up neatly in my arms, and I felt her slight body slacken into mine, giving itself over to the warm comfort that surrounded her, and I never felt so close to someone in my life. Through tired eyes I took a breath and kissed her neck.

"Goodnight my beautiful Gracie," I whispered in her ear. "You are true to me."

She let out a little breath that smiled forever, signaling that she had heard my voice as it echoed faintly through the distance of her dreams. Then she nuzzled a little closer to me, and I nuzzled a little closer to her, and together our bodies said goodbye to the evening.

We lay like that all night. I didn't know if she ever remembered.

CHAPTER 8
— WINTER BREAKS —

When I awoke the next morning Gracie was gone. I checked her room, then the rest of the house — as much as I could access at least — but there was nothing, no sign of her, not even a note. It was different during the day, much of the mystery surrounding the place seemed to disappear with the presence of sunshine, and standing once again in the living room I admired the beautiful view of the valley as it stretched far and wide past the big glass window that stood brilliant at the front of the house, acting like a large aperture that opened upon the city, altogether gleaming and pleasing to the eye. I thought it rather strange that she would just disappear without a word like that, but I figured it wasn't too much unlike the Gracie I had come to know, and I promptly determined that she must have got an early call or some other business to justify her absence — yes, surely that must have been the case — then, momentarily satisfied, I looked deep into the cloudless blue sky that hung crystal clear in the daylight, fully expecting her to contact me by days end.

On the ride home I never felt so happy, or so bewildered. I could hardly believe what had happened, and I pinched myself and shouted several times as I crossed back over the 101 to make sure I wasn't indeed dreaming. It was all so absurd — absolutely all of it — nonetheless, I held the girl of my dreams in my arms last night, and that gave some kind of new and real purpose to everything. I ran the events of that magical evening over and over in my mind until I had them solidified perfectly in my memory and had no more doubts about them, then I did my best to let them be, attributing my good fortune to being a genuine and true person, and I felt a great sense of valor course through my body then tingle across my skin, and I felt completely fearless with the world — I felt like a man.

I sat at my desk for the rest of the day, earnestly desiring to create something beautiful with my newly found inspiration, but despite my genuine efforts, they were — at least momentarily — endearingly hopeless. It was too soon, for my mind's eye was completely filled with her, and any attempts to do anything but sit and stare at the phone eagerly awaiting her call proved completely useless. I was far too strung on what I considered to be true love — a feeling which I found to be both completely wonderful and completely annoying considering its immobilizing effect — I could literally get nothing done, so in a sense there was nothing at all to do, but as the slow, steady hands of the dial reached six o'clock, and the call never came, I began to doubt the unshakeable faith that I previously had, and the thoughts that felt so sure in the morning didn't feel so sure anymore, and once again I began to contemplate Gracie's sudden absence, and again considered that I had been completely wrong in my reasoning, and that perhaps I had lost her. Then I remembered the voice, and what it said to me, and I felt my paranoia creeping in with every passing moment that the phone stayed silent, so, finding the thoughts completely false and artistically unhealthy, I quickly took action to shake them, and figured a good walk and some cool air on my face should do the trick. "Surely, there is a perfectly logical explanation," I thought, "surely." With that, I threw on my favorite jacket and plunged back out into the cool November.

It was a calm evening on the Boulevard, for it was only a few days until December now, and I could already feel the effects of the approaching holidays upon the city. They were, after all, just weeks away, and the town felt emptier now. People began to go back to whatever perspective places they called home — those little, podunk towns scattered flippantly across the country — and I wondered if I would drive home to my town this year, but that was contingent on a variety of factors that I did not yet know, so I quickly disregarded the thought, opting to focus on more immediate forms of distraction. Those people who were out, however, seemed to be in good spirits. That was probably because it was Thursday. I always found Thursdays to be good for walking. They were the perfect mix of routine and weekend anticipation, and there was all of Friday, Saturday, and Sunday to look forward to, which were all good days as well. I began feeling light, and walked back up to Franklin Avenue to buy an espresso and a small bite to eat, and I thought of all the wonderful things that would happen in the upcoming year — of true art, of true love, and of Gracie Garrison — and how incredible it would be to experience all of them.

**

The next morning there was still no word from Gracie — no call, no message, nothing — I decided I would give it another day before I started inquiring, but when that day came and went as well, I decided I would give it a week, and so on and so forth until two weeks had passed and there was still no word. I felt distant from her, and surprisingly, as a result, I was getting a great deal of work done. As my longing for her increased, so did my concentration, and out of my aching heart I found some of the most beautiful prose imaginable, full of truth and raw feeling, and the stimulation of seeing my emotions immortalized so exactly onto white paper acted as my temporary romance, and for the first time in a long while I experienced that artistic satisfaction that comes with real sacrifice.

It was mid-December by the time I felt I should inquire. I was truly distant from her now, and I knew that I could speak to her without getting emotional, which was of paramount importance, for there was no use getting emotional with girls, and I knew from past experience that it would backfire on me the moment I reasoned to do so. Ironically enough, despite this knowledge, that deviant emotion of mine still found a way to get its fangs in me with Gracie. To what I considered to be no fault of my own, I couldn't think when I was around her, and whatever guard I managed to construct out of life was shot dead the moment she landed those violet eyes on me. I was a sensitive person by nature, and ridiculously impatient, but I was finally learning to embrace the healing aspects of time that I typically resented so much. After all, I was on a roll artistically, and I figured I could ride that as long as it inspired me, and let it serve as my justification. I began making calls. I called Gracie's house first, which was the only logical thing to do, but of course there was no answer, so I called again just for the sake of it, but knew it was completely pointless, and sure enough there was no answer a second time — it just rang, and rang, and rang. Even if Gracie was home, I couldn't imagine her ever answering her phone, not unless there was someone else there to do it for her, and even then I wouldn't expect her to take it.

Next I called Maxwell Price, figuring if anyone knew where Gracie would be, it would be him. The phone rang five times, then I jumped suddenly at his booming voice before realizing it was only a recording, so I proceeded to leave a message.

"Hi Maxwell, this is Conrad Arlington. I hope you are well. Listen, I'm inquiring to see if you have been in contact with Gracie recently. Long story short, I spent the evening with her a few weeks back and I haven't heard from her since. I feel a bit bad about everything because we never had a proper goodbye, and, well, I was hoping to speak to her before too long. I'm sure you understand. You can reach me at my home number when you have a moment. I appreciate it, and I hope your holidays are going well. Speak soon."

I hung up the phone with a certain satisfaction, and I felt that it was a good, strong, professional message. Surely the phone would ring at any moment. I would get to the bottom of this, and Gracie and I could continue our blossoming relationship — he never called back.

I spent the rest of the afternoon making inquiries and placing calls, so many in fact I was certain that I had contributed to a substantial increase in line traffic at the operators' station that day, and I half expected them to start picking up the phone and addressing me by name. I had called all of Gracie's friends I had met from the previous evening — Bobby Finch, Alice Button, and Harry Vanderford — of which only Harry answered, and was surprisingly pleasant considering the way we left things the other night. He said that he had not seen her, but told me he would let me know if he heard of anything, and also informed me that Gracie was extremely hard to get a hold of, which only further added to the realization that finding out Gracie's whereabouts could — and probably would — take even longer than expected. I then tried Gracie's again that evening, hoping that at least Evie might be home to pick up, but there was no answer. I then called all my friends and all my acquaintances from the past year — other writers, actors, industry folk, restaurant owners — anyone and everyone I could think of that I thought may have heard of or might have had a connection to Gracie. About half had heard of her, the other half hadn't, and the ones that did were either amazed altogether that I was even trying to contact her or knew next to nothing about her, other than that she was a socialite of sorts, and they all had different theories about what she did in her personal life. I thanked them all for their time, and for the few that I actually cared to see again, I shared with them my condolences and desires to catch up. From there a few returned the gesture with an empty promise to get 'coffee sometime,' which, from my experience, almost always meant never.

It was deep into the evening now, and I had exhausted the majority of my resources. My mind was swamped with useless information, useless leads, and useless, mindless babble. Gracie had suddenly become even more mysterious than ever, and I had difficulty controlling the grandiose thoughts of where she could be or what she was involved in — some beautiful and magnificent — others terrifying. I felt myself becoming obsessed with finding her, and even though I knew I should give it a rest, call it a night, and focus my mind on something constructive to ease myself into the evening, my curiosity wouldn't have it. The more I tried to let it go the worse it became, until I was literally pounding my head against white paper on my desk like I was trying to knock an unshakable thought from my brain, or punishing myself for not contacting her sooner. "I was so close with her," I thought. "I was so, so close with her. What went wrong?" There was really no explanation at all, and the only thing left to do for the day was to try and create something good from it, so I reached into my desk for a fresh pencil, but instead my fingers touched something small and square. When I pulled it out I was face to face with a business card, black letters over plain white, with the word 'Actor' scribed under the name — it was the business card of Benjamin Trask.

Seeing his name on that card was like a flashback, and in a matter of moments what seemed so distant all came rushing back to me — the strange meeting at Gracie's, the magnificent cocktail party, the conversation on the balcony, the hallway, the back room, the rumors, the information — the information, yes, the information. He had offered to speak to me more about Gracie, and wanted me to call him that very next week — I never did.

I stared at his personal contact at the bottom of the card. It was completely clear what I had to do, and what I was going to do. I picked up the phone and placed the call. It rang twice.

"Hello."

The voice was clear and strong on the other end of the line, so much so that it was slightly unnerving, and it took me a moment to find my own.

" Hi — Benjamin?"

"Who is this?"

"It's Conrad — Conrad Arlington — we met earlier in November, on the balcony, at Gracie Garrison's house. The cocktail party—"

He cut me off confidently, and I could picture his sinewy jaw muscles guffawing masterfully along with his angular face. "Conrad! Of course I remember you. How could I forget? I was disappointed that you never called."

I wasn't expecting him to call me out so soon, but he didn't seem angry about it, and I reasoned he had every right to do so if he chose to exercise it, which he apparently did.

"I am sorry about that," I answered, hiding my embarrassment. "I got caught up."

"Quite alright, quite alright. I'd be lying if I said I wasn't used to it."

"How so?"

"It's LA, my good man," he said with a laugh. "We all get caught up from time to time. Don't beat yourself up about it. "

I figured his idea of getting 'caught up' was the act of making plans and then breaking them, and I realized my personal definition of the phrase was actually quite the same.

"So, what can I do for you, Conrad?" He continued. "Still want to know all there is to know about Gracie Garrison?"

He asked it rather matter of factly, and again I was surprised at his promptness.

"Yes, actually — how did you know?"

"That's why you're calling, isn't it?"

"The truth is I am. Nobody seems to know anything about her."

"Don't worry, you're not the first person to call asking about Gracie," he said with a hearty laugh. "It might take some time, but sooner or later they always call. I can hear it in the voice."

He sounded very arrogant saying it, and I didn't like the idea of being grouped together with a bunch of random strangers I had never met before.

"Benjamin," I said curiously. "Don't take this the wrong way… but why on earth would people call you… to ask about Gracie?"

"Why?" He said in shock. "Because we dated of course."

"You dated Gracie?" I found it surprising.

"Yes, for a few months, did I not tell you?"

"No, you didn't."

He chuckled lightly. "You sound surprised."

"I'm sorry, it's just — I didn't know."

"Quite alright."

"I hope you still don't have feelings for her." It was a stupid thing to say, but I meant well by it.

"Not at all. It was well over a year ago now. No harm done."

Suddenly it all made sense. That's why he was on the balcony that night, that's why he cringed when I mentioned Gracie's name, and that's why he was so eager to tell me false and ridiculous rumors about her. Although he said otherwise I seriously doubted whether he ever got over her, because I knew I probably never could.

"Well then do you mind if I ask what happened?"

"You can ask her, not me." A stain of bitterness carried over the line, and then he caught himself with a slight pause. "Irreconcilable differences, I imagine."

I didn't quite know what he meant by that, but judging by the entire nature of this conversation I figured it must be something just as mysterious and alluring as my attempts to find her, and I had little doubt to who was at fault in a relationship only lasting two months. Regardless, the conversation had gotten rather unpleasant — he had just been reminded of his loss, and I had just realized I was talking to a past romance — I had to be extremely careful with what I said from here on, and with what I believed, because, whether I liked it or not, he was probably my best chance at finding her.

"Listen, you wouldn't happen to know where I could reach her do you? I've been meaning to talk to her."

"Why?" He asked coldly.

I wasn't about to tell him I had spent the night at her place. Even if it was rather innocent, I knew he wouldn't believe it. I had to think of an alibi, and think of one quick.

"It's about a film project."

"A film project?"

"Yes, a film project, I've been writing you see, and I think I have the perfect role for her."

"Uh-huh," he said, not making much effort to hide his disbelief. "Conrad the writer. Yes, I remember now..." he paused, figuring his response. "What's the film about?"

"It's a noir — a modern noir — it's about LA."

"I see. Any roles for me?"

He was just toying with me now, and I didn't like it.

"No. I'm afraid I don't have any roles that fit your description, but I will be sure to let you know if I decide to write any."

"Sounds good — what's Gracie's role? Don't tell me she's the femme fatale."

"No. She's the innocent victim." I retorted harshly, for I was at the very brink of it now, and I was all but done talking to this moron. All I wanted to do was find out what I needed to know about Gracie and finish the ridiculous conversation.

"Ooh. That's new. How does she die?"

"She doesn't die. She gets kidnapped."

"Even better. What happens to her?"

He sounded sadistic, like a small child who grew up without any love whatsoever, and I figured he must have more bitterness towards Gracie than I ever realized. I decided right then that I wouldn't carry it on any further.

"I haven't wrote that part yet."

That took the wind out of the conversation fast, and I could feel his growing excitement fall flat on the other end of the line, and I seized my chance to salvage some of what I'd lost.

"That's what I wanted to talk to her about you see — developing her character — I want to get her feedback on what I have so far."

"Well, that sounds alright," he said rather pleasantly.

For a moment, I thought I had won.

"I could pass it along for you if you like."

"I was really hoping to do it myself. You know, it's more professional that way."

"It doesn't matter, trust me. I've been in the business a few years"

"I've been in it for a few myself," I said, aware that the game was indeed still going, and finding it even more difficult to hide my sudden dislike that was finding its way to the forefront of my throat.

"Then you know how it works. Just send it over to me, and I'll pass it along to her."

"I still prefer to do it myself. It's how I like to do things."

"She would prefer that you send it to me first. I used to read all her scripts for her — still do sometimes — she trusts me."

That was a bold faced lie, and he knew it. He was doing everything he could now just to see me snap, so rather than give him the satisfaction of breaking my temper, I decided to do the opposite with a cordial but prompt goodbye.

"I'll contact her another way. Thank you."

I was about to hang up, when I heard a ridiculous fit of laughter on the other line, cut with exclamations of my name through heaping hoots and guffaws.

"Conrad," he roared. "Conrad... Conrad... please... please stay on the line... I couldn't help myself... I'm sorry my good man... I'm sorry."

He continued his hearty laughter like a maniac, and I realized the whole charade was part of some greater sick joke, and I guessed it wasn't the first time. He seemed like he was well practiced, and I wondered how many other poor fellows had fallen for the same trick.

"You were joking," I stated flatly, finding nothing funny about it.

"I was, good boy. I was."

"Uh huh. Don't tell me that was the actor in you."

"It is, my good man, oh it is," he laughed. "It was just… it was just too easy."

"Right."

"I'm sorry," he said, sobering. "I'll help you. Of course I'll help you. I do hope you'll forgive that little outburst. I don't do it often."

"So it's just me, then?"

"No. No of course not," he said rather seriously. "Like I said, there have been many callers, and you caught me at a particularly good time in the evening."

I knew what he was hinting at, and it became apparent that he had definitely had a few.

"Drink much?" He asked.

"Don't we all," I stated, consciously choosing to lighten my tone.

"Good man," he said agreeably, trying to redeem himself a bit. "Listen, I feel I went too far—"

"I wouldn't worry about it," I said, cutting him off. "It's LA, we all get caught up from time to time."

"That's the spirit," he said thankfully. "Listen, let me buy you a drink."

"That would be fine." I took care to make it sound like an inconvenience.

"Good. Good. Lets meet at the Chateau Marmont. I've been staying in a suite there. Have you been?"

I was very aware of the Chateau. It was nothing new around town that it had long been the who's-who of places to see and be seen, and although I had been a few times before for the occasional drink or business meeting, I had never stayed there, and reasoned he must be doing well for himself to be doing so.

"Of course." I put effort into sounding casual. "When?"

"This Sunday — at seven — in the lobby."

My stomach dropped. That was nearly four days away, and although it wasn't that long, I was eager to locate Gracie as soon as possible, and I knew if I had to wait it would be the longest four days of my life.

"I was hoping to speak to her sooner," I said easily. "Can you do an earlier time?"

"I'm afraid that's the earliest I can do, busy schedule these days."

"That should work then," I stated, keeping calm and hiding my disappointment. "In the meantime, if you happen to speak to Gracie, would you have her contact me?" I was grasping at straws now. "It's a really great project, and I wouldn't want her to miss it."

There was a pause on the other line, followed by a sly, knowing chuckle. "I don't think that is going to happen, good boy. I'll see you Sunday."

I felt belittled, but I would retain my dignity. "See you then," I said as evenly as I could.

He hung up.

I let the phone drop from my ear and held it aloft for a few more moments. There was no doubt about it — he knew Gracie better than I did and that was a fact. As much as I liked to believe that I was one of the only men she ever let get somewhat close to her, I had to seriously consider the possibility that I could be very, very wrong, that perhaps I was just one of many young men who had drifted through her life, following the same formula as the man before me, and the man before him, and the hundreds more that would come and go after us — there one day, then gone the next, like a single speck of sand moved by the wash of the sea — and I never felt so vacant.

CHAPTER 9
— SUNDAY EVENING AT THE CHATEAU —

To my delight, the weekend came and went remarkably fast. As ridiculous as it sounds, my sudden bout of hopelessness supplied me with a great deal of inspiration. I spent the next few days vigorously laying it out on paper, finding it best to capture it while I had it, for I knew the moment I found Gracie it would definitely leave me as quickly as it came, and there would be a whole new perspective in which I would be seeing the world. There is no such thing as creating something out of nothing. The raw materials have always been there — this incredible vigor, this vitality, this life force — supplied by a God of some great and unlimited power, so everything done by human hands, including the hands of The Last True Artist, is more or less an elegant assortment of this matter — His beingness — and the reality of it was that my longing to be with Gracie was both elegant and assorted, true and tangible, for my heart was aching just as much or more than it ever had before, and as long as it was operating all I had to do was simply allow myself to be its conduit, letting it flow through me, trusting that my impulses came from the art itself, and the less I questioned it the better. It needed no shape, no form, it was pure, raw, truth, and I welcomed it openly when it was there.

This attitude carried me quickly into Sunday evening. Time was different when operating from a place of inspiration. Certain moments were longer, others shorter. Days began to blend together like ingredients in a cocktail, and life became altogether more timeless. Sure enough, when I looked from the paper to the clock, I realized I had only an hour before I was expected at the Chateau. Indeed, I had fell into such a flow over the weekend I had practically forgotten all about my meeting with Benjamin, and spent the next thirty minutes or so scrambling to look presentable without running the risk of being late.

It was just a few minutes past six-thirty when I got into my coupe. I hadn't driven it for a few days and I found the air a bit stale, so I rolled down the window to let some of the evening in. I could tell it had been a beautiful day, picturesque in every way that was California, with a glowing skyline that mixed a perfect blend of golden yellow and deep orange that hung ambient-like on the horizon. I took a right off Gower, and headed west down Sunset which turned out to be a straight shot the whole way, and for a moment I wondered how I was making such good time. Then I remembered that it was Sunday — there was hardly ever any traffic on Sunday — and I caught the lights well so it all made sense. By the time I hit the strip it was fifteen minutes to the hour, and I felt rather foolish for feeling needlessly rushed, then I kicked myself for not spending a few more minutes in the bathroom, for I had nicked myself a few times shaving, and knew that the Chateau, of all places, was the last place on earth to show up to looking like anything but one's best self — other than that, I thought I looked damn good.

I veered right off Sunset onto Marmont Lane and pulled up to the grandiose hotel that stood marvelous on the hillside, every inch of its eternal grandeur immortalized forever against the backdrop of the evening twilight. I thought of all the great artists, writers, actors, directors, and thinkers who had come before me, and I wondered if it felt as magical to them as it did to me now, and what memories lay hidden behind its walls that had been created because of it. Figuring this would be the first of many successful evenings to the Chateau in the upcoming years, I didn't think much more of it, for whatever mysteries were worth pondering now would still be worth pondering later, so I threw my key to the valet as if I had been there every night for the last three years, and then I thought of Gracie, and how lovely it would be if she was on my arm, then I stepped onward up the drive through the glooming nightfall.

When I reached the lobby, it was five-till-seven and Benjamin was already there. I spotted him in the back corner on a leather couch near the window. He was reading a stack of white paper between sips of scotch, which I could only guess was a screenplay, and from the looks of it I figured it was more likely that he had been holding up like that all day than had he actually arrived early and was waiting for me. Seeing that he was engrossed, I looked around the lobby. Indeed it was marvelous, with red carpet flooring beneath gothic overhangs that was the quintessential blend of true elegance and old Hollywood glamour. Low-lit lamps cast ambient shadows across the Victorian and European style furnishings, creating mysterious silhouettes from the bodies of secret couples and socialites that wined and dined in strategic clusters around the room, as to appear both perfectly desirable to those who mattered and perfectly unattainable to those who did not, crafting the highest possible illusion of complete exclusivity in the surrounding space. I even thought I saw a young starlet getting kissed beneath one of the shades, but I could not be sure, for she was whisked back into the shadows by her young lover as quickly as she alluded him, and I did not get enough time with her face.

"Benjamin," I called as I neared the couch.

Benjamin Trask was sitting under a lampshade. As he rose to greet me, I noticed that his youthful grey eyes reflected the exact color of his well-fitted suit.

"Conrad," he said enthusiastically. "I thought you'd never come."

"It's just seven now."

"It's just a figure of speech of my friend, just a figure of speech…"

He paused for a moment, and I had difficulty telling whether he was serious or not… he had that way about him.

"It's good to see you," he continued.

"Likewise."

We shook hands.

"In all honesty, I wasn't sure you'd make it." He sat back down on the couch.

"Yes, you mentioned that — why?" I took a leather chair opposite him.

"You didn't call last time you said you would, if you remember."

I didn't know why he was bringing that back up, and I figured it was either, one, to make him appear busy and therefore more important, two, to make me feel bad right off the bat in order to get the quick upper hand, or three, that he just forgot altogether, and if that was the case then he had a very complex case of short-term memory loss.

"Yes, we discussed that on the phone. I think we referred to it as 'getting caught up.'" I chose to make light of it.

"Oh that's right, that's right," he said quickly. "It's all coming back to me now. If you knew me better, I think you would find me to be good for my word at least ninety percent of the time."

We shared a quick laugh. If it resulted in finding Gracie I was willing to go through the motions.

"Not to worry," he continued. "There's a reason I wanted to meet here, you see I have a suite just upstairs— "

"Yes, you did mention that,"

"I did?" He actually sounded surprised, and I couldn't tell if he was faking or if he was just a really good actor, and then I considered that short-term memory loss was most definitely plausible. "Suppose I did," he mumbled after a short lapse, resorting back to his scotch.

There was a moment, and then by noticing his own drink at his mouth, he offered me one in return. He called over a waitress and had her bring me the exact drink I got at Gracie's cocktail party the night I first met him — a scotch and soda — and he did it without blinking an eye. I then realized I was dealing with someone much smoother and more cunning then I had previously given him credit for, and then add to that the fact that he was holding down a sizable suite at the Chateau, and dated Gracie for a decent amount of time, well, it made him rather formidable. If it meant that I had to play a game in order to find out Gracie's whereabouts, then I would play it, and I would win.

We talked for a few more minutes about the state of things, and I took care to nurse my drink slowly as he railed through a few more. He told me that a certain prominent director was doing a film in the first quarter of next year, and he was in top consideration for the lead role, hence the reason for the screenplay he was engrossed in just minutes earlier. I offered my congratulations, and we went on to discuss a bit more about each of our recent successes for the next half hour or so, as seemed to be the custom when catching up with industry folk. By the time the conversation finally began shifting towards Gracie, Benjamin was on his third cocktail since we started that evening, and he cut right to the chase.

"Conrad," he said rather airily. "There is no project is there?"

"What do you mean?" I asked, attempting to appear aloof, for I knew exactly what he meant, and I thought he would have the decency not to bring it up.

"The noir script you were talking about on the phone the other day," he continued. "That's not why you really want to talk to Gracie."

To my dismay, it was clear that he did in fact remember the totality of our conversation from the other day, and I felt my stomach burn as I realized he'd been toying with me earlier.

"It's funny that you'd remember that, since you seem to remember nothing else from it," I snapped, a little more aggressively than I would have liked, and I thought for sure the tension would only escalate from here, but he didn't react like I was expecting him to — he was not hostile — instead, he leaned back against the couch and took a good, long sip of his drink like something much deeper was bothering him.

"It's just that..." he began after a moment. "Gracie's not an actress."

"What do you mean? Weren't you the one who told me that she had been on the look out for a starring role?"

"Don't get me wrong," he continued thoughtfully. "She's an actress, sure — she acts — I'd even go as far as to say she's quite talented, but she's not a true actress. She's not anybody you'd bring any serious material to. You seem like a serious person."

He must have sensed my confusion, for he sat back up on the edge of the couch and gave me his full attention.

"Let me explain. Gracie is a bit, well... how do I put this..." he paused, taking his time to chew a nail rather than use the wrong word. "Gracie is a bit flighty."

"I think I got that," I stated flatly. Flighty was the one thing, if anything, that I was certain about with her.

"I even hear she's dating a musician now, poor girl."

"Really?" I was concerned, but attempted to show indifference. "I haven't heard a thing about it."

"Well, I don't know if it's true of course. Who knows what's true anymore with her, but the thought alone is a goddamn tragedy."

"Why do you say that?"

"Why my good man," he stated coolly from behind a drink of his scotch. "Musicians are the scum of the earth."

He was so relaxed in the way he said it — all reclined back against the leather couch with his arm dangling neatly over the side, twirling his drink — that he almost had me convinced. I had my own experiences with musicians in Hollywood, and based on them alone I didn't necessarily disagree with him completely. In fact I wanted to agree with him, for I was taken with the image of Gracie dating some talentless musician, lost in the gaudy trenches of complete and total obscurity, and then I remembered how Gracie liked music, and how if she was really dating some musician — whomever he was — than there must be at least one thing about him that was good, even if he was talentless, and then I thought myself as being narrow, and I reasoned to take a more neutral approach.

"I have my own opinions about them," I stated plainly. "I wouldn't call them the scum of the earth — in fact, if I had the pick of the lot I'd probably choose to be a rock star."

"More sex?"

"I didn't say—"

"That's what you were thinking, wasn't it?"

He had me nailed down. Without indicating, I took a deep breath and steeled my nerves. "An actor much more accomplished than either of us said that once." Without having to read him further, I knew he knew whom I was referring to. "I think his word speaks for itself — but yes, I'm sure sex had something to do with it."

"Well, they *are* the scum of the earth," he retorted bitterly. "Sex or no sex, anyone can play an instrument, Conrad. It takes no talent to do it."

"That's a statement. What about Beethoven?"

"There's brilliance sure — as there is in all things — but that is few and far between, and it sure as hell doesn't exist in all these talentless hacks on the Boulevard. A few stray notes and a bunch of loud noise and they think they're worthy to call themselves artists. It's ridiculous!" He laughed heartily, and truthfully, and I knew he really thought it to be just as funny as he made it out to be. "Tell me something... when you think of Hollywood, what do you picture?"

I just stared at him as my face fell flat, for I was annoyed with the way the conversation was going, and the last thing I wanted to talk about was a bunch of musicians — talentless-hack musicians according to him — and I wanted to move back towards Gracie as soon as possible.

"That's not difficult — the studios of course — the film industry."

"Exactly. Then why would someone move to Hollywood and become a musician?"

"To follow a dream I suppose, just like the rest of us."

In that moment he got very serious. He leaned in very close, and poised his fingers together, holding them in front of his grey eyes as to pierce my very mind with them. "No," he whispered with a slight smile, as if he was letting me in on secret that only the enlightened ones of the world knew. "They do it, because they can't do what we do. They can't be truthful. Instruments can be learned, Conrad, but the portrayal of real truth — human emotion — takes talent, talent that they don't have, and they will always be last in line because of it." With that he fell back into the couch, and, as if to congratulate his own brilliance, stretched his arms out lazily along the backrest. "And that, my friend, is why someone becomes a musician."

There was a moment where we both said nothing, and before I called him on it, I wanted to give him a moment for all that effort, for what it was worth, I felt he earned it.

"You sure you're not jealous?" I inquired shortly after.

"My good man," he said with a haughty chuckle. "The last thing on earth there is to be jealous of is a musician, so much so that I find it impossible."

I just looked at him.

"Acting is truth," he stated confidently. "Writing is truth on paper — I mean look at you, boy. What you do is sheer genius — and at your age."

"I wouldn't call it that," I stated, not liking to be burdened with the responsibility of such a word.

"Well, believe it, because it's true," he stated in absolution. "It takes one to know one, and what you are is a genius, Conrad, so you might as well get used to it."

I detested him more by the second, especially this arrogant bout of self-proclamation he was putting on. "The way I see it," I started with a good deal of resentment aimed specifically at him. "There's only one genius — God — the rest is just make-believe."

To my dismay this had the opposite effect, and was apparent when he boomed out in a kind of victorious laughter. "Excellent! Most excellent!"

"What's so funny?"

He laughed for a few more moments, and then managed to pull it together enough to speak. "Why, your inability to take a compliment, of course. It's completely savage, Conrad — brilliant — but savage. It's perfectly representative of what you are. I just complimented your genius by comparing you to myself, and in return you threw us both under the bus in favor of some mischievous deity that may or may not exist. With what I'm getting you'd likely throw your whole family under as well, if it meant diffusing a basic compliment."

"They all live out of state, so that might take a while," I scowled.

He laughed again and shook his head, apparently pleased with something. At minimum, it was clear he was impressed.

"I see you're really getting it," he chuckled. "You're learning to ride the Holly-go-round. Very good."

"I told you I'd hold on."

"Holding on is one thing, my friend, flourishing is another, and you have a long way to go."

"I wouldn't know anything about it then." I was unamused.

"Have you ever heard the term 'fake-it-til-you-make-it'?" He asked.

"Yes, and I detest it, almost as much as I detest that stupid statement 'paying your dues'," I said coldly. "But perhaps you could tell me more about it, since you clearly think so highly of yourself."

"Like I said, savage." He finally fell silent and took a drink of his scotch, and for that I was thankful, but there was a staleness to the air now, a staleness created by topics best left untouched, and to my frustration I didn't know how we had gotten there. For better or worse, the conditions ironically mirrored my situation with Gracie almost exactly, which was the complete opposite of what I had set out to achieve. Then, with the sudden remembrance of her name, the beauty of her face followed, and the feeling of how much I truly missed her, and once again I felt powerfully compelled by my objective.

"I believe we've gotten off topic," I said as enthusiastically as I could, momentarily staying my pride. "If I spoke out of turn, I apologize."

Benjamin smiled slowly and sat up. "I've been looking for something to pull me out of that god-awful script all day, and here you are… if anything, I should be thanking you."

"The script's not good, then?"

"Just because it has an inflated budget and a big director doesn't necessarily make it an enjoyable read," he reflected, almost painfully so. "I'm sure you could write better."

"I don't know—"

"You could," he stated absolutely, looking me in the eye. "And don't ever apologize for good conversation again, Conrad. It's beneath you."

There was a moment, and I knew we were both back on the same page. It was time to continue.

"Alright," I started. "You were saying something about Gracie being flighty."

"Right." He snapped up from the couch as if he had never got sidetracked at all. "She can't be counted on for anything, you see. She can't be trusted."

"Explain," I said, cutting in. I still didn't like the idea of anybody talking bad on Gracie, and I once again felt it was my personal responsibility to protect her dignity — especially after all we had been through the other night — then I once again remembered what I was trying to accomplish, and the look on Benjamin's face told me I wouldn't get anywhere with flippant demands, so I made the conscience effort to digress — "I mean… explain, if you'd please."

He eyed me with a moment of uncertainty, and then his expression once again softened as he consented to continue. "Well, as I mention before, Gracie and I were seeing each other for a couple of months earlier this year."

"—Yes—"

"Everything was going quite well at first. You see, like you, I also thought I was in love with her."

"I never said—"

He casually held up his hand, effectively waving off my feeble defense. "There's no use in denying it my friend," he said lightly. "She's a beautiful and intriguing woman. There's no shame in it."

He paused for me to respond, but I couldn't disagree, and having nothing to say I simply nodded in consensus.

"As I was saying, everything was going extremely well, and I couldn't have been more happy. Indeed, I thought I had met the perfect woman. I was a young up-and-comer teetering at the edge of stardom, and she was all desired and beautiful…"

He paused, and in doing so gazed off pensively toward one of the medieval chandeliers that glowed hauntingly against the wall. Then after a moment, his jaw muscles pulsed slightly, and his mouth cracked a small smile, and I knew that whatever fond experience it was that his mind was replaying in his memory, he wished he could be back there. His grey eyes glazed over as the memory reached its climax, and then he blinked, and it was gone. He took a steadying breath and set his attention back towards me.

"I guess you could say at the time we were quite the item. Everywhere we would go people would stop and stare…. it was wonderful… it was really a wonderful time…" He took a drink of his scotch, and the emotion passed.

"How did you meet?" I inquired. "If you don't mind me asking."

"Not at all," he said, straightening his grey blazer as he leaned back coolly into the couch. "We were introduced, by a mutual friend."

"Who?"

"Bobby Finch."

"Bobby Finch — the art dealer?"

"That's right. Do you know him?"

"Vaguely." I wasn't at all about to tell him how we met. "I actually tried to call him the other day — same day I called you."

"Any luck?"

"No."

"That's not surprising," he said with a chuckle. "He's a hard man to get a hold of — that Bobby Finch — I'm surprised you even got his number."

"Try the operator. They'll connect you to his office just fine."

"Which office?" He posed the question with raised eyebrows over the rim of his glass, with an air that was both curious and condescending.

I adjusted in my chair, nursing a small drink. "So he introduced you."

"Yes, we were both in New York at the time. I was there auditioning for a play on Broadway, and Gracie was there for fashion week. Bobby just happened to be in New York that weekend — he spends most of his time in Paris you see, he's hardly ever in LA — did you meet him in LA?"

"Yes."

"When?"

"At a gallery opening, back in November."

"Hmm," Benjamin narrowed his eyes. "Was I there?"

"I'm sure you'd remember if you were."

He looked at me, curious and annoyed, then, as if deciding to think no more of it, continued with his story. "Anyway, I suppose it was fashion week, so it wasn't too coincidental that he was there. I really don't care for fashion week much. I don't see a use for it. Yourself?"

"Never been," I said, honestly unamused.

"You're not missing anything. I can tell you that," he stated, his haughty, arrogant guffaw once again returning to his voice. "A bunch of models everywhere. Never trust a model."

"Yes, you've said that before."

"Well it's true. A bunch of talentless air heads the lot of them — beautiful sure — but talentless, just a step above a musician, and as you know that's not saying much."

"Gracie's a model, is she not?"

"Don't get me wrong, there are exceptions, but for the most part talentless." He took a strong, defiant sip of his scotch, and once again his eyes glazed over, but not in the pleasant way that I saw before. This time it was sullen — bitter — and it was probably reinforced by several bad experiences. Regardless, by this point he had had a good deal to drink, and despite his remarkable tolerance it was beginning to show.

"So Bobby Finch was in New York." I made it a point to push the conversation forward.

"Right," he said, realizing he had slackened his pace. "And he was having a party at his gallery that weekend. Gracie was of course invited — they go way back, I have no idea how far — and Bobby had somehow heard that I was in New York so he personally phoned my agent to invite me. He prides himself on entertaining high profile people, like he's trying to be the next Andy Warhol or something ridiculous. Anyway, I thought it was pretty swank at the time, I admit."

"Uh huh," I said with a slow, unconvinced nod of my head, taken by how truly pompous and arrogant Benjamin really was. I never got that impression the night I first met him at Gracie's, and I'd be lying if I said I wasn't a bit disappointed. Then again, a lot can happen in two months, and perhaps his recent success had gone straight to his head — he also wasn't nearly as drunk the last time, but that was a poor excuse.

"So," he continued. "I arrived at the party not really knowing what to expect, but I've got to tell you, I had never seen so many beautiful faces."

"I get that idea," I interjected.

"Interesting man, Bobby Finch — odd but interesting — I figured he kept good company, so he must be nice enough. He instantly took a liking to me, almost strangely so, and he kept telling me somebody was coming that he wanted to introduce me to, because — his words — he thought we'd make a 'neat pair.'"

"You don't say."

"Well, I don't know what all this 'neat' nonsense was about, but all that didn't matter the second she walked in the door." He smiled again, but this time it was true and genuine, and I knew exactly of whom he was thinking.

"Gracie," I stated — saying her name felt good.

"That's right," he said, nodding his head with real conviction, and I knew that for the first time in a while we were both in total agreement. "Gracie Garrison walked through the door that night, and well, the rest is history."

"You fell for her."

"I did, my good man, I certainly did." he acknowledged my statement with a smile. "She was the most beautiful, lovely, alive girl I had ever laid eyes on, and I told Bobby I had to meet her immediately. Within ten minutes we were sipping champagne and discussing the origins of abstract art, and she was giving me the most difficult time imaginable. I simply stated that Pablo Picasso was without a doubt the single most important individual to modern day expressionism, and Gracie, she seemed convinced that Jackson Pollock was the most important individual, but she didn't ever say why other than she adored his paintings. No matter how much I tried to persuade her otherwise or how much logic I used to support my argument, she wouldn't have it." Again, that same genuine smile spread across his face, even wider this time.

"I had never met a girl so stubborn — or so challenging — I found everything about her to be positively addicting."

"So you began dating?"

"Yes, she eventually agreed to go on a date with me, but only after a month of persuading on my part once we were both back in LA."

I felt a small leap of victory arise in me when he said this, and I chuckled to myself when I realized it took him a month of begging to get a date with Gracie, when she had, in fact, called me personally for one. It was a basic, adolescent pleasure stemming from my lower nature, but what the hell, he seemed to so enjoy making everything a competition, and with that in mind I took a great deal of satisfaction in knowing that I had just one-upped him.

"If she did have any reluctance," he continued. "I was so thrilled when she finally said yes I wouldn't have even noticed. I had never spent so much time courting a girl before, and I don't think I ever could again, but I'll tell you right now, it was worth every minute I put into it."

I wasn't much interested in hearing the details of their romance, and with the way things were going it was apparent that he would be perfectly fine talking about his past memories with Gracie all night — the point had come — I had built enough of a rapport, he had had enough liquor, and it was time to start prying.

"Benjamin, you mentioned earlier that she couldn't be trusted... what did you mean by that?"

That took the wind right out of him, because all the blood seemed to rush out of his face as he held his breath, and he turned a temporary, pale white that was a little more than subtle.

"I did?" He asked.

"Yes, you did."

"Yes, well, suppose I did," he began in his semi-formal, half-reluctant way that he resorted to when he knew he had been caught, and wanted to save as much face as he could for it. He found temporary shelter behind a deep pull on his drink, considering his options, and seeing he had none, consented to look back in my direction, taking care to avoid my eye line. "What do you want to know?"

"I want to know why you said it."

"See here, I won't be forced."

"No one's forcing you," I said calmly. It was important to keep my focus and cut him off logically. "You called me here to tell me about Gracie, did you not?"

"Perhaps—"

"And you told me you'd help me on the phone the other day. You told me to come by the Chateau for a drink."

"I suppose I did, yes."

"Then unless you're pulling another one over on me — and if that's the case its completely tasteless — then I take it you weren't planning on having me drive all the way over here, on a Sunday evening, just to waste my time. Correct?"

"No. I don't waste people's time my friend. It's not like me. It's unprofessional." He straightened his blazer and sat up to his full height. "Purely second rate, third rate even."

"Well, so far you've told me a great deal, but a great deal of nothing — nothing that really helps me make sense of things on my part — so I'd ask that you'd at least honor our original agreement and tell me why you think she can't be trusted."

Benjamin took his time, considering my rationale behind a sip of scotch, and I could tell that the alcohol was definitely slowing his ability to process, but not necessarily hindering the result. As egotistical as he could be, he was also a logical man, and when he wasn't joking I recognized that he was always one to honor the rules of a good argument, even if it meant momentarily staying his pride. For what it was worth, I couldn't say that about everyone I knew, and at least, for that, he had my respect.

"Well… where should I start?" He asked, rightfully consenting to the rules that he himself set up.

"Why don't you start from the beginning — whenever it was that you began to notice anything peculiar."

"Peculiar," he burst out impulsively. "Strange is the better word for it."

Then Benjamin got very quiet, and very sober, and looked around at all the low-lit silhouettes scattered about the dusky lobby like they had all been waiting in earnest, listening in all evening for this exact moment to arrive. Then he leaned in, and got very close to my face. "I'm about to tell you things that I've never told anybody," he said in all seriousness. "You can't repeat what I say here, understand? Not to anybody."

"I won't say a word," I stated, rather shocked at the sudden change. He definitely had my attention now, and I was no longer able to hide my intense curiosity.

"Nobody knows. Nobody finds out. Period. If it ever got back to her — if it ever got back to whom it concerns — she would know where it came from, and that's it. I'm not sure exactly what would happen, or what could happen, but it's not worth it. Understand? It's not worth it for either of us. I only tell you because I said I'd tell you. I've always been a man of my word, and I won't be seen any differently."

"Of course," I said, doing my best to appease his insecurity, for I was on the very edge of my chair now. My senses were heightened, and my heart felt like it was going to lurch through my chest. The whole lobby seemed to close in around us, and I knew that whatever I was about to hear it had been worth the wait, and the whole evening suddenly felt perfectly justified. Seeing that he had gotten his point across, Benjamin eased back slightly against the dark leather couch and took a thoughtful sip of his scotch, contemplating exactly how he should start.

"I had been seeing her three to four nights a week for about a month," he began articulately. "When I started to notice… patterns… with some of the company she kept. Naturally, that brought up all sorts of questions with me, but I never dared to ask. That was one of her rules you see. You never ask questions."

I was all too familiar with that rule, and I remembered how Gracie had successfully worked it into our first conversation over the phone at the beginning of our first evening, making me promise it to her before she agreed to go out, and then how she used it on me later in the night to avoid me when I desired to communicate with her most.

"You said that was one of her rules — so she had others?" I asked, calmly enough to cloak my personal association in mere curiosity.

"Yes." He didn't elaborate, but looked at me as if doing so would be particularly difficult. "Well, what were they?"

I left him no choice, so he rolled his eyes and shook his head — it was still difficult.

"Oh, let's see, there was a whole variety of them — 'you mustn't snoop, you mustn't get curious, you mustn't wonder how I feel about things, you mustn't have any expectations' — more and more as time went on, but I found all these to be eclipsed by her central rule that you were to never ask questions, so I figured the others pointless."

I was about to speak when he remembered something.

"Oh, and there was one more she mentioned later on — 'you must never speak of love' — and then after seeing the expression on my face she added — 'for a great long while.'"

"I see," I said, for I saw a trend in what Benjamin had mentioned so far, and it seemed to me that all of Gracie's so called 'rules' were set up in order for her to keep a certain distance between herself and the people she was seeing, but the real question was 'why?'

"Yes, I was completely enamored by her," he continued. "I just figured it was the way she liked to do things, like a test of some kind, and I thought that if I passed and then continued to impress her, we might eventually get married. That's definitely what I wanted anyway — it's always hard to find a good woman, especially in this industry — anyway, a few more weeks went by, we started to get a little more comfortable, and then she began to grow passively disrespectful towards me. She wouldn't return my calls, she'd act like she was constantly busy —which of course, wasn't true, — she'd lie over just about anything, and she was constantly late, not just a little late, say ten, fifteen minutes, I'm talking hours. Whole hours, Conrad."

"That's a long time," I added, seeing that he was getting worked up.

"Damn right it is!" He blurted out. "I didn't know why she was doing it. It made no sense. Everything seemed to be going so well. It was positively aggravating." He dove into a drink of scotch, leveling himself out. "However, I wanted to honor the rules, and I figured it was just her way of trying to get me to break them and fail the test. Well, I wasn't going to give her that satisfaction, and being a man of an even temperament I chose to simply ignore it, believing that it would all go away and she'd be back to her normal self once she realized that I could not be shaken by any of her childish games."

He paused his fit of bitterness, and the cute house waitress that had been floating around the lobby all night stopped to top off his scotch. This time she just left the bottle.

"She didn't stop did she? — The games?" I asked as the waitress left.

"No, good man. She didn't," he said with a deep sigh. "In fact, it got much, much worse."

I waited in earnest while he primed himself for the inevitable with a crane of the neck, a stretching of the brow, a long drink, and a deep, deep breath.

"One night, I had a little too much to drink, and when we got back to her place I decided to call her on it — her behavior, that is — I asked her why she was being so flighty with me. She responded like I was ridiculous for even bringing it up, like I was insane for even asking. Can you believe it? Me?! For asking her?!"

He looked desperately beaten, like an old man who had been dominated by his wife for an entire lifetime and was all out of answers.

"I told her how it made me feel," he continued. "And I asked her if she loved me, because if she did she would stop — she would stop immediately." He stewed, heavy, as if doing so could still change the outcome.

"Well, what did she do?" I asked, breaking the silence.

"She laughed in my face."

I nearly burst into laughter! I had to stifle myself with a heavy drink of scotch that I began to choke on immediately, falling into a fit of hysterical coughing which I couldn't have been more grateful for.

"I do say my good man. Are you alright?" He asked, taken aback.

"Yes — yes, yes." I barely managed to speak between the suffocating coughs. "I'm fine."

"Are you sure? Do you need a glass of water?"

"No — no really — I'll be fine in a moment — it's just a passing — it's just a passing thing."

"Well, then, if you insist," he said with unamused intrigue, sinking back into the leather couch. "Are you sure you're alright?"

"Yes — yes, I'm fine — absolutely I'm fine." I continued to cough through the last bits of liquid caught in my throat, and I pictured the surprise on Gracie's face when he had asked her for her love, and I couldn't stop smiling.

"I'm sorry about that," I said after a moment. "It seems that I've — 'cough' — it seems that I've had a bit to drink."

"That's only your second glass," he jeered.

"Really?" I asked, faking surprise. "Surely it must be my third."

"It's only your second. You've only had one refill."

"Well, it feels like a third. You'd think I could trust my body to know better."

"You'd think, but it's only your second," he stated coldly, at last realizing that I was truly laughing at him.

"I've hardly eaten anything today, I suppose that could be it," I diverted quickly, for he had more information — information I desperately needed — and I wasn't about to lose it over an impulsive laugh and a petty disagreement.

"That will do it," he began with a great deal of self-assuredness. "It's not good to miss meals, Conrad. Look at you. You're too skinny. Women love muscles my good man, so does the camera."

"I've been writing a lot lately," I said, dismissing the annoying comment. "Good thing I don't need much of a body for that."

"Do you know how many times I eat a day?" He interjected with a proud smile.

"How many?"

"Six."

"Six times?"

"That's right. Keeps the metabolism up. Makes the body lean."

"Right," I stated flatly. The truth was I couldn't have been less interested in whether he ate once, twice, or fifteen times a day for that matter, but I had found my chance to appeal to his ego, and I knew I might not get another. "I bet Gracie appreciated that," I said with a quick change of direction.

"Ha," he began with a haughty grunt. "You think she would, wouldn't you? It's her loss."

"What do you mean?"

"My good man," he said with a laugh. "We were never intimate."

"Intimate?"

"We never made love, Conrad."

I stared at him in a strange disbelief. He noticed and seemed rather amused by it.

"I'm sorry, were you under the impression that we did?"

"Well, yes, I suppose." The truth was I absolutely thought they were, so much so that it was never even a question in my mind, but until then I had chosen to spare my mind by not entertaining the idea.

"And what would make you think that?" He prodded.

"It's just the way of things, isn't it?"

"You would think — you would think, wouldn't you? But we never were… it's her loss." He finished with a strong drink, and he looked like he could kill.

"If you see it that way," I said.

"What was that?"

We both looked at each other, and each man knew the other desired the same thing.

"I said, 'if you see it that way,' that's all."

"That *is* the way I see it." He stared at me, rolling the ice cubes around in his empty glass, taking his time. "Do you want to be with her?"

I just looked at him.

"Gracie doesn't sleep with nobodies, Conrad," he said as if it was a commonplace. "Surely you know that by now."

That was a low blow, and any sympathy I had building for him was tossed right out the window. He also left himself vulnerable to a devastating counter if I chose to exercise it, for with a great deal of harnessed resentment he had just admitted to me that he had never reached that highly treasured level of physical intimacy with Gracie either, and with that information I knew I could destroy him. I could lay waste to his fragile ego and leave him as nothing more than a ball of wallowing self-pity drinking himself to death in the lobby of the Chateau Marmont, but I had nothing to prove to this man, and, with only Gracie in mind, I made the hard choice of letting it level out. "Yes, I'm beginning to get that idea."

With that, Benjamin burst into another ridiculous bout of intense, overbearing laughter. Although he'd want to appear smooth on the surface — and by most accounts he was doing a good job — I was far enough down the line with him that I could tell that he was pushing in order to give himself room to recover. "Idea!" He projected. "My good man, it's the truth!"

I wasn't amused by his laughter, which I found to be entirely overdone, and I didn't like to be belittled, which I felt like he was doing, so I just waited for him to say something else, which he eventually did.

"I can see you're not following."

"No. I'm not."

"Let me think of an example," he said with a new lightness, and suddenly he was sober and as dapper as can be, for whatever it was that Gracie did, it was so visceral for him that it literally took a physical affect, like a drug, or alcohol, or any other substance that causes the chemicals in the body to shift back and forth. "You know that Maxwell character she runs around with?"

"Yes. Maxwell Price."

"Why do you think she keeps him around?"

"I haven't the slightest idea," I said, flippant. "Because she likes him I suppose."

"I like a lot of people my good man, doesn't mean I give them a key to my house."

"You asked the question."

"I'll tell you why," he said with a knowing smile. "Because it's safe."

I thought his answer was stupid and found no reason to respond.

"Tell me something," he said leaning in. "How many women do you know that look like her, running around with a man that looks like him?"

"Not a lot, but it can happen."

"Well surely it's not for sexual reasons."

"I wouldn't consider it. I happen to know that's not part of the equation."

"And I happen to know he hasn't much money, so that's out."

"I wasn't considering that either." I didn't like the idea of money being a staple factor in relationships, and even if it were the true way of things, it didn't mean I had to like it anymore than I did, which was not at all — my tone made sure to convey that.

"Then what on earth's the benefit?" He blurted out. "An unattractive man with no money and a beautiful woman spending so much time together, with no consideration to sex whatsoever? The very thought of it is ridiculous. Don't tell me you haven't had questions."

As much as I wasn't a fan of his self-righteousness, I couldn't deny that he had a point. The fact was that I had been curious about Gracie and Maxwell's relationship since I first saw them together at the bar that night, and now that it was being discussed openly I saw no reason to hide my true feelings. I knew that whatever it was that kept them together could be the key to unlocking the mystery of Gracie's alluring psychology, which I considered to be in itself a form of true art, and to go into it would be a magnificent experience indeed.

"I have to admit," I said. "I've always found their relationship to be a bit — well — odd."

"Odd isn't the word for it," he said angrily. "It's downright sick, that's what it is."

"I didn't say there was anything wrong with it," I stated defensively, surprised at his dark choice of words. "She keeps odd company, surely they can be friends."

"Friends!" he blurted out louder than he had all evening, his grey eyes bulging from his head. "Conrad, it's emasculating! That is what I had to deal with in our relationship — men like that!" he continued ardently. "A woman meets a man that isn't interested in her sexually, she submits to his will, and instead of becoming lovers they become friends. He fulfills all the same needs for her minus one that she then begins to forget about, and suddenly she feels as though she doesn't need to sleep with anybody —

ever — in order to be satisfied. Not even those that she apparently loves. It's a goddamn epidemic."

"Surely you can't be serious?" I said, astonished at his absurd conviction.

"I am," he said strongly. "In fact that was the singular point of downfall in our relationship. That man — whatever he is."

"So Maxwell was who you were referring to earlier. The company you found to be disagreeable — the pattern, I think you called it."

He sat back into a contemplative drink of his scotch, and I knew I had hit a nerve.

"There were a few others I didn't care for," he said after a moment. "But he was by far the worst of them. He was the reason for all her... unnatural behavior."

"Unnatural?" I chuckled. "Have you ever just considered that maybe she simply wasn't interested?"

"Impossible," he snapped coldly.

"It's alright," I said as neutrally as I could, for I of all people knew better than to take a swing at a man's pride, especially when he was clinging to something that was lost, and in this case no good could come from it. "People can be different, it doesn't make either of you any worse for it."

"It makes her worse for it — that's a fact."

"It's not a fact, but it is a bold statement, and I don't see how either of you are better than the other."

Suddenly, he somehow once again managed to drop into a haughty bit of laughter that could have been considered sincere if he hadn't been so sinister just moments before. "You're alright, Conrad," he said with a chuckle. "You're positively alright. Your steadfast belief that people are inherently good is extraordinary, and that makes you likable. I'd say you'd be damn close to winning me over, if I wasn't so jaded."

"I don't think all people are inherently good," I stated truthfully. "But I do think some people are."

"Good boy, you've been defending her all evening," he said with a knowing charm.

"You've given me no reason not to so far. I don't see Gracie here to defend herself, and I've always been somewhat of a devil's advocate."

"That's very noble of you." He spoke to me like a child that just did something good, and wanted to reward me for it.

"Besides, all I have is your word." It was difficult to hide my building aggravation. "If it's no good, then what am I even doing here?"

"Like I said… likable," he said with a dropping smile and much less conviction.

"Why would you say that about yourself anyway?" My frustration was growing, and I was eager to get the spotlight off me and back on the subject at hand. "That you're jaded? What kind of man says that about himself?"

"I said it, good boy, because I am." He dropped his head in a personal defeat. "I don't see the use for people anymore, not like I used to anyway. I too once believed that people were good and bright — especially women — yes, I used to think women were the light of the world." Then back to his previous thought — "I couldn't place it before, but now I've got it — you're like a still good version of me."

"I sincerely doubt that," I mumbled on his high note, for I didn't like being compared to someone I found to have a disagreeable nature, but he mustn't have had heard me because he continued as though he hadn't.

"Well, I don't believe that about them anymore," he said with an air of darkness that put him right back on track, and his eyes narrowed with a sudden evilness nearly as menacing as his sinewy jaw muscles that now pulsed more rapidly and foreboding than ever. "Now all I see is darkness when I look at them. Corruption. Wickedness. They're the weaker sex for a reason, and they'll bring down the whole damn kingdom if you let them."

"That's a cynical way to look at things. It seems to me you're bitter."

"Bitter? Ha! Damn outraged is what I am," he stated defiantly. "I'm outraged at the whole damn thing. I'm outraged that I ever had to consider it. In fact, I'm outraged that I even have to have this conversation! — Although I shouldn't be, it's her own damn fault you know. She never had any restraint, and I doubt she ever will. There's not the least bit of logic in that girl. Not one damn bit!"

"There's no use in getting mad about it now. Gracie's not a creature of logic. So it will do you no good to speak of her like if she was."

"You seem to know a lot about it," he snapped.

"I know what I know," I stated, holding my ground. "Besides, women are more emotional in general. Surely a man such as yourself knows that by now."

"Well damn her logic, and damn her emotion," he stated in absolution. "With me she had the world. She could be in here, now, sipping scotch right next to me in this marvelous hotel, but instead she's out there running around with some washed up musician not good enough to shine my shoes, and that damn Maxwell character — brainwashed to the nines — I knew he was no good the moment I laid eyes on him. He's a damn fake. "

"He's always been very agreeable with me. I'd even say he's rather pleasant. Just what exactly happened that makes you despise him so much?"

"What? Are you his advocate now too?"

"No, but I think your bitterness is making you ignorant, and it doesn't reflect well on you, or your character, and least of all your position." I stated calmly, feeling perfectly justified.

"Yes, well, I have my reasons."

"Let's hear them, then," I said with a surprising enthusiasm. "The way it stands right now you have no argument, and I don't believe that is what you brought me down here for."

"It's most certainly not," he mumbled in a neutral tone, which could have gone either way depending on the state of the listener. "Say, what is it to you anyway? I don't usually take meetings, and this is why. Here you've had me going on all evening, enticing me to go much further into detail than I ever initially desired to, and you haven't even told me what it's all about."

"I have my reasons."

"You know you're good at that," he countered.

"Good at what?"

"That — taking peoples words and turning them against them — you have a good memory. It's an excellent weapon for debate, and you've spared no use of it tonight."

"Yes, well, I suppose its only fitting, being so likable and all."

He burst into another fit of his pompous, drunken, half-stupid laughter, in which I could only sit and watch as it played itself out. "Touché, my good man! Touché!" He exclaimed, his laugh leveling out. "There it is, just when I thought I had you, you've done it again. Bravo!" He situated himself a little further back into the couch, like he was under the impression that he had just experienced a small victory, or some other kind of misinformed triumph he had resolved to fabricate in his mind. "So tell me, just what is it that's going on between you two anyway?"

I was promptly out of patience and stared at the gloating young man in disgust, sitting there, all haughty in that grey designer suite that was completely expensive and completely devoid of any real character at the same time, a juxtaposition which I found to be a completely accurate reflection of his personality. All his youth, all his good looks, and all his effortless charm would eventually fail him without any true virtue, and in time he would see that his physicality would become subjective if he were in the business for any real respect. There was something true there, but it was buried far beneath a false self-realization that I hadn't the time or the tolerance to deal with any longer. If logic was the only thing he understood than I would treat him like an accountant, or a mathematician, or any other person who's profession relied solely on theory

rather than art, and I hated to do it because I believed
he was a good actor, and I liked actors for the most part.

"Here are the facts," I began directly. "You brought
me here because you said you could help me. Well so far,
you've hinted at many things but have revealed next to
nothing."

"I've told you personal information," he interjected
defensively.

"True, but very little of it is fact — philosophies,
opinions, sure — but no facts."

"My good man, I've been honest, open. I've told
you everything I know."

"Not everything," I stated quickly. "I want to know
why you are avoiding talking about Maxwell Price."

"I said I'd talk about Gracie, not that floundering
moron," he snapped.

"You said it yourself that he was the reason behind
all her behavior. I see that as being directly involved."

"There you go again with your tactics." He waved
his hand, trying to dismiss his agitation. "Why do you care
so much anyway?"

I looked him hard in the face. "You said you'd help
me."

"So what? People say a lot of things, and don't
think you're any different. From the way it sounded over
the phone I thought this was going to be a good bit of
gossip over a couple of drinks, and it's turned out to be a
damn near wrestling match. And for what? For some
lonesome, near-sighted attempt at self-fulfillment? For
some empty, hopeless quest for true love? It doesn't exist
man! She's gone. Forget about the girl, because you can be
damn well sure she's forgotten about you."

"I just need to know... what happened to her," I
stated as slowly and calmly as death — my hands shaking,
my resolve complete.

"Why?"
"Because—"
"Because why?"

"Because I love her, dammit!"

My voice rang out like a shot in the dark, and the little silhouettes whose sleek profiles were illuminated under the gleaming lampshades all evening were now turned towards me, and through the stillness I saw nothing but shadows where their eyes should be, and I felt completely watched by them. There was no movement in the room, only silence, broken by the faint 'clink, clink' of ice as Benjamin twirled his drink. Then all at once motion returned to the lobby, and the profiles of the little clusters floated back around into view, revealing well-defined noses, and mouths, and bangs, and cheekbones that rested high against the eminent low light, and then the soft chatter began again... and then it was over.

"Ah," he said softly and knowingly. "Now we're getting somewhere."

I just sat with my decision, my cards all out on the table.

"So," he started in again after a moment. "The writer thinks he's found real love in the city."

"Right now, yes," I stated, regaining my composure. "I can't help it, and I don't know enough about things yet to tell me otherwise."

"That's honest of you," he stated sincerely. "I do respect you for it, and I can tell now that you mean it — that you feel it, that you *really* feel it! That's what it's all about good man, *real feeling*!" He clenched his fists together while he said it, as if he just encountered a source of inspiration for one of his many acting roles, and then he relaxed them again with a chuckle. "I used to feel it too you know — what you're feeling right now — I've only felt that feeling once in my life, and yes, it was with her. I just wished I would have had the same courage to call it out when I felt it, because then maybe things would be different, and maybe I wouldn't be sitting here alone." He leaned back into a drink, and I knew that behind all that success, and all that cynicism, and all that decadence, and all that resentment, and all that pomp, and all that was grey

about that blasted designer suit, there sat a man lodged
in a great deal of loneliness, who had many regrets in his
still short life, and I had a feeling Gracie was just a small
part of the greater whole. "I admire you, Conrad... after all
that's wrong in the world … I admire you."

He let his drink fall sorrowfully from his mouth,
and I almost pitied the once vibrant man who sat in front of
me, the one who just moments before boasted brightly
about having the whole world and everything in it save for
the one, single girl that was his only downfall. For a
moment I felt like patting him on the back, telling him it
was okay and that everything would be all right in the end.
Yes, for a moment I contemplated being just like every
other chum he undoubtedly chose to surround himself with,
the kind that told him exactly what he wanted to hear when
he wanted to hear it, thus relenting his personal remorse,
but only for a moment did that feeling last, because all at
once a great deal of loathing rose up inside of me, and all at
once I detested the pathetic creature in front of me,
squandering his talents in an undignified wallowing of self-
pity, already speaking of the 'good-old days' that had
passed him by even though he could be no more than thirty
on his worst day — it was utterly pathetic — I would shed
no tears for him, for if I was to help this man I could only
offer him the truth — I, Conrad Arlington, The Last True
Artist could offer this man the truth — something far more
valuable than any forms of wealth, or fame, or glory, or
expensive suits, or parties, or women, or rare scotch. Yes, I
would offer him the truth, and in the end he would be
higher for it.

"Then you can start by doing something about it," I
said.

"It's too late, good boy," he wallowed, defending
his defeat. "She's gone."

"It's not too late—"

"Did you hear what I just said?"

"Yes, and you're wrong." My voice was clear and
confident. "You're completely and utterly wrong, and the

very fact that I have to sit here and witness you wallow in your own self-pity is pathetic. It's a completely pathetic experience. "

"Perhaps you speak the truth again, good boy, perhaps that is what I am — pathetic."

"Would you prefer I tell you how great you are? How everybody loves you? How everything is going to work itself out in the end?" I tried to rouse a sense of pride in him, but none came, he just looked down into his scotch, feeling completely sorry for himself.

"That would be a nice start," he mumbled gravely.

"Well I'm not going to do it," I stated strongly. "You have no sympathy here, and I'd be doing you an injustice if I gave you any. The only thing standing in your way is yourself, and at the end of the day your life — your art — lives and dies with you and you alone. No one else can be responsible for it, and no one will. From one artist to another, *know* that what I say is the truth." I was on a roll now, and after sitting there all evening, listening to all his nonchalant, self-righteous opinions on things, it felt good to let off some steam, so much so that I found it difficult to stop. "And you'll stop being so terrible to yourself in front of me, understand, or I'll get up and go right now. Do you hear me? I won't stay to be around it. You want to talk about emasculation. You're emasculating yourself, and it's sad to watch, it truly is."

My voice trailed off, and he sat there in his defeat, head down, still unable to face himself — I had made my point.

"How old are you anyway?" I asked.

"I'll be twenty-eight next month." He spoke to the floor.

"You'll be twenty-eight next month." I repeated it back to him slowly. "Does that sound as ridiculous to you as it does to me?"

He didn't respond. He just touched the five-points of his fingertips together in a triangle and kept his focus downward.

"Do you remember the first time you saw her? At that party, in New York?"

He looked up, fingers to his lips, face scrunched in concentration. "Yes."

"What did she look like?"

His eyes glossed over with a sheen of deep grey, and his breathing became free and light again, like it was being drawn from some deeper place is in his body, and thus he took his time, drawing on the memory for support and encouragement. Then his mouth opened, and I knew only truth would be spoken, and I readied myself for it.

"She had golden hair," he said slowly. "Her hair was all done in gold."

He fell quiet, and I just looked at him, for in that phrase existed the very soul of Benjamin Trask, and I could not bring myself to do any differently.

"I remembered its texture," he continued. "It was matted, washed even, dried over in a natural stain that I would not call perfect — no — it was the imperfection that made it perfect." He blinked his eyes a few times as he gazed into the darkness, licking his dry lips that had cracked from too much scotch, re-creating the image in his mind. "And she wore a simple black cocktail dress that was so plain, but on her it was flawless, yes, flawless... it was the most flawless dress I had ever seen." He breathed for a moment, and then another moment, and then another moment still. "She looked like a fallen rose pedal, all alone and quiet — distant — upon the sullen ground."

Silence again took the room, but this time it was not by a shout, or by a whisper, or any other audible devices known to man, but by our mutual appreciation for the dearness of a girl, which lingered on forever within our midst.

"She had an effect on me." He started up again with a full body nod. "Still does, I suppose."

"I'd say she might."

We both chuckled slightly, but no tension was relieved, for there was only an understanding that now existed between us as we listened to the chatter of the surrounding lobby that went on in clinks of crystal, and light whispers, and the little, faint laughs of young women as their bright tenors rose above the rest and then fell just as suddenly, quickly dampened against the dark. I took a sip of my own drink, then checked my watch, then took another sip, and after nothing transcribed I decided that the conversation had abruptly reached its end, that I had gotten all I could out of the remorseful man, and it was time for me to go.

"Benjamin, I would like to thank you for the pleasant evening…"

I took my motion to leave, bending slowly forward off the leather chair that I had not moved from in nearly two hours.

"It was October the twentieth of last year," he began, speaking up. "It was a Saturday."

My body immediately dropped back into the stiffness of the leather, reclaiming its original position — attentive, alert — ready for anything.

"There was something in the air that night — something rich — I can't be certain what it was. It was like, a thick liquid, clear as crystal, and I felt detached somehow. I parked my car as usual and waited, but it didn't take long for me to know that something was different. I had never made it to her door before. She was always out and on her way down by the time I parked, and any questions, even though forbidden, were never necessary. I waited for exactly two minutes, and when there was no unlocking of her door, no sound of her heels descending the stone steps that preceded it, and no Gracie flowing marvelously downward in one of her free evening gowns, I knew she desired that I call on her, and so I did."

He paused to clear his throat, reassuring himself that it was okay to continue, and I held my breath.

"For the first time I ascended the steps to her marvelous house, and I was overcome with a feeling of being watched that grew heavier with every step. I stopped

on the stoop, and I remember it was like — like a portal
of some kind — and I knew that whatever awaited me on
the other side would be terrific. I knocked three times.
There was a pause, and then unsuspectingly a man's voice
boomed from the other side. It was not unlikable, it was
rather friendly, or so it seemed, so I entered, and that's
when I saw him."

"Maxwell," I stated.

"Like I said before, I didn't like him the moment I
saw him," Benjamin said darkly. "He had that big grin on
his face, like an orangutan would if it could smile as wide,
and I was disgusted."

He continued promptly, seeing I would object.

"I can see from your expression that you want to
ask why. Rightly so, but I have no definite answer for you,
other than sometimes you just get a feeling with people,
Conrad, and I had one of those feelings with him." His face
remained dark for a moment and then brightened as his
mind shifted focus. "But then I saw her, all blasé and cool
on that black velvet couch, and all that went away for a
moment, yes, for a moment, all that went away — do you
remember that couch?"

"Every detail."

"Of course you do, of course you do," he mumbled
softly, reassuring his memory by checking it against the
concreteness of mine. "I sat down in the chair at the far end
of the room. Maxwell was at the front of the room by the
big window, and Gracie was of course on the couch. He
offered me a drink and began to pitch me some ideas for a
film. I knew right away that it was no good, for no amateur
worth his salt would try and pitch a project on a Saturday
night, but to appease Gracie's wishes I did my best to sit
and cooperate. This of course, did not last long." He paused
and emptied his scotch.

"What happened?" I asked after a moment.

He steadied himself, and looked me coolly in the
eye. "I called him a damn fake."

"You actually said that?"

"I said it earlier, and I'll say it again — the man's a damn fake and there's nothing anyone can do to change that."

"Well, what did he do? What did Gracie do?"

"Gracie, of course, did not approve. She flew up off the couch... and she said... things... she said terrible things to me." The ice cubes rattled in his glass as he went to refill it, for he was visibly shaking. "We broke into an argument right there — our first real argument — I had never seen her angry like that before, never in my life. She was screaming. She was screaming so loud it was terrifying. Then I began screaming. I told her that man was using her, and that I knew a swindler when I saw one, and then she screamed even louder. Screaming for me to get out. Telling me to get out and to never come back. I pleaded with her to reconsider, that I was trying to protect her, but she wouldn't listen, and the way she looked at me in that moment... she looked at me like... like I... like she didn't even recognize me anymore... like she never recognized me... like I never even existed... like I was dead to her."

In one motion Benjamin downed an entire double pour, and even through the shallow darkness of the lobby I could see his sinewy jaw muscles bulging bravely against clenched teeth as he stared, wide-eyed and vacant into empty space.

"What did he do?"

Benjamin poured another double and downed it even more ferociously than before, amplifying the fumes of alcohol that went in waves before him. "The bastard didn't say a word... not a goddamn word." A certain darkness coursed through Benjamin's voice that was much greater than just a deep hatred — it was a loathing — a loathing cloaked in death, and it hung in the air like black clouds on a cold Sunday morning. "He just sat there, sat there like a king on a throne, a king that already had his victory."

I stared at the broken man before me, all that glory and all that prestige now clouded in grey — faded — like painted boards under a heavy winter. He stared back, and a mutual sense of loss connected us in that moment. It was at a loss for something that we both never had, never could have. The kind of loss that was created to simply exist on its own — to torture, to maim, to cling, to hurt — and in the center of all its beauty it prevails, cold and alone, a dark and wretched speck in the brightness.

"You see Conrad, he empowers Gracie to be as dangerous as she can be, nothing more." He looked me dead in the eyes now, and I felt the pressing of a final verdict. "Power. Sex. Wealth. Beauty — she has all these things — she has everything, absolutely everything, everything that can destroy us, and she will do it." He paused. Certain. Defiant. He centered in. Poised. Ready. "She will do it, because she can. She will do it, because she has the perfect and complete ability to do so. She will do it, because men let her — men like you and me — and it won't stop, not now, not tomorrow, not next year, not next century... no... no... not for a very, very long time." He let that sit, his grey eyes bright and alive within his reality. "And that, my good man, is all I know about Gracie Garrison."

He dove into his drink for what must have been well over the two-hundredth time for the evening, and I knew, without any sense of doubt, that he had indeed just revealed his defeat. A certain hopelessness washed over me, and the darkest corners of the room closed in all around like a stifling lid, and the soulish yearnings of desire and truth screamed out for vindication within me, but none came. The present absence of my bright and beautiful Gracie was made completely known to me, stronger than ever, so strong that my lungs tightened in my throat and chest, cutting off all breath. Oh God, how I wanted to hold her in that moment! I wanted to hold her forever, high above the endlessness of loss and death! High above the treacherous throes of inconsistent emotion! I wanted to pull her into me! I wanted to smell her! I wanted to taste her! I wanted to touch her! I wanted to feel her face in my hands!

I wanted to hold her bright, blue gaze as it swam perfect and complete, lost in the depths of mine! I wanted to caress her lips with my fingers! I wanted to feel the soft flesh of her warm and perfect skin! I wanted to kiss her everywhere! Her eyelids! Her nose! Her cheeks! Her mouth! I wanted to see her fully, all golden and silver in the pressing darkness! "Be with me Gracie! Be with me now!" My soul cried out in a state of absolute need. Then my body reacted, and I turned in my seat towards the entrance of the lobby, fully believing I'd see the last testament of true expression cross the shadows in a display of dazzling, shimmering light. Yes! Yes! My Gracie! May you live forever! And may the God of some marvelous heaven ever hold you in his hand! The perfect one! The only one! Gracie, my love, come and find me! Come to me now and forever I will hold your hand! Your little hand, yes, your perfect and lovely little hand, how perfect it is, and how wonderful! And then my eyes dimmed, for there was nothing, nothing but the wake of a hallow gloom, washed out and bleak against the deathly silence, and then there was nothing still.

"It was a dark day for me, Conrad," said the man in the grey suit. "The darkest day of my life."

We sat like that for a great long while, the Chateau alive and dancing all around us…

CHAPTER 10
— THE THREE POOLS —

The last days of December came and went, and after it so did January as well, during which the loneliness and isolation my body felt from the absence of Gracie's presence began to mend. The reality was I had formed a kind of dependency on her, and now that the bright vividness of her face was beginning to fade, so was my art, for her image had been the sole source of my inspiration for some time, and as that image began to blur, so did the integrity of The Last True Artist, and I found myself in a state of total desperation. I needed to feel again. I had to. No Gracie meant no true art, and no true art meant death — death to The Last True Artist — and I could not allow that to happen.

I was not with out action, however, for I had continued with the greatest of efforts to track her down. One particular evening in January, I finally managed to get a hold of Bobby Finch. He was at his private home address in New York, and I obtained his number by throwing on my most expensive suit and taking an afternoon trip down to the same gallery Gracie took me to on that beautiful night back in November. I strolled confidently through those big double doors, consciously suppressing the still aching memory of Gracie's hand as it had rested so perfectly in mine the last time, and while doing so, I spotted a sleek, pretty, middle-aged woman lounging near the front desk sipping on what was undoubtedly some offshoot of the Manhattan cocktail. She wore upon her face the poised, tight lips and arched neck that was indicative of Beverly Hills aristocracy, and it wasn't until I spoke that she even bothered to lift her gaze, considering me with her cold, bluish, deep-set eyes, analyzing me like a promiscuous boy in a lingerie shop.

"Are you the owner?" I asked with a sort of commanding charm, in the same way that I imagined

Benjamin Trask might, whose character I shamelessly used as a reference point.

"I am," she said flatly, but I saw her eyes brighten a little, and I knew that she had at least temporarily bought the approach.

"Excellent, then you can help me. I'm looking to invest in some art, quite a bit actually."

"Are you a collector?"

"That's right. I've recently come in to a sum of money and I'd like to expand my collection."

"How much are you looking to invest?"

"I'd rather not talk numbers at the moment," I said like a true-blue capitalist. "But I can assure you, if the piece is right, when it comes time to sign on the dotted line, I will make the buy."

She sat up a little straighter in her seat — I was winning her over.

" Very well, Mr…?"

"Arlington, Conrad Arlington." I didn't mind using my real name. By the time she caught on to me — if she did at all — it wouldn't make any difference.

"Very well, Mr. Arlington, take a look around the gallery. If you see anything you like, you let me know and we'll talk numbers."

"That would be fine," I said as if it were expected. "The experience of buying each piece is important to me, and I'd like to speak directly with the artist if possible — Bobby Finch — I've been told that you could put me in touch with him."

A coldness returned to her eyes, and I could tell I had aroused some suspicion. "Bobby Finch is an art dealer. If you want to see his collections, I'm afraid you'll have to speak directly with him."

I chuckled a bit, not back pedaling at all. "That's exactly what I plan to do," I proclaimed defiantly, guffawing with such an overbearing intensity that it would put Mr. Trask himself to shame. "Now put me in touch with him now."

She recoiled slightly, shocked at the command, and for a moment she began to obey as she reached for the phone, but then becoming aware of what she was doing she managed to regain enough composure to stop herself.

"What makes you think I have that information?"

"Of course you have it. You're the gallery owner."

"Yes, well, that's private information Mr. Arlington. I'm afraid Mr. Finch only deals through select galleries — such as this — and with extremely high profile clients."

I purposely let my patience decrease, for this was highly unacceptable behavior. "See here, I'm looking to make quite a large buy. If you're worried about getting cut out of the deal then you are clearly misinformed. Now put me in touch with him immediately. I just spoke to him at the opening in November and I don't see this taking any longer."

She must have been a highly competitive woman, because in spite of my dominating certainty she still managed to maintain her disbelief.

"You were at the opening?"

"Of course I was."

"Well, you see, I put together the guest list that night," she retorted. "A list of very important people. I remember everyone from that list, Mr. Arlington, everyone except you."

"That's because I came with someone."

"Yes? With whom?" For a moment, she thought she won — I did too even — but honesty to some extent had gotten me this far, so I thought it best to just stick to it.

"Gracie Garrison — I came with Gracie Garrison." I put no inflection in the name, just let it sit — drift through the lofty gallery, resonating off the walls and filling the corners with its music.

Then, it happened. The woman suddenly perked up, snapping to attention as if she had just made a fatal mistake and looked to correct it as quickly as possible. "Why yes," she stuttered. "Of course." Without reaching for the phone she got up and went behind the desk. She took a small pair of keys off her person and unlocked a small safe, in which she pulled out a black binder that she promptly opened. With delicate and articulate hands she slipped on a pair of reading glasses, began flipping through the pages of confidential information until she came to a particular page located somewhere in the middle, then looked up at me with surprisingly soft and inviting eyes. "Do you have a pen, Mr. Arlington?"

***

With Bobby Finch's direct number in hand, I drove back through town towards the hills in the crystal clear daylight of winter, fully enjoying this small victory, and commending my skills as a compelling and convincing actor. Finally, the information I needed! I had it in my hands! And hopefully, along with it, the whereabouts to my most prolific inspiration — the golden girl herself — I could practically feel her racing back to me with each block as I climbed higher and higher up Highland Avenue.

I threw open my apartment door in sheer triumph — surely, any moment now — I marched steadfastly to my room, sat down at my desk, took a good, strong breath, picked up the phone, and placed the call. It rang five times.

"Hello?"

Even though I spoke to him for only a minute at the gallery that night, I recognized the high-pitched cadence of Bobby Finch's boyishly whiny voice immediately, and was struck with the image of a slim, almost feminine figure completely and comfortably stretched out in some posh, high-rise apartment in the center of Manhattan, overlooking the entire city as it moved tirelessly below him.

"Hello, Bobby Finch?"

"Yes, who is this?"

"This is Conrad Arlington. We met—"

"How did you get this number?"

"I got it from the gallery. The gallery that you opened in Los Angeles this past November."

"Which one?"

A surprised laugh left my lips when he asked, for I was stricken with his commonality.

"Tell me which gallery, or I'll hang up," he demanded promptly

"No, please," I said quickly. "The gallery just off second and La Brea. We spoke. I was with an associate of mine. Gracie Garrison."

"Gracie!" He burst out in a dramatic ecstasy. "I just love her! She's perfect!"

"Yes, she's a good friend of mine—"

"Absolutely perfect! Gorgeous!" Then he paused for a moment. "What did you say your name was?"

"This is Conrad Arlington. We met at the opening. Gracie introduced us."

"Conrad!" He burst out as if we were old friends. "How are you? I hope Los Angeles is treating you well."

"It is, thanks."

"Excellent, excellent. That's just so very excellent. I love to hear it when my friends are successful. It just makes me so very happy."

"—Yes—"

"Well, what can I do for you? You're looking to purchase some art I suppose — invest some of those entertainment dollars." He let out a laugh, quickly applauding what he thought to be his own wittiness.

"Actually, I was—"

"I can tell you right now I'm moving a few pieces around — hot pieces, very hot pieces Conrad — right now I have them going for a cool hundred K, but that price is sure to double in the next few years."

"What I wanted to—"

"We can talk numbers later, there's no rush," he interjected. "I can always knock a few thousand off for a friend. You'll want to fly out and see the pieces this weekend before they go, I can do Saturday."

"—Mr. Finch—"

"And if you're looking to invest a few million, I have a few hot pieces that I think will triple in the current market — hot pieces, hot pieces, Conrad."

"Mr. Finch!"

"Yes?" He halted abruptly, his train of thought singed.

"I'm actually not looking to purchase any art — at least not at this time — but I assure you I will be looking to buy very soon. I'm calling about Gracie Garrison."

"Gracie!" He exclaimed again, so loud this time that I could feel the reverberation through the phone, and I figured my assumptions about the posh, high-rise apartment were probably true. "I just love her! I just love her to death!"

"Yes, you see, I just got back into LA recently," I lied, "and I was wondering if you know where I could reach her?"

"Let's see... the last time I saw Gracie Garrison... was... Ah! I just saw her three weeks ago."

"Three weeks ago? Where?"

"She was here. In New York."

"She was in New York? Three weeks ago?" I asked pointedly, desiring to be completely clear, for I didn't know Bobby at all, and without imposing too much judgment I deemed it very possible that his perception of real time could be a little bit off.

"Don't act so surprised," he said lightly. "Gracie loves New York. She's here all the time. And she's perfect! Just a perfect little creature!"

"Right," I said, trying to figure out my next move. "Do you know where she is now?"

"I have no idea." He sort of whined the phrase as if it wasn't worth wondering. "She could be in Paris for all I know."

My heart sank. "Paris?" The question left my lips in a hopeless breath. "She told me she's never been to Paris." My voice dropped out, and it must have been very true — very true and very powerful — so powerful that it pulled all the light from the room.

"Oh Conrad, you sound sad," Bobby stated with concern. "It's okay, I'm sure she's fine. Don't think she's run off and died or anything."

I couldn't answer, for in that moment the dam of my absolution broke, and I was unable to respond. Truth and pain flowed through my entire body, until it found its way into my eyes which welled with hot tears, the kind of tears that come from loss, death, far removed from the cool, blue tears of light that pooled in Gracie's clean, bright eyes so many nights before. No, these were white-hot tears of true retribution, and as they screamed to the corners of my eyelids and stung the folds of my skin like forever would if it was made of ash, I was entirely immobilized by them.

"My God, Conrad, is something wrong? Has something happened?" Bobby's voice was a panic, for he also feared for Gracie's life.

"No, no." My voice forcefully returned to me, but only by necessity. "Nothing's wrong at all. It's just been some time. She was a good friend, and I would very much like to speak to her again."

"Oh, thank goodness!" Bobby burst out in another bout of ecstasy. "You gave me quite the scare, Conrad, quite the scare. Please don't do that again."

The emotion had passed, and the previously whiny inflection returned to Bobby's voice in full cadence. I suddenly felt completely annoyed by the neebish dealer, so much so that I wished the pain would return, just to spite his pitiful and trifling reactions which I found to be completely overdone and unnecessary, and the fact that he was taking giant, gasping breaths that boomed deafening over the line, was particularly aggravating.

"I don't intend to," I stated flatly.

"It's right you shouldn't." He said with pure, sickening apathy. "I can tell that you're somewhat of a romantic."

"Suppose I am." My irritation was boiling now. It wasn't long before it would brim over.

"Oh Conrad, sweet Conrad," he said with a nauseating tone. "I love romantics. I have a particular fondness for them."

"That's nice."

"It's a beautiful thing, Conrad, a truly beautiful thing. It's how I make my money, after all — romance that is — it's where all the true art in the world comes from. The romantics, the brilliant ones, and all their great pieces." He paused for a second, as if deriving some kind of surreal pleasure in the way the statement happened to form words in his mouth, and he wanted to make note of it. "But you have to protect your heart, Conrad. Romance is a fragile thing, a beautifully fragile thing, and we don't want you getting hurt — well, not too hurt that is, a little hurt is good sometimes, a lot of good can come from a little hurt, and lots and lots of money — but still, be careful with your little heart, dear boy. Be good to yourself — yes?"

I didn't like most of the words in that statement. In fact, I liked just about none of them. The phrases 'little heart' and 'dear boy' I found to be particularly annoying, and in a quick twist of fate I would have liked nothing more than to reach through the line and wring his scrawny neck so that he could never speak to me with that pitiful voice ever again, but, as I had done so many times before in the still-short span in which I had called life, I digressed into something most would consider to be more socially appropriate — "yes, I suppose being good to myself would be the proper thing to do."

"It would be, dear boy, it would be."

That damn 'dear boy' again.

"Well," he continued with haste. "I really must be off. If you happen to get a hold of Gracie please have her call me for there are always things to talk about."

"What kinds of things?"

"Things, Conrad, things. Oh, there are so many things. Things all the time."

"I would very much like to know what those things are," I insisted.

"I'd love to Conrad, but I don't have the time."

"Well make time!" I commanded with absolute authority.

His voice wavered. "I-I have to go—"

"Don't you dare hang up that phone!" I interjected, and then I waited. The line did not go dead, but rather hung in silence, along with the faint, cool 'hum' of the connection.

"I'm sorry, Conrad, but I'm afraid I can't help you, and I don't think anybody can."

"What aren't you telling me?" I asked, slow and discerning, and completely menacing. "What do you know about her?"

"I-I wish I could help you—"

"Then help me!" I commanded once again, then desperation entered, and my tone lessened to one of a great need. "Please Bobby, she's been gone for months, I'm very, very concerned. If you can't tell me where she is, then please help me try and understand."

There was no response on the other line, only silence that spanned the three thousand miles between us like a ray of light spanning the glassy surface of an endless sea.

"She's dear to me, Bobby," I started with all sincerity. "So very dear. Please, help me understand."

The silence hung another moment, followed by the faint smacking of unsure lips moving across the line, but no voice rang forth, as if the decision had moved towards agreement but the words would not come, and through that line existed a great deal of pain, and sorrow, and remorse for memories gone by, memories so rare, and so thinly brittle that the slightest touch could trigger the grandest of eternal collapse. What those mysteries were that floated high and suspended in the air only the higher beings of existence could possibly try and fathom, the deepest things of the spirit, and like fire courses through the golden meadow I suddenly felt the energy grow hot, and I knew it was too late. The last charge of The Last True Artist had failed, and lay dismal and destroyed on the lonely battlefield, along with old hopes, true grandeur, and pools of broken glass.

"Wait, don't hang up—"

The line went dead. I tried back ten times but there was no answer.

***

The phone fell from my ear, and darkness took me. I awoke in some kind of strange dream, and in that dream there were three pools — one of gold, one of blue, and one of silver. I stood at the edge of the middle pool — the blue pool — and as I stared into its surface it shimmered like hot glass, and from that glass arose a figure from the water. As the figure took its shape it completed the form of a woman, then that woman moved towards me, strolling perfectly across the glass, and as she did the surfaces of the gold and silver pools ran over across the surface of the blue pool, adding their luster to the magnificent figure, with the silver wrapping itself around the waist of the torso in a gleaming shawl and the gold creeping up the chest, and then the neck, and then the featureless face, and mouth, and finally coming to rest on the head of the figure, in which it formed into golden locks of bright, shiny hair that fell perfectly down, and came to rest at elbows length, just below the slight shoulder blades. Then features began to develop — lips, a nose, a mouth — and eyes, big, bright eyes like fire from a distant sun, eyes so bright that I couldn't even look at them. I had to cover my own eyes so I was not blinded, and then the fire subsided, and burned a low-lit blue, and I was left breathless, for before me stood the everlasting figure of Gracie's body, all golden, and silver, and a glossy blue, and in her eyes existed a perfect spirit, one of endless life, truth and love, beauty and perfection. Indeed, she was the most perfect spirit in the universe, and in that pool she stood, looking at me in a way that was completely good, lovely, and correct. Then in a burst of inspiration and a silent laugh she twirled, summoning me to join her on the surface of her sacred pool, far away from all the pain and suffering of the distant shore, that of a mortal life and a quest of worth. Thus with a courageous foot I stepped out upon the glass, and to my delight it held strong, like a diamond would if it could be woven as tightly, and it was with even steps that I approached her presence, standing just feet away, looking into the eyes of what reflected my own soul burning back at me. I reached out, once again, with a courageous, trying hand, and grazed her slight hips in a way that said, 'I need you,' and as my fingers touched her glass form her figure became flesh, and her warmth and scent surrounded me, and her eyes solidified into human eyes, and her hair fell down in what became strands of mortal hair, and her lips became a bright rose, and with all the hope, and love, and truth in the world, I pulled her into me and kissed her mouth, and it was perfect, as perfect as life must have been at dawn's first light, and once again I was filled with purpose, and I was complete. Then, suddenly, her body recoiled from me, and fell trembling back against the endless pool, and as I reached out for her she fell further from me, so I screamed her name but no voice came forth, only a single ripple that spread across the surface of the violet glass, moving towards her at a dooming speed, and then she turned, and she ran, but the effect was too fast, and in moments it overtook her, sending her crashing to the ground, and then she turned back and looked at me with the most hopeless smile, the kind that built nations, and moved mountains, and melted the hearts of kings. Although I ran with all my might towards her I had achieved no forward motion, and my screams lay silent — still upon the glass — then her perfect body began to crack, and her smile turned to pain, and then with eyes of a glossy blue her everlasting figure shattered into a million fragments, and I screamed forever across the lake as I fell to my knees. Then with the velocity of an earthquake the pool cracked and split at the place where her body went, and then all at once the entire surface of the pool shattered, and I fell beneath it's distance, lost, and gone, and devoid of truth forever… and then my eyes opened, and I knew it was only a dream… it was only a dream…

***

It was past midnight by the time I awoke on my bedroom floor. My clothes were damp, and my face stuck to the carpet as I lifted my head, tearing the fibers from where my sweat had dried. I sat up and looked around my room. Everything was black, so I waited to let my head clear. My ears were ringing horribly, and my brain was pulsing against the inside of my skull like it was being pounded from within by a hammer. I felt completely wretched, weak, thin, and I realized I had eaten next to nothing for the last few days. My already gaunt frame had become almost waif-like through the middle, and regardless of my need for sustenance I had no appetite. The very thought of food made my stomach turn into knots so tight that I felt my body might cramp and implode on itself, so I decided to remain just skin and bones, skin and bones in the night, and then I remembered the dream, and the great pain returned. It was heavy now, so heavy that I felt it might crush me — reduce me to nothing in the remorse of lost love — there were no tears, for all my tears lay wasted and spent in the threads of my bedroom floor, and now there was only agony — agony and a deep, deep torment.

I pushed myself off the ground and stood in the center of my room. It was quiet, dark, and except for the ringing in my ears I knew that I was completely alone. And, God, that pounding! It was like the Almighty Himself was beating me through the sides of my skull. The pounding increased as my blood rushed back to my head, and in one surge it threw me stumbling back on my bed in which I collapsed under its enormous weight. I heaved dry sobs into my pillow, terrible sobs of pure frustration, and then all at

once it hit me — all at once I knew exactly what I
wanted — and in a blind stupor I threw myself onto my
feet, and clutching my head I stumbled from my room into
the dark.

The cool night air felt good against my hot face as I
walked down Franklin Avenue, and what little it did to ease
my throbbing mind I welcomed openly. I felt haggard,
exhausted, and I shivered as the still damp clothes that hung
like blank drapes over my withered body grew frigid in the
evening, and I felt completely stupid for forgetting to throw
on a jacket. I laughed bitterly at my own foolishness, for I
must have looked like a runaway the way things were,
unshaven and thin and worn like the long winter that
surrounded me, and I didn't even care. It felt good to be
cold. I wanted to be so cold that my whole body would go
numb, and perhaps then I would just waste away, waste
away on the Boulevard under the shallow listlessness of the
night, next to the broken, the used, and the ones who's
souls had left them.

After about fifteen minutes I reached my
destination, and I felt my flesh leap with the possibility of
relief. I walked through the double doors on the corner like
the entrance to a kingdom, and danced through the aisles of
gold, and clear, and dark brown potions like a sanctuary
filled with open music. I grabbed a bottle of light brown
scotch on a back shelf and stumbled towards the counter,
where I threw it down in complete and total absolution — I
was going to buy this potion, this potion that would heal
my soul, and I was going to drink all of it.

The clerk told me the price, and I laughed at him
like he was a fool, completely disgusted with his existence.

"I don't care how much it is. Just give me the damn
bottle."

He repeated the price, and I laughed again as I
reached for my wallet, but it was not there!

"Dammit! I forgot my damn wallet."

The clerk jumped at his chance to tell me off, and reached to pull the bottle back behind the counter with a snide little smirk that I found completely loathsome.

"Wait," I exclaimed. I still had on my watch that I wore to the gallery that afternoon, and with no discrepancy or hesitation whatsoever I pulled it from my wrist and slammed it down on the counter, snatched up the bottle, and turned to exit. I didn't even bother looking back to gauge his reaction — I could have bought thirty bottles with that damn watch.

***

Half the bottle was gone by the time I stumbled the half mile into downtown Hollywood, its lights streaking all around in colors of blue, red, and a decadent white. The drink had gone directly to my head, and as my body had leapt from my bed an hour or so before in its anticipation, I knew it had not failed me. I felt good, light, relieved — forever numb — just like I wanted, perfectly content with my failure as I stumbled down the five-pointed names of the immortal, sparkling blurry against the plush lines of the marbled sidewalk. Yes, this was the resting place for The Last True Artist. Here I would die, I was sure of it. I stumbled past the dives and haunts, jeering bitterly at them, pulling on the hot liquid, allowing it to churn, and burn, and whisk my pain away into a deep, dark oblivion.

"Say, give us a pull, would cha?"

I looked through foggy eyes towards the ground and saw a homeless young man about my age. His clothes were ratted and torn, and hung wretchedly off his gaunt frame like the remains of a gutted scarecrow. His hair and what little he had of a beard were caked and mucked with dirt — he was a vile specimen, no doubt about it — and next to him sat a little dog that stared up at me with big black eyes that held steady as the rest of its tiny body quivered and quaked around them. I suddenly felt a wave of sympathy for the two urchins, and then I hated them for making me feel that way, and then he ventured to speak again.

"Here now, you don't need all that," he said with a devious little smile. "Share a little drink would cha? Share a little drink of whatcha got. Help out a kid that needs helping."

I just stared at him, all decadent and sick against the Boulevard, and suddenly I detested everything that he represented, and I wanted nothing more to do with it. "Take it," I said as I held out the bottle. "I have no more use for it."

"Just a pull will do," he said, taking it gleefully. "I'm not looking to put you out."

"You already have." With that I turned to be on my way.

"Say, thank you, Mister!" The boy called out, and his little dog barked, sharing in his simple pleasure. "You're a true friend, ya hear! A true friend! Many blessings to your night! May you find a girl and may your dreams be fulfilled!"

I walked for another ten minutes or so down the Boulevard, and despite the cold the drink kept me warm, and I felt reckless in spite of myself. I began to see women, all sorts of women as they passed me, and my body suddenly felt awake and alive in a way that I had not felt since that night at Gracie's apartment, only this time it was different — this time I felt like a ghost — empty and vacant against the Boulevard, and I never had such a hollow need for fulfillment. I veered off the sidewalk and walked towards a familiar nightspot, one that I had passed many times in the years before, but purposely avoided for the sheer vanity of it — the pretentiousness of it, and all the connotations in that damned word— this is where young Hollywood came to play, and tonight I would compete with the best of them.

I walked right up to the velvet rope and demanded entry. The promoter, a tall, blonde, modelesque woman gave me a once over, then looked me directly in the eyes with a calculating stare, but I was not intimidated. I looked right back with all the dominance in the city, for I knew her kind, and I knew what she really wanted, and I would not be denied. Her eyes softened, and she looked down towards the ground, and for a moment I saw nothing but a little girl. She nodded her head and the big security guards that stood enormous and still like stone gargoyles on either side of her lifted the rope, and I walked past it, moving forever forward into my glooming peril.

I threw the double doors open with an excessively aggressive shove — the kind that gives real substance to an entrance and makes a presence known — but to my dismay, the place was so packed that no one really noticed, so I stuck my chin up in the air as high as I could and walked distinctly into the social. The space was dark and hollow, with a low-lit ambiance that attempted to recreate the literary and artistic atmosphere of the Golden Age, but there was no truth there, only a ghostly crowd of posers and fakes, talentless fiends and talkers, broke producers and aspiring actresses that were little more than prostitutes in disguise.

I walked through the crowd like a hawk, like a lion on the prowl, for I had had my share of drink, my share of pain, my share of heartbreak, and my share of truth. All I wanted now was one thing, and as I searched the hungry crowd the ghosts feasted their little eyes upon my flesh in little gazes that wandered up and down my body, to my waist and then to my eyes again, and I met every single stare, daring them to touch The Last True Artist, daring them to make their desires known, for in my body existed enough talent to destroy each and every one of the vacant souls that existed within their ninety-pound frames — I had a love in me that they could not possibly imagine, depths that they could not possibly fathom — I was a higher being, a true artist, and one kiss from my lips would end any and all existence of their surface little lives forever, but they would not get it, no, these weak ones would not have me. If I was going to lower myself I would at least have the best on the Boulevard that night, and only the best, so I walked around the entire room until I found the most beautiful girl there — the girl that looked most like Gracie — and I approached her in absolution.

I walked up to her and looked her right in her deep, blue eyes. She was a beautiful, petite girl, about Gracie's height, with a dainty, smooth complexion and blonde hair that came cascading down in long, stringy waves that indeed made her a creature to behold. No, she was no Gracie, I knew that immediately, there wasn't the depth behind the eyes that Gracie and Gracie alone possessed, and she wasn't nearly as elegant, but nonetheless she was the most high-profile girl in the room by a long shot, and tonight it didn't matter. Tonight it was about filling the empty void, the vessel of loneliness, and I would make her mine simply because I could. I could have her and any other girl I wanted, for I was the one that they could never have, even in the deepest recesses of their dreams I represented all that was unattainable for them. They simply were not built to co-exist with greatness. They weren't capable of handling such powerful truth inside of them, and tonight would be the only chance they would get in their entire lives to be with a higher being, to be filled to overflowing with infinite talent, truth, and brilliance, and all but one of them would fail.

I continued to stare at her, and she stared back. A few moments passed, and it felt like forever. Finally, she looked down and up again in a little smile was completely open.

"Hello," she said in a cute British accent that would have been enduring if I allowed it to be.

"Hello." I returned the gesture with a bright, sensual smile, and I didn't take my eyes off her.

She giggled, then looked down at her drink, then back up again. "Are you going to tell me your name?"

"No," I said calmly, and her little body began to tremble.

"Alright then," she said softly. "Would you like to know mine?"

"No," I replied, and her mouth dropped a little, and her blue eyes dilated, and I knew right then that I had her.

I continued to stare. She stood frozen, enamored like a scared animal caught in some distant light. Then I moved slowly and smoothly forward, taking care not to startle her, and as I did I saw her chest begin to rise and fall more rapidly with every inch, and I saw the color of her slight neck begin to flush a scarlet red, and then with the boldness of a conqueror I reached out a courageous right hand, grazing her hip as I reached around the small of her back, and I felt a shiver run through her body that transferred to mine, giving me all confidence, and strength, and power in the world, and then in one motion I pulled her into me, until her abdomen was flush against mine, and I felt the steady rhythm of her hot breath as it ran in waves across my face, and then in her eyes I saw all desire, and I looked from those eyes to her trembling lips, and then I thought of Gracie, and I kissed the girl.

I kissed her long and hard and deep, and I tasted every corner of her entire mouth until I was sure that I had possessed her very soul, until I was sure that I had made such a deep impression on her that she would desire me above all other men for the rest of her life — a desire that lasted forever — and when the day came that this beautiful, unknown creature would inevitably have to compromise and give herself to a lesser man, and when her union with him would be complete, I would be the last thought in her mind as she lay next to him upon her bed at night. Before she closed her eyes she would remember the day that she kissed The Last True Artist, and with my image she would dance into her dreams, the places just beyond the limits of her reach, and it would remain that way, for she would never be rid of me, never, not for the rest of her life, and she would hate me for it forever — I wanted to know what it felt like to do that to someone.

I disengaged, and she drew in a breath of pure submission, and I felt the distance of her lips tremble as every fiber of her body still screamed to connect. Then without speaking, without breathing, and without even blinking, I turned on my heel and headed for the door, and I didn't look back. I didn't have to see her to know what I left behind — a little blonde girl, standing there with breathless tears and a broken heart, and I never felt so evil.

I plunged back onto the Boulevard and hot tears streamed down my face. It felt good to be awful. It felt good to be horrible. It felt good to be wicked. I had taken from a girl — a beautiful girl — the vitality of her very soul, and by doing so I had filled my own ghostly void like a ghoul. Yes, that's what I was now, I was nothing more than a blood-sucking ghoul, and I was satiated, and I was justified. I had taken what I wanted because I could, that was all. This was my existence now, this was my sick and terrible fate, and I would continue to prey on the weaker beings of the world, the bright young things whose only desire was to attain in a lifetime what I was given at birth, quenching my unquenchable thirst, stalking, and taking, and hurting, and killing until there was nothing left of me, indeed, until I was nothing more than dust on the ground.

Then suddenly, my weeping stopped. It stopped dead as if stabbed through by a stronger power even more evil and more deceitful then its predecessor, and once again I felt the Great Arlington Pride rise up within me, and I felt a great rage that ignited like an oil well would if it were set ablaze in my stomach, illuminating before me the horrors of my internal agony "How dare she!" I thought to myself, as my heart raced with heavy, pounding thumps threatening to pulse right out of my chest in an explosion of terrible, hot blood, and my anger burned in the indignant retribution of my coming wrath. "Nobody does this to me! Nobody! How dare she walk out on me like that! How dare she disappear! I am Conrad Arlington! I am The Last True Artist! I am the greatest talent that ever lived! I am the hope for mankind! And who is she? She is just a girl! She is nothing! Nothing! Nothing but golden dust! Golden dust thrown into the world and scattered poorly across the Boulevard! She is weak! Brittle! Used up and washed! She is a fool for leaving me! And she will pay! Yes, she will pay! And when she sees me strolling arm and arm with the next golden girl under the brilliant lights, she will loath the day she met me! She will burn with desire, but she will not be satiated! She will come to me, and I will turn away! Yes, I will turn her away! She will try and captivate me with her beauty, but I will turn her away! And her golden hair will fall in my presence! And her blue eyes will fade! And all her elegance, and all the mysteries of her youth will be made known to me, and I will turn her away! Yes, Conrad Arlington, The Last True Artist will turn her away, and she will remember me forever!"

I took a final gasping breath and collapsed against a marbled pillar on the edge of the Boulevard, and I was completely sick. Then, as if I had never shed a single tear in my life, hot drops began flowing from my eyes, and deep, wretched sobs surged straight from my heart and coursed through my gaping mouth, and I felt more true pain than I had ever felt in my life. I was a fool! I was a sick, arrogant fool! I had become the person I hated most! I had fallen from the graces of the beautiful and bright! I had let terrible blasphemies enter my world of truth! Unspeakable blasphemies! I had screamed pain and suffering against the perfect one, and I would never be forgiven, no, never! I had done it. I had hurt my Gracie, my sweet and beautiful Gracie. I had hurt her in my mind, and I would never be worthy to stand in her presence again, not as long as I should live and never, never again. Then suddenly I hurt, I hurt inside like I had never hurt before, and I felt my already brittle bones being bent and twisted and popped to the point of snapping, but they would not break, and in a single dry heave and a great shout I keeled over on the Boulevard, falling against the cold marble of some forlorn name, and then darkness took me, and I was finished.

CHAPTER 11
— SPRINGTIME FOR THE ARTIST —

I somehow managed to wake up in my bed the next morning. I didn't know how I got there, and I didn't know why, or when, or any of those nonsensical questions that really have no relevance after a night of indulgent behavior. For all I knew I could have taken a cab, or walked blindly up the ten or so blocks necessary to reach my door, or perhaps I was taken home, taken home by some good Samaritan who saw a man in a desperate state of need, but I doubted this highly, and the thought of a faceless person having access to my apartment was so uncomfortable that I quickly pushed any thought of it from my mind. I was alive, that was all that mattered — tattered perhaps, broken even — but I was alive, and in time I would mend, or so people liked to say for a dose of broken encouragement.

The last month of winter hung around the village in a bittersweet ambiance that couldn't be counted on for anything. One day it would be sunny, crystal bright, and seventy-five degrees outside, and the next it would be cold, overcast, and a little more than fifty. I hated the cold days, but I didn't judge them too harshly, believing that the sporadic changes in weather were all but an accurate depiction of what had come to match my personality exactly — an endless wave of ups and downs, lost hopes, and listless remorse — and as quickly as Gracie's brilliant face would leave me, it would return just the same in an explosion of color so vivid and pure that powerful, rushing waves of emotion would flush over me, threatening to send me to the ground at any moment, and I would have to steady myself upon my desk with a great effort to keep from succumbing to it.

I began taking walks again. The truth was I had seldom taken any walks at all since Gracie's disappearance earlier that winter and had spent the majority of my days in my gaudy apartment, staring at a blank page for hours, attempting to create, and then hating myself for being unable to do so. Oh, the frustration of having no inspiration! Oh, the quiet and the fruitless waiting as the hours turned from day into darkness, and then suffered through the wan twilight of the early morning. Indeed, it was good to be outside again — out amongst the trees, and the sunlight, and the living — and my body thanked me with big, deep breaths of cool, crisp air that filled my lungs all at once and then flowed lavishly out of my pores, taking all directions, cleaning out the old and corrupt and replacing it with what was good, clean, and bright. Yes, it was time to start over. It was time to dream again, and if Gracie never came back to me — if I never saw her quaint and perfect face again — perhaps it would be for the best.

These outings increased with such vitality that I eventually began to forget about my past pains and troubles completely, not in the way that one might imagine it to be, in which the hurt simply subsided until I felt well again, no, it was nothing like that at all, for things had changed a great deal, and I simply didn't feel as strongly about anything anymore. There was something beautifully sad about it — that is, the loss of true feeling — on one hand, my internal suffering was dampened considerably, which made everything around me more beautiful than before, and everything inside of me quiet and hollow to the point that I was barely aware of my own identity or the fact that I was indeed still a person. I felt empty, stretched, like I was entertaining some new arrogance and all the bliss that could come from it pushed outward past my face and skipped my body entirely. On the other hand it was completely awful, so awful that I could have been suicidal if I could still feel deeply enough to be so. My art was gone. Vanished. Nothing was present anymore, and without it I felt like a purposeless grain of sand lost in a sea of aimlessness hopes, and so I began to hate hopes, and hoping, and in doing so I despised the very meaning of hope all together, for I saw no reason for them — these purposeless, aimless hopes — without talent and inspiration they were nothing more than a lifetime of torture for the common man, false grandeur for those who knew nothing. I would pass them on the Boulevard — those young faces roaming up and down — and their uselessness was terrible, so terrible that I laughed at their pointlessness as I passed them, for indeed they knew nothing, nothing more than what their pathetic eyes could see — no purpose, no truth, no meaning — and it was aggravating to feel myself falling even a step lower down towards them, and so it was that for the first time in my life I felt like I was becoming a member of the aimless generation — the aimless class — and one of the most horrible existences I ever previously thought imaginable was becoming my reality. I no longer had any purpose. No reason to exist. My dreams were dead. And without Gracie, and without true art, and with all my tears and feelings spent, there was no goodness left in me anymore, no truth. Without those essential qualities that made me who it was I aspired to be — who I was created to be — I was nothing more than another one of those ghosts, wandering the Boulevard in search of some vacant actuality, and I reasoned the right thing to do — the true thing to do — would be to remove my unusable presence from the face of the earth, and let the new, clean, and bright fill my corrupt, empty space and make use of the precious existence I squandered day and night with my constant, conceited application of deep aimlessness, loss of direction, and hard, long pulls on that wretched bottle that the weaker beings of the world turned to. I was one of them now, and no matter what anyone said — my friends, parents, or the bright young hopefuls at the bar who foolishly drank to their hopes of some unfathomable glory that existed in the most naive recesses of their seductive minds — in my eyes, the truth was clear. I had simply become a waste of valuable and limited space, and it was time for me to go.

I gave it some thought, and determined that if I was not well on my way to once again fulfilling my purpose as The Last True Artist by the second month in spring, then I would indeed remove myself from the face of the planet. I was fully aware that this demand was extreme, but I believed in my inherent nature as an extreme person, and any kind of action, thought, or movement that sent me into a place of real feeling was better than the despondent, dismal dejection of my current state. I also believed it would put some personal pressure on me to perform, and in return jump start the hard-wired human code of limitless self-preservation, and through that code I might find the means to once again create art I felt true enough to justify my now pointless continuation — yes, this was exactly what I needed — it was damn near perfect! This is what I had to do. I was a survivor. I needed to survive. Not only that, I needed to create! I was Conrad Arlington, The Last True Artist, and without creation I was nothing! And with creation I was everything! Those were the stakes that the universe had laid upon me, the stakes for The Last True Artist, the stakes that would propel me into the ultimate realm of inspiration — life and death — it was everything. I was everything. And I would forever live fully or die trying.

**

It was the first day of spring — it was a Wednesday — I had exactly one month to create true art, and I would do it, or I would die. I went out and bought the finest blend of coffee money could buy, I sat down at my desk, took a sip, picked up my pen, put it to paper, and then I sat. I sat so long that I thought my eyes would bleed. It was so frustrating that frustration itself led to an even greater rage, the same class of rage I felt that night on the Boulevard, and although I didn't write more than a single letter — 'I' — at least I felt something, and believed without a doubt that I was heading in the right direction. However, to my unexpected dismay, this did not stop, but instead went on and on and on and onward still, and pretty soon three weeks had gone by and I had not written a single word. My already gaunt frame had lost a vital five pounds from the stress, and I had become so thin that I literally looked like death itself. My cheeks became sullen in such a way that they reflected the state of my internal paranoia like a mirror, and gazing back into that reflection, I became aware of the pressing reality that I had only one week left to live, thus launching the fires of pitiful self-preservation, and with no art to cool its sting, I fully felt the desperate agony of my internal monologue. "I must create! I must create to live! Oh, Gracie come back to me! Come back and give me your inspiration! Come back to me and let me feast on your blue eyes, your golden hair, your porcelain skin! Oh beautiful one, where have you gone! Oh look at me, now! I am nothing! Nothing anymore! And soon I will be gone! Gone forever! If only I could see you one last time! If only I could hold you in my arms like that night in your room! If only I could take back those terrible things I said and tell you how I really feel! If only I hadn't been so cruel, you might still be here! If I took you physically, you would be here! Yes, you would be here if I had you! I was a fool to not have you! I was a fool to honor you! I was a fool to not reduce you! I was a fool to not treat you like dust! Damn true love! Damn it to hell! It is dead! True love is dead! There is no romance! Only flesh! Only bodies of emptiness! Only ghosts on the Boulevard! Empty ghosts! Damn them! I hate them for existing! Oh true love! Why must I want you? Why?" I fell to my knees in the middle of my room, and I never felt so alone. Then I wept bitterly.

***

The day had come, and I took to the morning in all seriousness, for indeed I had not written one true word, said one beautiful thing, or done anything worthy of artistic note for the entire first month of spring, and in the quiet of the afternoon I secretly prayed that the phone would miraculously ring and it would be Gracie's sweet, timeless voice on the other line to rescue me in my waning moments, but none ever came. No ring. No voice. Only silence in the low-lit square of my headroom, and it was now time for my soul to disembark. This was to be the moment of The Great Passing — The Great Passing of The Last True Artist — and nobody would know about it. There was to be no one. No grand audience. No cheers and no shouts. The ignorance of the world would make it blind to the passing of its only hope, and my coming death would signal the end of the entire artistic age. All true art would surely die with me, and with me all true art, and all creation in the world would be no more, for I was indeed Conrad Arlington, The Last True Artist, and without me the world could not possibly continue to renew itself, it would simply be no more, lost and fully unaware in its endless depravity.

As I had done only a few times since arriving to Los Angeles, I put on my best suit and walked out the door, for I was headed to the Boulevard, to the battle ground of my moral acquisition, and today I was going to finish the great war that had been raging inside of me since the day my bright eyes opened and became conscious of reality. I became aware of every color, every sound, and the grand palms that hung majestically over Franklin Avenue like a preserving canopy became vivid and marvelous, and I was taken by them as they cast tiny, inviting shadows across the sun drenched pavement. Yes, this is what it meant to truly feel — to experience a true feeling of connection with the world — and it took me until death to get there.

I walked slow, cherishing every last moment of my life on earth, but still, within five minutes I managed to hit the strip — the same strip that I had walked on so many occasions before, when I was feeling bright, and hopeful, and good about the world — and it was so much more grand and quaint then ever now. As I passed the little shops and nooks that would serve as the very haunts for those who would speak about me in the tune of myths and riddles after my final hour, I thought they were absolutely perfect, and I would have liked nothing more than to sit down and have a final cup of coffee or one last cold pint, pondering the afterlife for which my spirit was about to join, but it was too late, so I walked onward in my cowardice towards the only reality I ever knew.

"Conrad!"

A voice shot out behind me — a female voice — surely it was my mind, surely it was my decadent and terrible mind playing tricks on me in my final moment, but no matter, it could not stop me now, there was no more truth left in me for it to latch onto. Onward!

"Conrad!"

The voice rang out again, clearer now. No. No! Be gone devil! Be gone now from my mind! You are not the voice of truth! Be gone before I smite you out! Onward!

"Conrad Arlington!"

I stopped, and I turned, and my eyes went wide, for in my line of vision it was none other than Evie Clark, sitting slender and marvelous outside my favorite French bar, hailing me with a white table napkin that she held cool and aloft in her graceful hand. "Conrad Arlington, is that you?" She asked softly, her voice so sweetly real that it overloaded my senses immediately, and it was all I could do to keep from toppling over right then onto the sidewalk.

"Why, yes," I said stupidly, all too taken by the shock of it. "Hello, Evie."

"Conrad," she said pleasantly. "I haven't seen you in so long."

" —Yes—"

"And look at you. You're all dressed up."

"Yes — yes, I am — yes."

"You look good, Conrad," she said with an admiring smile that flowed perfectly into her captivatingly dark, doe eyes. "You look very, very good."

"Thank you, Evie." I felt completely absurd saying it, and I thought those might have been the most interesting three words I had ever uttered in my entire life.

"Would you like to sit down?" She asked, gesturing to an open seat across from her, and suddenly I became very aware of my body, and I felt completely stupid and exposed standing there lucidly in the middle of the sidewalk.

"Evie... is this real?" I asked, leaning-in, dreamlike, still fully believing that Evie's slim figure which sat cool and graceful in front of me could absolutely be a projection of my mind — some last ditch, clinging effort made by the completely difficult, completely stubborn condition of human self-preservation, a condition which would not at all agree with my intention to depart.

"I think it is, yes." She giggled slightly, and I thought it might have been the most beautiful thing I had ever seen.

I stood for another moment, completely awkward in my body, and then in one impulsive motion I took the seat across from her and resolved myself to sit.

"Where were you going?" She asked, curious and intrigued.

I didn't know what to do. My mind felt torn between a state of desperation and survival. It must have been a very neurotic display, because Evie couldn't stop smiling at me, and I was becoming increasingly frustrated at my inability to decide.

"You don't have to stay if you don't want to. I didn't mean to interrupt your day—"

"No," I snapped much too strongly, and I finally felt my body give, and I realized that what I was feeling was a sense of good — that's right — a sense of good, of well-being, both right and grateful, and I liked it. I eased back in my chair, drew in a deep breath, and looked at Evie sitting all pretty across from me like a goddess might if she decided to spend her afternoon sitting in the sunshine on Franklin Avenue, and I was stricken by how appealing she looked, and I couldn't believe I never visualized her this way before. "I would not die to day," I thought to myself. "Perhaps soon, but I would not die today."

"I was just going for a walk," I said quickly, and I felt a sense-of-self return to me. "I like to dress up sometimes. It makes me feel better about the world, wouldn't you say?"

"Very much so," she said with a delightful, little laugh. "I didn't know you cared so much about fashion, Conrad."

"I don't, but I care about life, and I think fashion makes life better for the most part."

Evie laughed.

"And I have nothing against models," I continued rightly. "No matter what anybody says otherwise, I simply won't believe them."

"Well maybe you should." There was a certain look in Evie's eye, and I hadn't felt alive like that for a very long time.

"Perhaps you're right," I said coolly. "I think I'll start today."

We shared another laugh, and I must have smiled the first genuine smile I had in months, then our eyes connected, and I felt myself fall completely into them.

"You look good, Evie," I said with true conviction. "You look very, very good."

"That's what I said about you," she giggled.

"You did?"

"Yes."

I looked at her suspiciously.

"Yes, just moments ago, right before you sat down." The smile on her face was so big I thought it might consume every inch of her entirely perfect face.

"Well, then it seems you caught me," I said, and with that we smiled at each other into the evening.

***

The days in spring rolled by and Evie and I began seeing each other. I never quite got that about women and intimacy, why with some it flowed so easily and with others hardly at all, but whatever power it was that was passing between Evie and I could best be described as effortless. My inspiration had returned in full capacity, and the Great Arlington Pride that continually threatened my existence and every relationship I had ever known was at least, temporarily, dormant. Once again I had found my reason to live, to create, to be, and as long as that existed I resolved to keep my judgmental little eyes off that which had so often been the Achilles' heel of all my self-sabotaging behaviors – that was my pride – with the body being depression, self-animosity, melancholy, worthlessness, and spite, and the head being a great, great wrath. The truth was, I didn't know why Evie was put into my life, but her touch cooled the sting of being alive in this nowhere city, and I was grateful for it. Even so I was fully aware of the oddity of it — of how we met, of how she lived with Gracie for a time, of our estranged interactions at the end of last year, and how she tried so hard to be indifferent to me — but for that first month none of that mattered. As we began to grow more comfortable with each other, and our passion for each other became deeper and deeper, a lot of those mysteries began to reveal themselves on their own accord, whether they were completely true or only slightly or not at all, I did not know, for that was the world these women lived in, a world of greatness, and parties, and endless champagne, and I was only a stranger on the edge, standing off near the corner by the window.

The granddaughter of a wealthy steel manufacturer, Evie Clark — to put it modestly — was the definition of old money. Her father, James E. Clark, a domineering man and self-described playboy, met Russian-American model-actress Yelizaveta — in English, Elizabeth — Karelin at a film premiere in New York. They had a tumultuous relationship to say the least, the kind fueled by drink, infidelity, and copious amounts of money, but nonetheless, they were in love, and after three years of endless decadence and forlorn affairs from both parties, they finally found it in their hearts to commit to each other, and thus they were married, and so Evie was born.

Having wealth and privilege from a very young age, there was no doubt that Evie's perception on reality was somewhat skewed — or perhaps it was just mine, or perhaps it was both, it didn't matter — the fact was that Evie Clark had a certain way of relating to the world, one that was both glamorous and beautifully tragic at the same time, and I always found it to be completely fascinating. According to her, she never developed a relationship with her father who — between his continual philandering and glorious escapades — quite frankly, "never had the time for her." She also found it impossible to get along with her judgmental and calculating mother who "demanded the very perfection out of people that she struggled forever to attain," and, as a result, was simply "all too unpleasant to be around, awful really."

At age sixteen, Evie left her estate in New York and moved to Los Angeles to begin her modeling career that "had always been so readily available to her," and it was — according to her — "the easiest decision she ever made." Naturally beautiful, she came into success almost immediately. Of course, given her name and status this was inevitable, but I had no doubt she would have made it regardless, for Evie was a hard worker when it came down to it, and she had a way about her that was altogether impossible to ignore, which was continually signified by the greedy eyes of both men and women that explored her body on the streets and the bars and the haunts she vacated, and it was only by some chance encounter on some strange, sunny afternoon that I was no longer one of them. It was her kindness that spared me — the kindness that existed inside of her — and I owed her my life. Indeed, she was all I had, she was everything to me, everything in the world, for what was once gold, blue, and bright had been shaken from my soul, and replaced with something tender, warm, and safe, and I had no intention of letting that go, not for all the gold, and blue, and brightness in the world. I had found my girl. She had found me. My art followed that which was dear to me, and that which was dear followed my art, and our hearts beat softly against our spirits in the clearest way, and together we became what was lovely — something deep, something quiet, something complete in the stillness of our tender evenings — and we both could not have been happier.

It was on one of these very evenings that the topic that had been burning at the center of my soul for so long would find its way into formation, for the reality was that I knew this day would eventually come to be — it was not strange — and by the time it was finally upon us I felt it flicker like a candle in the dark, and my body gave into its fluttering drifts, and I could not have been more powerless among them. I took a sip of wine as I laid propped up in the corner of my bed, and with a steady breath of confidence I readied myself to chance the question that had been dancing on the tip of my tongue for the last week, and it was this particular evening beneath the cool glow of my lampshade that I finally found that confidence to do so.

"Do you remember Gracie Garrison?" I asked in the most nonchalant way I possibly could, but regardless, the question still hung thick in the silence of the room like fog hangs heavy in the stillness of a bay, and I could not have drunk enough wine to ready myself for the aftermath to come.

Evie slowly lifted her head from my chest as her big, brown eyes fluttered open. "Yes," she said with the softness of a dove. "Of course I remember her, she was my best friend." There was a moment that I felt completely watched and judged — just a moment — and then it slackened. "What about her?"

She was able to hold my gaze, but somewhere deep within the lovely darkness of her eyes I could see that there was fear there, true fear, the kind of fear that comes from uncertainty, and the difficulty in which she tried to hide it made me wonder all the more, until I myself felt like a drifter in those eyes I had come to know so well, and for a moment I considered if it was wise to continue, but I steadied myself and pressed on all the same.

"Nothing important," I said calmly, stroking her hair. "I was just wondering whatever happened to her that's all. It has been some time."

Evie sat up and looked me square in the face with all the need and want in the world, and her lovely eyes shimmered big and dark in the gleam of the shallow lamplight, holding tears against their deep pockets until they threatened to brim over at the slightest advance, and I felt completely guilty for breathing. "Have you been thinking about her?" She asked innocently as the tears broke from one side, followed swiftly by the other.

"No, no, of course not, Eve," I said, quickly calming her. Evie then fell against my chest, and I held her for a moment as the emotion passed. "What makes you think that anyway?"

"It's just that... it's just that," She was no longer able to speak.

"Evie, dear... whatever is the matter?" I propped her up and leaned her against my shoulder. "Did I say something wrong?"

"No, no, you didn't say anything wrong, Conrad." She coughed lightly through a little sob. "It's just difficult for me that's all. It is very, very difficult."

"What's difficult?"

"Oh I knew you'd ask it! I just knew you would!" She stated, getting frustrated.

"Ask what?"

"About her," she snapped. "You'd ask about her!"

"Gracie?"

Evie nodded and began to cry again, this time falling against my shoulder. I felt completely terrible, but I also had no idea what on earth was the matter, and the tact it would take to coax the truth out of the sweet, sensitive creature on my shoulder would have to be perfect indeed, for she mattered more to me now than anything, all life was with her, and despite her love I still needed to know what I needed to know in order to move on and accomplish the great things I was destined for, so I held her tight, and kissed her neck, and whispered soft and lovely things in her ear, and then I held both her hands in mine so that she was completely safe, and with a final nudge, she turned her face towards me, and she opened her pretty mouth that would unveil the secrets that nobody ever knew about the golden girl, until that night when they were released into the dark, and I, Conrad Arlington, The Last True Artist would bear witness to them. There was no fear present, only truth, only trust, and I would never let her go, not for the purest gold or the deepest blue in the world, for she was fragile in that moment — so completely and wonderfully fragile — and I would hold her together, yes, I would hold her together forever, and tomorrow we would wake up with each other perfectly free and in love, finally clear of this tumultuous weight that still hung over us, the mysterious power of that golden name, ever-threatening to crush us with its memory, yes, we would face it together and be rid of it at last, so Evie took a breath, and she spoke, and thus begins the tale of the mysterious truth, the glorious beginning, and the enchantingly complicated existence of Gracie Garrison.

Evie Clark met Gracie Garrison on a fashion shoot in London at the age of eighteen. They were both up-and-comers at the time, and they were both equally desired. Evie, of course, with her elegant, flowing body and deep, sophisticated complexion, and Gracie — she was the 'it girl,' the icon, the trendsetter — and they were perfect for each other. The blonde and the brunette, the bright and the graceful, and together they turned cities upside down. In the words of one high-profile fashion editor at the time, they were "the most obnoxious pair I had ever seen, but we loved them for it. We absolutely loved them."

"Our competition was limited," Evie said, and as she flipped her hand and fluttered her eyes towards the ceiling, I saw a bit of the model in her come out, and it was powerful. "It was never really an issue."

I knew this was true, for they were so different in look and poise, yet equally so alluring. If anything I figured they would have complimented each other in front of a camera, but according to Evie — "We were hired for different things. They never wanted us in the same room," she said with a little laugh. "They couldn't handle us in the same room."

Indeed, they were almost inseparable, and as the months passed, and as they traveled the world going from shoot to shoot — the airports, the flights, the hotels — from one champagne breakfast to the next with boxes and boxes of cigarettes in between, they began to rely on each other — or rather, Evie on Gracie — for Gracie was always the dominant personality of the two — alive, loud, and demanding, with moments of fragility in between — there was an ever-present liveliness to her that Evie indeed did not have, and I too, could testify to that fact. Evie's heart was as soft and as vulnerable as a newborn child's, thus explaining her indifferent façade that she so often wore, including the night she first met me, and for a short time thereafter. It was to protect herself, nothing more, to shield herself from all the awfulness, and betrayal, and hurt in the world. It had been years since she let anybody in, indeed, since Gracie herself left her as long, and I was there to encourage her to let go, yes, to encourage her to trust in the truth she had inside her. There was so much truth in that girl, so much total and complete truth, and I encouraged her to pull down her polished exterior and let people see who she was, because that is what the people of the earth fell in love with — what I fell in love with — and her beauty was the gateway to her hurting soul, and for now, only I could see it, so I pulled her close, and I kissed her tiny forehead, and in the safety of my arms she found the strength to continue into the gleaming center of the deepest pain she ever knew.

When they were both twenty-one, Gracie and Evie moved in together — into the same grand loft, the one overlooking Studio City.

"It was during this time that I began to see... certain tendencies," Evie stated carefully. "In Gracie's behavior."

"What kind of tendencies?" I asked, and once again I felt a great curiosity rise inside my chest, and there was nothing I could do to suppress it. Evie hesitated, so I gave her a little nudge with my head to continue, signaling that it was okay.

"She," Evie stammered. "She's a liar, Conrad. She lies." Evie's eyes glazed over, for it was difficult for her to say that about someone, especially an old friend. "Oh, I hate gossiping Conrad. I hate it so much. It's so evil."

"Yes, it is," I agreed. "But there is no gossip here, Eve, only truth. This is troubling you a great deal, and it's good to talk about it."

"I'm not sure it is."

"It is, Eve, it is," I said in reassurance. "You don't have to say anything you don't want to say, but know you are safe with me." She looked at me with eyes of pure trust, and I had my permission to continue — "What did she lie about?"

"Everything. She lies about everything, Conrad, absolutely everything. I don't even know what's true anymore."

"Well surely there must be some truth," I stated in confidence. "Everything must come from somewhere."

"Not with her," Evie stated, and her eyes became more serious than I had ever seen them, and I could see in them that she was truly afraid. "She's bad, Conrad. I hate to say it but Gracie's a bad person. She's no good. Please don't push me further."

"Just tell me what you know about her, Eve." My patience waned as my desperation for the truth increased. "It's only words."

Evie looked at me with more vulnerability than I had ever seen in a girl, and it killed me to look back. "Please don't push me further, Conrad," she asked again, this time pleading.

"It's only words, Eve," I stated again. "Just say it, I want to know."

"I asked you not to push me further."

"Well there's no reason for it. It's only words."

"Please don't push me further, Conrad" She said with more power this time — power singed with tears.

"I want to know!"

"Please don't do this—"

"TELL ME!" I screamed, and instantly all hope was pulled from the room, and her bright face fell like death as her eyes pooled over, and I knew that I had just broken her trust, that I had truly become nothing to her, just another ghost in her distant past, and I had sacrificed everything for a girl that was now gone to me. I had given up what was real, true, and tangible for some faded memory of love gone by, and then desperation fell like a sword from my body, and the beautiful creature in front of me was laid upon it.

Evie managed to hold back her tears, just long enough to utter her words — "If you make me do this, Conrad... if you make me say these things, I will leave you. Do you understand? I will leave you, and you will never see me again."

I just looked at her, and I could not utter a sound.

"Oh, don't you love me?" She suddenly burst, pleading with so much need that I couldn't even stand it.

I looked up at her pretty face, and I made my choice. "Yes," I said, but I could not lie. "But I love her more."

Death fell upon the room, and I once again felt the absence of true love as it was lifted from my presence, and my body screamed in such wicked agony that I thought I might die as I gazed up at what I had destroyed, and it was horrible. It was the most horrible thing I had ever felt since feeling, and I knew that I had done what I most feared — I had broken the heart of a girl I loved — I had destroyed a beautiful spirit, for her eyes were darker and more glossy than I had ever seen them, and her silky hair fell in waves over her shoulders that threatened to destroy my very existence, and I knew that I would forever pay for this moment, and in my heart I would have given up my entire being to never have had to experience it.

I thought then that Evie would then get up and leave the room immediately, forever removing her blameless existence from my self-destructive presence, but she didn't. With inner strength that I didn't know was there, Evie flicked back her head and raised her chin to its full height, accentuating her perfectly structured face as to show me not only what I was losing, but who I was truly dealing with, and she became more powerful in that moment than I had ever seen her, and I had already lost.

"Very well," she began. "After tonight you will never see me again, Conrad, and I can only hope that you don't spend the rest of your life alone."

Evie got up off the bed and moved across the room to the drink stand, where she poured herself a hearty glass of wine that she downed in one gulp, then proceeded to pour another, even fuller than before. She then sat down in a chair adjacent from my bed in the best possible way any model could, and I felt our relationship change immediately. This was now a transaction, nothing more, a transaction between acquaintances, and I took her in fully for the last time, and I felt like a nonentity within her dark stare, but I no longer cared, for in my mind existed the blue and the golden, the fair and the bright, and in the stillness of the night the dark and lovely became nothing in her presence.

"Gracie has always thrown parties," Evie began, steady this time. Her guilt was gone completely and any fault was mine and mine alone. "Lavish parties, the best parties in town. The problem was — and Gracie has always had this problem, ever since I've known her — she could never keep money. Never. She would spend it as soon as she earned it, so naturally, after a while I began to wonder where she was getting all this money. She wasn't modeling much anymore. She didn't fancy herself a model. She always thought she was better suited for the screen. She borrowed from me for a while, but as she never paid me

back I eventually had to refuse her access to my funds.
Oh, it was horrible. She would go into terrible fits — the worst fits you could possibly imagine — she yelled and screamed, called me terrible things, told me I was fake. Worthless. She was so abusive, but I loved her you see, I loved her…"

Evie broke off, long enough to wipe the faintest trace of crystal tears that formed in the corners of her big eyes, and I could only look at her.

"Oh, don't be so quick to judge me, Conrad," she snapped. "You would have done the same thing."

"Perhaps I would. Perhaps I wouldn't," I said calmly.

"You would. You've already shown that tonight. You would do anything for her, and I think it's pathetic." She stared at me with all disgust, and I didn't hate her for it. No, I did not hate her for it, I embraced it, I liked it, for I deserved to be despised for what I had done, and I opened myself up to take the full hit, to feel all of what it could do to me — I wanted to be destroyed by it — tears formed in my eyes as my mouth quivered, and I did not retaliate, for I had no grounds to retaliate on, so I looked her square in the eyes — those big doe eyes that burned at me like death — and I dared her to continue.

"Gracie talked me into it a few times — giving her money, that is — she just had a way with words, and she knew how to hurt me so bad. She could be so vicious sometimes, so cruel, and I longed for the kindness and appreciation that followed when I gave in. It was like… it was like a cool glass of water after a long day in the sun, and there was little I could do to resist it." Evie cocked her head to the side, for she was remembering the coolness of those words, and I spared her my urgency. "Then the day came when I finally said 'no,' and after all the anger, the bitterness, and the name calling —after all the terribleness — she finally realized that I wasn't going to budge, so she stormed back to her room in a rage. I didn't see her for several days after that."

"So she was using you for money," I implied. "Is that what you're saying?"

"Well, it's not like she ever had any, at least not enough for her lifestyle." Evie took a large gulp of her wine. "Even with my modeling I have always counted on my trust, Conrad. There's not that much money in the business — not enough to live like I do — and Gracie has always been far more excessive than myself. My parents have always been generous in that way, and as far as I know Gracie never had the same luxury."

"So when the money dried up," I continued, "and you stopped writing checks, then what did she do?"

"Well, she got it from somewhere, didn't she?"

"How so?"

"Well, the weekend came around, and nonetheless, there were people, weren't there? And wait staff, and appetizers, and neat gifts, and boxes and boxes of the most expensive champagne money can buy."

"So she got the money…? How?"

"I don't know how, Conrad," Evie snapped. "If I knew I would have just skipped the whole damned thing and told you."

"Do you think she was lying to you all along? About not having money?"

"It's a possibility," she shrugged. "Anything's a possibility with her."

I didn't like the way Evie said it, and once again I felt myself defending a girl I hardly knew, and despite my own foolishness I was helpless to resist. "I loved her so hard," I thought in my mind. "I loved her so, so, hard, and I might die before she ever even knows it. Indeed, I am a fool! And if I am I don't care! I am Conrad Arlington, The Last True Artist, and I will fight for true love even if it is the death of me!" It was the most foolish justification I had ever fathomed, no doubt about it — pure insanity — but there could be no reason when it came to dealing with the lovely things of the world, and if it was all just a dream, some distant, forlorn dream that had no heavenly substance whatsoever, than I would truly die trying to make it real, and perhaps then my greedy body would release me.

"Well it has to come from somewhere," I stated in agitation. "Perhaps she was just playing you the whole time. She saw a weakness in you and she exploited it. People do it every day. What do you need all that money for, anyway? God knows you didn't earn it."

Evie looked at me with the most ruthless glare, and I felt her dark eyes might consume me as they fell upon me like the end. Then in one fluid motion she got up from the chair and bee-lined straight for the doorway.

"No!" I yelled, lunging for the door, slamming it closed just in time to stay her swift exit. "I'm sorry. I'm sorry."

Evie stood up to her full height and looked me right in the eye, for she was always taller than she appeared to be when she was upset, and her anger made her formidable.

"I am wicked, and I am cruel, but I am desperate, Eve, please, you must help me, if only for the last time. You never have to see me again, but please, just tonight, stay and help me." Tears flowed from my eyes like a child. "I am tortured, Evie, tortured in ways that you can't possibly understand. My very existence is one of a tortured soul, and there is no vindication for me. Please help me. If you don't help me tonight, I will surely die. Please."

I was on my knees against the door, using my full body to block her exit. She just stared at me in a way I had never seen before, and I felt from her nothing but pity.

"My God, Conrad," she said, seeing me clearly. "You do love her." True knowledge filled her eyes, and I didn't know who felt more pain in that moment, but we shared a likeness in our suffering, and that was perhaps the closest Evie and I had ever been.

I couldn't speak — I no longer had the strength — Evie rolled her eyes up towards the ceiling, and pulled her lips in tight as if contemplating doing something she knew she probably shouldn't, yet still felt compelled to do otherwise, then in one swift moment she spun on her heel and moved back towards her seat. She sat down quickly, hands in her lap, her eyes sharp and vacant as she stared off into the air, and I knew that she had never had someone love her like I loved Gracie — it was an impossible love — she didn't realize that level of love even existed until she met me.

I couldn't get up, so I just leaned against the closed door watching her, for as long as Evie was in the room I needed nothing else, and I would stay like that as long as was necessary, until the very truth I needed floated from her mind into the nighttime air.

Evie sat at the edge of her seat, poised and strong. "If you speak of my family or my money again I am gone, is that understood?"

It was an ultimatum, and I had no choice. "Yes," I managed a single breath to fuel that single word — the word that my whole life hung upon.

Evie blinked a few times rapidly, and her nose twitched up and down like a rabbit's might if it were testing the quality of a bit of food, and then, as if by impulse and nothing else, she made her choice and spoke into the ether of that sacred space we shared together.

"I have an idea where Gracie gets her money, Conrad." Evie stated, bold and flat. "But I don't think you want to know. I'm afraid it might crush you."

She looked from the air over to me, and I could not be reduced to any less. Then Evie's eyes signaled the truth on their own, and there was no need for me to speak. She then once again faced the wall that was a quarter turn away from me, and uttered the words I had perhaps always feared.

"She gets her money from boys, Conrad, boys like you." She said it quickly, and then rode its momentum as it moved like a reaper into the room. "She tries you out for a night, sees what she can make of it, and if she doesn't get the result she wants she moves onto the next one." Evie looked directly towards me. "You are nothing to her, and you've always been nothing to her, just like the rest." Evie started to weep again. "She consumes them, Conrad. She consumes them, and now she's consumed you, and it's so heartbreaking I can hardly stand it!"

My mind bobbed wearily against the inside of my skull like an apple bobs on top of the water, and as quickly as the vile words left her mouth, I felt the Great Arlington Pride rise like a fire within me, and within a split fraction of a moment I was on my feet, and my retribution had no end.

"You're a liar!" I screamed.

" —No— "

"You're a liar! And a fake! And you are nothing compared to her! Nothing!"

"Oh, can't you see it?" Evie pleaded in terrible sobs, dropping to her knees on the floor. "Can't you see her for what she is? I was trying to protect you. I was trying to push you away from her, but you fell for her just like everyone else, just like every other bright young boy that has ever laid eyes upon her."

"No!" I screamed. "You were jealous! You were jealous of our love!"

"There was no love, Conrad! There was never any love! She was using you like she used me."

"There was love!"

"There wasn't!"

"It was the truest love that ever existed!"

"It never existed!"

"It did!"

"No!"

"SILENCE!" I screamed as I moved towards her, and that was as close as I had ever come to striking a girl in my entire life.

Evie just held her face aloft, bold and courageous, shaking and trembling, ready to take a hit that she did not deserve, for evil itself had made its home in me, and I was wretched for it. Realizing what I was about to do, I collapsed backwards up against the door, and slid down it into the shadows, terrified of my own existence, for this was the second time in my life that I had no justification to go on living, for indeed I was terrible, I was a terrible, terrible soul, and I longed for the deep, gasping breaths I took from the air to betray me, that I might have no more source in which to draw life, and then I would die, and the world could be rid of my awful existence forever, and then perhaps I would find peace.

Evie looked at me from across the room, and in her deep breaths, and big, heartbroken eyes, I was no more. "I too have loved, Conrad. Yes, I too have loved. I have loved completely. Countless times I have loved completely, I have loved more than you can possibly understand." Her voice was truthful and calm, and never had I heard a voice that was so painfully beautiful — indeed, it was perfect — for what it was, for what it could be, suspended forever, in the power of some eternal moment. "And what hurts me the most, is not that you fell in love with Gracie — no, I have seen that too many times. Countless times. Countless times she has taken loves right out of my arms. No, that's not it at all — what hurts me the most is that I thought you were true, Conrad, and you're not."

The words landed upon my chest with so much weight that I felt it cave. Surely this was it. It would be only moments now before I suffocated completely and my spirit said goodbye to the earth, and the relief would be great.

"Don't you see?" She continued. "You were everything to me, everything that was a boy. Oh God, I loved you so much, Conrad. Oh God, I would have loved you forever..."

"It can't be," I stated in disbelief, for even in the depths of her grief my insatiable mind did not stop its ceaseless wanting. Indeed, it would never stop, for it only wanted one thing, and I would see no mercy in the end. "What we had was true. I know it... the way she looked at me... I know it was real."

Evie's breath stopped, and I heard her heart break. Her big eyes flowed freely, and I saw every emotion in the spectrum of humanity pass through her body in perfect fragments, and I prayed that whichever one she rested on would be the last thing I ever witnessed, but by her graceful and elegant heart she chose sympathy, and every word taunted my very soul, for I had broken a girl's heart, and there was no death like the death I deserved.

"It was true for all of them, Conrad," Evie stated through the tears. "I watched it with every single boy, and I am truly sorry." Tears of mercy flowed from her eyes, tears that I did not deserve, and I felt each precious drop burn my heart as they hit the ground.

"Why?" I stated weakly, and I felt the fight leave me, for there was nothing left to fight for — there was nothing left of me — just skin and sallow bones upon the dusty floor.

"I don't have the answer, Conrad," Evie said. "She can do it, that is all I know, and because she can she chooses to — she's done it her whole life." Evie paused, composing herself, and with a final stroke of empathy her dark eyes met mine, and I knew that I would never see her again, and I wanted to die. "I'm sorry," she said, and then she lifted herself from the ground, and moved across the room to the door.

"Wait," I said in desperation.

"Get out of the way, Conrad. It's time for me to go."

"No, please, just stay a while Evie," I pleaded. "I don't want to be alone right now. Please don't let me be alone right now."

Evie yanked the door open and I fell helplessly to the ground through the frame. She then stepped over me like something obtrusive on a crowded sidewalk, and began moving down the hall, and just as she was about to turn the corner, I found one last bit of strength.

"Wait!"

Evie stopped at the end of the hall, turned, and I saw in her eyes that she no longer knew me, and this would be our final word.

"You said it was an idea," I stated from the ground, wretched.

She just looked blankly at me.

"You said you had an idea where Gracie got her money," I called out. "You said it was only an idea... does that mean you could be wrong?" I stared at Evie with the utmost need, and by doing so I gave her power over my life.

Evie stared back at me, but there was nothing in her eyes, indeed, not a single emotion that creates a person, and with the grace of some forlorn spirit she lifted her mouth, and that was it.

"Goodbye, Conrad."

With the turn of her head she was gone, and I continued doomed and broken, lost forever, trapped, running through some endless dream.

CHAPTER 12
— SOLITARY OF GREATNESS —

I spent the last two weeks of spring confined within the walls of my apartment, and there was nothing left of me. I had completely lost all sense of time, and the days turned into nights, which turned into days like a rotating lamppost set outside the closeted shades of my bedroom window. I had lost all appetite, and my weight had plummeted considerably because of it. My diet consisted mainly of coffee in the morning and alcohol from the afternoon onward, as I found it increasingly difficult to process solid food, and it was only out of necessity that I was able to choke down two to three spoonfuls of raw peanut butter a day to avoid starving completely, a process I found to be altogether horrible and completely taxing. In absolute truth, I missed Evie like life itself — I missed her breath, I missed her touch, I missed her lying next to me — to have something so good, so sure, and so healing suddenly ripped and cast from me was emotionally and spiritually devastating, and I felt my soul depart with her presence. Add to it the enraging and embarrassing fact that it was basically self-inflicted, and, well, I had the human makings of an absolute wasteland. I was completely spent, in fact, I was so completely and totally spent that even the thought of ending it all was too emotionally corrosive to conjure, and I loathed the Almighty for laughing at me, looking down from the heavens above with that eternally-boyish, glowing face of His and laughing at me for the choices I made that had gotten me to where I was, so I became nothing, just a body without a mind, content to physically waste away in a dark and stuffy room.

This went on for a great while — it was timeless really — and as in all things under the sun, it took its effect on me. Eventually, what once hurt so terribly found a way to become distant and despondent, at least enough to lift me up to see the light again, so, on some bright summer day in

June, I threw on a pair slacks that were now two sizes to large, cinched them up tightly with a belt, and walked back into the very world that nearly killed me.

I stood at the edge of the street, and it was completely strange, for I had missed the beautiful transition — that transition between spring and summer that I loved so dearly — and I felt my eyes well with tears in its absence. There was energy in the air, that same, vibrant energy that always floated through the village in season, cool and lively on the upper end of Hollywood, but it was different now — I was different — and the California sun that fell hot upon my pale skin solidified the difference. Summer was truly here, and oh what a beautiful time of year it was! A beautiful time for the brilliant and the bright, the young and the gifted, and I used to be one of them, but no more. Now I was just old and alone, old and alone and without any inspiration to call my own.

I went back into my apartment and threw on some longer clothes to keep the sun off, for I was no longer accustomed to its rays, and en route was instantly struck with how truly gaudy the place had become in the previous weeks — it smelt stuffy and dead — and I knew that if I were going to end it all now was the time, for those desolate weeks — still enclosed within the doors and the walls and the ceilings of that ill place — was as close to death as I had ever been, so I threw open every window in the house to let the air in, and on the coattails of a summer breeze, doom finally found a way to leave me.

I plunged back into the summer sun, for I was going on a walk, and that was the end of it. I was going on a walk, and I was going to eat real food, and I was going to live again, and nothing was going to stop me. I rounded the corner out onto Franklin, and instead of going east as per my usual I headed west — southwest in fact — for due below me stood the pinnacle of my moral acquisition, the town that had built me up, glorified me, then laid waste to my entire life, and in this tired frame that floated skeletal and slim upon the hot sidewalk I would stand. Yes, I,

Conrad Arlington, The Last True Artist, would stand in
the center of the town, and I would finally submit to
everything I fought so hard to destroy.

I took joy in my steps as I walked down Franklin,
and I smiled at the way my slight muscles pulled and
stretched with the motion. "What a strange thing it was to
be alive," I thought. "What a completely strange thing." I
looked to my left as I approached Argyle Street, and I was
taken by the sight of two delicate girls strolling arm in arm
out of a grandiose French style apartment building
overlooking the freeway. I stopped moving immediately,
and my breath left me as I glanced back and forth between
their lovely blonde and brunette heads. I tried to shout,
"Evie! Gracie!" But no words came, only sadness, and as
their slight and graceful bodies strolled happily east
towards the village I knew that it wasn't them — it couldn't
be — for nothing was ever as perfect as the sight of them
together, and I would never witness that again, not as long
as I lived, so I turned on my heel and continued towards the
Boulevard.

It was a little past noon by the time I dropped down
into Hollywood. The sky was clear and bright, and a cool
breeze rolled in over the town that fell like mist upon my
skin, and I was completely calmed by it. Then I felt my
stomach begin to rumble, so I dropped off into some low-lit
haunt for a quick meal, thankful for the darkness and
temporary shade. Despite my hunger, after a few bites of a
club sandwich I was completely full, for my stomach had
shrunk considerably in the last month, and it was all I could
do to keep down what little I had. I wanted to drink —
alcohol specifically — but despite my urge I managed to
stay my hand long enough to plunge back into the shining
daylight, and the dark and hollow thoughts vacated my
mind in the glorious rays.

I strolled along once more, taking delight at what it
was to be full — to be alive — and everything became
vivid and colorful again in ways I hadn't seen for a while,
and I noticed people, I noticed people all around me, and

they were beautiful, yes, they were beautiful — these people — so full of life and hope, and I remembered how I used to be one of them, aimless and true and full of some false purpose, and now I was simply beyond them, but I did not hate them, no, I did not hate them like before, I saw a reason for them now, I didn't know what it was but there was definitely some kind of reason, and so I let that be as I weaved through the surrounding crowds, and I remembered what it felt like to be good, and I wished so dearly that I was still ignorant.

I walked down to La Brea Avenue just as I used to do, taking in the stars that crowded my feet in their squared clusters of pink and gold, and I laughed at them, I laughed at them like they were the last remnants in existence that had any faith in themselves, for I realized they were nothing now, nothing at all, just stars on a boulevard that laid waste to great men, and they were foolish for it — the hundreds and hundreds of names within the confines of five points— they were all fools, limiting themselves like ants, living their lives for marble and stone, and I hated the fact that I wanted to be one of them, but no more, no more for The Last True Artist, there would be no more foolishness, only laughter, for fools lived their lives for marble, and concrete, and blue, and gold, and ashen stone, but it was all nothing now, nothing at all, and it would all amount to nothing in the end.

I made it back to Vine Street and stood at the corner of the intersection — I must have stood there for some time, because shadows fell cool upon my face now, shadows caused by the small cluster of towers that loomed over me, and I felt the chill of evening creep up my skin, and I shivered, watching as people walked up and down, as cars zoomed by with horns that honked all enraged and impatient, and I pondered what it was all for in a way that I had never done, for I was a different person now, the town had truly changed me into a completely different person, and what I had believed so strongly to be true on that one fine evening in November felt like the sliver of some distant dream, blonde and creeping, and sifting, and floating through the five corners of my mind, and I, Conrad Arlington, The Last True Artist, felt like I was none of those things, none of those things that were true, for within the last year I had loved, and I had hated, and I had cried, and I had fought, and I had hoped, and I had dreamed, and I had breathed, and I had screamed, and I had doubted, and I had believed in ways that perhaps no other human being in creation had ever done, and in that moment I realized that I was not meant to live upon this earth. No, I was simply beyond it in purpose and capacity, and I knew I would be alone forever.

I took a breath and looked up at the sky, and then I walked back towards heaven in the shallow brightness.

CHAPTER 13

— THE FALL OF THE GOLDEN GIRL —

Some time went by, and before I knew it was July. Despite the fact that I saw it as pointless, I began to write again, write like I had never written before, and I did so without inspiration, for I had just began the lethargic process of recording the way I felt about things that most people called 'journaling' — a disorganized, compulsive form of writing that I turned to in my lower moments — in hopes that someday I might feel a story again, and then, for the first time in some time the phone rang.

I stared at it, wondering if it was real, and I had a strange feeling — 'ring, ring!' — The feeling became stronger, and I felt like I should let it go, but damn my curiosity — 'ring, ring!' — I set down my pen, and I picked up the phone.

I listened on the line. There was wind — "Hello?"

"Conrad, it's Maxwell!" Boomed his deep, inviting voice.

"Maxwell!" I said in complete shock, and I felt my body straighten like it hadn't done in months. "Hello!"

"Hello to you, my friend! Listen, I'm sorry we've been absent. We've been gone in New York."

"New York," I stated, trying to act surprised. "Of course. Where are you now? I can barely hear you."

He laughed across the line. "That's because I'm driving, my friend, and we're coming to swoop you up."

"What do you mean?"

"I mean we're coming to get you."

"Now?"

"Yes now, old man. Put your shorts on, we're going to spend the day by the pool."

I was too confused to agree, and with his voice, all those old emotions came rushing back with such intensity I could barely think, and I felt that old pain return, the pain of losing someone dear, and my body wasn't ready to agree with it. "But I can't," I stuttered aimlessly. "I'm working."

"Nonsense," he retorted. "I'm with Gracie, she wants to see you. Now what's your address?"

The sound of her name went through me like a gunshot, and I was instantly terrified, and alive, and all of those things that she made me feel at the exact same time, for this was the very phone call I had been waiting for — praying for — for over half a year, and the fact that it was finally here was completely overwhelming. "Gracie, she's with you?"

"Yes, she's with me, dear boy! Where else would she be?"

"I-I don't know," I stuttered. "Paris?"

Maxwell's laughter boomed across the other line with such vigor and vitality that I thought the phone might explode. It was so strong that I almost toppled over in my seat, and had to pull the phone several inches from my ear to keep his expression at bay. His loudness aside, I was completely ecstatic, for I had been all pent up for far too long to be considered social, and circulate images of Gracie in her swimsuit began to dance through my mind faster than I could articulate thought.

"Paris!" He finally exclaimed from his laughter. "My good boy that's absurd!"

"Yes, I suppose it could be."

"There's no supposing, Conrad. It is. " Maxwell said, his laughter quickly giving way to seriousness. "Gracie's here with me now, and we are coming to get you. Now what's your address?"

I had only a split second to make my decision, but the choice was already decided for me, for no matter how much I wanted to protect myself from the great pain that awaited me, a glimpse of hope was all I needed to throw all that reason away, and enticing images of Gracie's slim body glistening and shimmering in the sun submerged my senses, and I remembered her smell, and her blue eyes, and all that blonde hair, and there was nothing I could do but comply, so I spoke my address, and thus sold my heart back into bondage for a single token of forlorn hope.

"Excellent my friend," he said with great enthusiasm. "I'll see you in ten minutes." Then he hung up.

***

Ten minutes later I was standing in my driveway at the base of the hills when Maxwell pulled around the corner in his silver, sports convertible. Now, there's not much distance from the end of my street to Franklin Avenue, but if there was, I could have spotted him coming from a mile away. Those big, oversized glasses, that cheesy smile, and that big sun hat that hung enormous over them both — he looked like the epitome of the corporate salesman on vacation — and if it weren't for Gracie, who sat beautiful and sun-kissed in the passenger seat, that's almost exactly what he'd be, for she was perfect, immaculate, and she glided up that street which bore her like a cool breeze on that hot summer day, and a lifetime's worth of grief was suddenly blown apart by some great light, and it was unreal — it was the most unreal thing I had ever experienced — and I thought surely I had died, surely I had not lived to see the sight I had dreamt of in the greatest depths of the night, and despite the hot sting from a self-inflicted pinch, her image became clearer and clearer, and then the car came to rest beside me, and all of her was vivid.

"Hi Conrad!" Gracie exclaimed out the window.

"Hi Gracie," I said stupidly per my usual, for I could not string together one thought, and the sight of her was beyond brilliant, indeed, so brilliant that I could hardly breathe.

"Good to see you my friend!" Maxwell said. "Hop in."

Lucidly, I walked around the car to the passenger's side.

"Would you like me to move for you?" Gracie offered as I neared.

"Don't bother," I said coolly as I threw my day bag lazily in the back seat, and then I hopped over her with as much finesse as I could muster, taking advantage of the opportunity to show off a touch of my athletic grace, which I reasoned she might find attractive. I landed in the back seat and I was enamored with my own feelings, for the hard fact that I was face to face with a girl whose image nearly killed me just months and weeks before didn't even exist for me now, but strange feelings made people do strange things, and I believed that I had — at minimum — pulled off the move in some fashion, for I swore I heard Gracie give a small little 'oh' as I did, as if taken off guard by my boyish decisiveness. I landed in the back seat with a 'plop,' and was staring at the back of Gracie's blonde head next thing I knew, and I smelt her perfume for the first time in months, and I had no idea how I found myself there.

We left my driveway and took a right on Franklin, then crossed over behind Hollywood until we hit La Brea, which dropped us promptly down to the west end of Hollywood Boulevard. The day was truly beautiful, and I felt suspended, lost in a sea of wind and warm sun and perfume, and I noticed that against all odds, Maxwell's enormous hat managed to stay on his head, and I couldn't help but smile. Gracie's blonde hair flowed perfectly back, tangling and mixing in the wind in the most perfect combination of golden blonde and light brown streaks I had ever seen, so I closed my eyes and let the soft smell of roses that emanated from them overtake my senses, and I breathed in the warm air, and I pushed all doubt and fear from my mind, and I imagined that we were together.

We took a quick left onto Fairfax, which dropped us coolly onto the Sunset Strip.

"Are you excited, Conrad?" Gracie called out, bright and alive from the front seat, loud enough so that her voice could trail back and reach my ears, and what a beautiful voice it was.

"Yes! Where are we going?"

"You'll see!" Maxwell yelled from the drivers seat. "I promise it's someplace grand!"

I didn't doubt him as we weaved our way through the steady, afternoon traffic that proceeded slowly west down the Strip, for there was nothing normal about these two — nothing convenient or trite — and I remembered the night that I first met them at the bar, and how I came to know them, and then the cocktail party, and how strange it all was at the time, and how magical and surreal and completely captivating. Then I looked to my right and saw the venue that Gracie and I visited back on that one magical night in November, and I remembered how we connected there, and how she held my hand as we moved through the sea of ghosts that looked to devour us, and I remember how she gazed at me, and how beautiful she was, and how her body fit so perfectly against mine, and I wished that we could have stayed like that forever. Then the car rolled on and I saw the Chateau that stood grand and gleaming upon the hill in the bright sunshine, and I noticed how different it felt now during the day, and how much plainer without the grandeur and the mystery that came in the evening mists, and I remembered what it felt like to be in the lobby, and how secrets seemed to lurk in every corner amongst the people and the lampshades, and I remembered Benjamin Trask, and his grey suit, and how truly heartbroken he was, and I remembered what I felt like at the time, and how I truly thought Gracie was gone from my life indefinitely, so I looked forward into the cockpit of the car, and I let my eyes wander up and down across her golden form. "Surely this is a dream," I thought. "Some lithe and graceful strange, strange dream... and perhaps I'll never come out of it... and that would be all right."

After ten minutes or so, Maxwell turned left off Sunset and we rolled into the driveway of a grand hotel that stood high and lofty overlooking the city. It was roughly nine stories high, with big gleaming windows that blazed a deep silver against the sunshine it reflected. Indeed, it was a sight to behold, for whatever happenings awaited beyond its great walls had been reserved only for the privileged few — the young, and the beautiful, and the extremely gifted — and I was not at all surprised that I found myself there, only saddened by the fact that I had let myself become one of them, so I stomached my remorse and exited the vehicle, and I knew that I would never be free again.

"This is it, my friend," Maxwell said as he gave his keys to the valet. "I hope you came hungry."

"I can't wait for you to see it, Connie," Gracie said playfully, turning to Maxwell who was unloading all sorts of unnecessary beach items from the trunk. "Oh, leave it won't you Maxwell?" She scolded. "Can't it wait 'til after lunch?"

"A man is only as good as the chair he sits in, darling."

"That's the most ridiculous thing I've ever heard, Maxwell, and you know it. "

"That might be so, my dear, but nonetheless, I am going to take it," he said deliberately. "And you'll just have to live with that fact."

"I've come to the conclusion right now, Maxie," Gracie said, throwing back her head. "I haven't any reason for you."

"And you love me for it."

Maxwell shut the trunk with a grin and the valet took the car away, and once again I was struck with just how odd their little relationship was. It was romantic somehow, but not at all sexual — no, not sexual at all — but nonetheless they had a way with each other that I had never seen in two human beings before, and I both loved and despised them for it at the same time, for I knew that the platonic way in which they went about life with each other was an impossibility for me, and I suddenly felt a great deal of anger against the passionate way I was fated to live life, the passion that very few souls were tasked to bear, and I once again felt alone, then Gracie smiled from the driveway, and I became perfect again.

"Are you okay, Conrad?" Gracie said, studying me, her blue eyes darting back and forth off mine, and I knew that she remembered everything.

I was breathless, for it was the first time I had looked her full in the face since her return that morning, and whether or not it was a dream, she was indeed the most beautiful creation I had ever seen, and the days and nights of torture proceeded by her memory were now justified completely by her porcelain countenance, and I found myself alive once again within the golden locks that enclosed her. "Yes, I'm okay."

"You're lying to me, Connie," she said with a smile. "I know when you're lying."

"I'm fine," I stated, and as beautiful as she was I hated the way she looked at me, for there was no mystery there anymore, only pity, a pity that comes from real loss, for she knew exactly how much she meant to me, and I felt like it was all nothing to her — all that feeling — nothing at all, just some tiresome speck in her spotless world.

"Hmm... whatever you say then." She gave me a look, and a slight smile, then girlishly flipped her blonde head, and left me with her back as she took her entrance.

Maxwell, who looked completely ridiculous with all the unnecessary items he was carrying, filed in behind her, and I behind them both, and together we crossed through the grand doors into the lobby. The inside was beautiful, with polished, hardwood floors dotted with eclectic, white pieces of furniture that only added to the ambient lightness of the entire space. Gracie moved quickly through it, and her eminent presence enhanced the space even more than it enhanced her, and everything about this inner world was made pristine, so much so that even the modelesque girl that stood tall and lovely behind the front desk stared in envy as she passed, and although she tried to remain irreverent there was no use, for her eyes betrayed her immediately, and all the other men in the world stopped and stared at the girl they could never have, and I pitied every single one of them.

We filed into the elevator en route to the top floor. No words were exchanged, only a cool smile from Maxwell to Gracie — Gracie to Maxwell — and then back again. I was struck with the feeling that they were able to speak in code, like they were planning some great and elaborate hoax against me, and that I should probably fear for my life, but then there was a "ding," and the elevator doors flew open, and Gracie led the way into the marvelous hallway.

We walked down the aisle until Gracie approached a large door, and I had no doubt this was the grandest suite in the place. She entered.

"William, we're here!" Gracie called as she floated fully into the foyer.

"William? William?" I thought to myself as I followed inside. "Why does that name sound so familiar?"

"Come on in! Make yourselves at home!" I heard a strong male voice call from somewhere upstairs. "I'll be just a minute!"

I stood somewhat awkwardly in the middle of the foyer while Maxwell dropped his cumbersome load off next to the doorstep. Gracie wasted no time, and began fluttering around the room like she owned the place, putting together drinks with no apparent realization that I was uncomfortable in the least, so to remain from feeling completely unimportant I took in the grandness of the space. Indeed, it was beautiful, with polished, dark, hardwood floors littered with black rugs topped with white and golden furniture. At the far end of the room stood a large glass window which single handedly lit the space by the warmth of the California sun, and for the sole purpose of something to do I walked towards it. My eyes widened in enchantment as I neared, for beyond its layer of crystal glass, all of Los Angeles spread out completely enormous and sweeping in its entirety, sprawling on forever like concrete waves on a silver sea, and I instantly felt a sense of greatness, for I was physically standing above the rest of the world, and I wondered what it must do to a person to see that every day.

The kitchen — which was perfectly visible from the foyer — was covered with stainless steel units dispersed by granite countertops that ran on a great distance, eventually ending abruptly at the bar where an equally long liquor cabinet sat with its doors wide open, inviting anyone and everyone to partake in its inexhaustible spirits.

"It's a beautiful room, isn't it Connie?" Gracie chimed out.

"It is," I agreed.

Having finally finished organizing his cumbersome load, Maxwell walked over and put a large hand on my shoulder, his deep breaths falling heavy upon my face. "Come, my friend, let's have a drink."

We sat down in the kitchen along the bar, where Gracie finished up the final touches on four large cocktails whose glasses I could have sworn were twice the size of regular ones, then she distributed them evenly amongst us, leaving one on the tray for the man upstairs whom I had not yet met, and was not so completely eager to be introduced to.

"Here you are, gentlemen," Gracie said. "Two Manhattan specials."

"Thank you, my dear," said Maxwell, taking his like it was the most desired thing in the universe.

Eager to quench my thirst, I took mine just as greedily and experienced a delightful sensation as the cool, hard liquid dropped adamantly down my throat in a single motion. It was delicious, and having gone almost half a day on an empty stomach, I found the effect of the alcohol on my system to be instantaneous. I felt the same coming from the others as well as we sat coolly sipping our drinks, and given the circumstances, I didn't think it strange that we exchanged few words. Gracie lounged beautifully against a dark wooden chair, humming softly to herself while Maxwell adjusted an odd piece of straw on his broad, flimsy hat that had managed to work its way out of place. I sat back and smiled while I watched them, feeling that I should utilize the time to say something bold or important, but I didn't, for no sooner had I placed the thought when a beautiful, modelesque girl with dark hair over a familiar, petite structure paced elegantly towards us across the foyer. She wore a brown two-piece that strung tiny across her tanned, sinewy frame, and I pictured a scene from a movie I must have watched years before, but I didn't have time to place it, because as she drew nearer she solidified herself into reality, and I saw before me a girl who was none other than Evie Clark, and I thought surely it would be the end of me.

"Evie!" Gracie exclaimed, rising up and running over to her as she slid open the glass door, throwing her arms around her. "I'm so glad you're here. It's been so long."

"Hi Gracie," Evie mumbled in her same, indifferent tone that she used when I first met her, and I prayed that she wouldn't look at me, that she wouldn't turn her graceful head only slightly to the right and lay her all-knowing eyes upon me, but she did. It happened. All time seemed to suspend itself, and her brown eyes went wide as she was held victim to Gracie's loving arms, and I was at her mercy, for before me stood the girl that had truly saved me — saved me from certain death — and to repay her I had broken her heart, and I deserved to be destroyed as punishment. It was an impossible situation. The very girl that had possessed me to such a degree that all of Evie became nothing in the shallow wake of her distant memory now had her slender arms wrapped firmly around my lost lover's neck, and the air became deathly still, and I thought I could hear a pin drop all the way down in the lobby, and I don't think I was entirely wrong.

"Hi," I said, holding up my glass in Evie's direction, doing my best to appear as irreverent as possible, and suddenly our roles had reversed.

Evie didn't say anything, in fact, she didn't really respond at all, just stared at me in an estranged way until Gracie finally let her go.

"How's the pool?" Gracie asked, ecstatically.

"Yes, how is the pool, Eve?" Maxwell doubled.

"It was good... it was nice," Evie replied slowly, still staring at me.

"Would you like a drink?" Gracie asked. "I just made my special Manhattans that you're so fond of. I could make another round if you'd like."

"No... no, no thank you." Evie said, finally letting me off, and I couldn't have been more thankful. "I'm very tired... I think I'll go lie down for a while."

"Do what you want then," Gracie exclaimed, disheartened, and as far as I could tell she remained unaware of the tension between us, either that or she didn't even care, which was entirely worse. "Do tell William to hurry won't you, it's been a long drive and he promised us lunch."

"William? William?" I thought to myself. "Where have I heard that name?"

"She won't have to, I'm right here," said a manly voice behind us.

"William!" Gracie got up, ran across the kitchen, and threw herself into the arms of William Montgomery, a mature looking man just shy of thirty, and then bang! Reality struck me like a ton of bricks might if it could be so powerful, and I remember exactly where I had heard the name, for it came from the lips of poor Alice Button back in the gaudy confides of her Westside cottage, and I remember how she aimed that name at me in what I thought was, at the time, just some fragmented title in the bouts of her insanity. Since then I had not heard the name, not once from anyone else, and I remember Gracie dismissing the name as quickly as it came up, and I could not have been more curious as to why.

The man holding Gracie in his arms had dark, tanned skin that stretched roughly over an athletic build clearly kept up through the benefits of natural exercise.

His dark hair was pulled back coolly in a ponytail, perfectly divulging his big, chocolaty eyes, chiseled jaw line, and a good amount of five o'clock shadow that would have taken me a week or more to grow. His outfit was reminiscent of something I thought a dark, renaissance painter might wear, with leather boots below canvas chaps, and a loose, leather vest that hung unfastened over a thin-white, fiber-cotton shirt, unbuttoned to the chest with the sleeves rolled up. Here was a man that appeared to have it all, and the sight of his strong, brazen arms wresting authoritatively around Gracie's waist gave me a certain distaste for him that I found difficult to shake, for I knew that before me stood competition for The Last True Artist, competition that possessed some kind of nameless talent — I didn't know exactly what, but it was there — and in that moment I felt the pang of some bitter jealousy run up through my stomach in a way that wasn't so different from the Great Arlington Pride that had streaked through me so often before, but still, this time it was different — perhaps even more wicked — indeed, it was so wicked that I thought I might not be able to control it, so I pushed my cocktail away from me, and gave myself some distance to subside.

"Hello, Gracie," William said with ease. He gave her a kiss on the cheek and let his arms fall from her in such an assertive way it made me wonder why all of life couldn't be as simple. "Hi, Maxwell."

"Hello, my friend," Maxwell boomed, and it was obvious that he approved.

"I'm sorry about the wait, I spent all morning by the pool and had to make sure I looked at least somewhat presentable."

Evie, who had waited out the introduction, continued on her path for the stairs, and I still wondered what she might do — what she was capable of doing — and I was terrified, then suddenly I became curious, curious as to why she herself was there, and then many scenarios began to flash through my mind, scenarios that were more dangerous to her than they were to me, and then I wasn't so afraid anymore.

"Where are you going?" William demanded from Evie in a way that somehow managed to hold its charm.

"I'm going to lie down for an hour," she said lucidly. "The sun, it just takes it right out of me." She then disappeared up the glass stairwell, giving me one final glance as she did, and in that final moment when her brown eyes met mine, a certain understanding passed between us, for this was life, and it was bitter, and cold, and as awful as hell at times, and I knew for certain that we were the only two people in the room that fully realized that, and then I looked at Gracie, and Evie was gone from my life forever.

William turned his steely gaze towards me. "I'm William," he said, holding out a strong hand.

Maxwell butted in. "Ah yes, William, this is Conrad — Conrad Arlington — we're in the process of going into business with him."

I felt like slapping Maxwell hard across the face, for I was enraged that he could say something so flippantly defiant after all the time that had passed, and I thought for sure if he knew what I had been through he would have at least been decent enough to hold his tongue, but then I thought about Benjamin Trask, and all that he had said about him, and I can't say I was so sure anymore.

"Conrad's a writer, William," Gracie added as she moved around the kitchen, never staying in one place for too long. "And he has lots of wonderful stories to tell."

"I see," William said in a knowing tone. "It's nice to meet you, Conrad."

"Likewise," I said, shaking his powerful hand. "This is quite the place you have here."

"Thank you. It's not much, but I find it relaxing in the summer months." He looked around modestly, sizing up his own space as if it was barely anything at all. "Come, let's continue our conversation over lunch."

William led us outside to a beautiful, airy patio located just above the marvelous rooftop over his suite. Los

Angeles spanned on forever around us, and the Hollywood Hills loomed to the north above all the glamour of the Sunset Strip, Los Feliz and Silverlake to the east, downtown and greater LA to the south, and Santa Monica beyond the confines of the decadent Westside — a prison for the once true and glamorous — and it was altogether breathtaking. We took our seats in flowing chairs centered around an elegant glass table covered by a large umbrella that blocked out all interference from the hot sun, and a few waiters made the rounds with cocktails, followed by a smorgasbord of French appetizers that were so delicious I was all but stuffed by the time they got to the main course. Maxwell ate heartily, making up for Gracie, who had heaped up a decadent plate of lentils, rice, and heavy amounts of seafood that she barely even touched, preferring rather to satiate her appetite with a number of different cocktails, that, from which I could tell, had little effect on her. Despite her wispy frame there was no mistake about it — the girl could drink — and perhaps more so than anyone I had ever met in my life.

"That was absolutely delicious, William, thank you," Maxwell exclaimed happily, leaning back in his chair to support his full belly.

"Yes, it was great, thank you," I added quickly.

"No bother," William said with a wave of his hand. "It's my pleasure to entertain. I don't have enough guests these days."

"That's because you're always traveling," Gracie implied.

"I suppose that could be the reason," William answered, pretending to be modest.

"Speaking of traveling, how was New York my friend?" Maxwell asked eagerly.

"Yes, how was New York, William?" Gracie added. "Oh, do tell me it was grand."

"It was just a bit of business, that's all."

"Oh, how I do wish to go to New York again, it's been so long." Gracie said in yearning.

"Weren't you just there?" I inquired, remembering the conversation I had with Maxwell on the phone earlier that morning.

Gracie looked at me in a quizzical, unsure way, and then broke into a bit of laughter. "Oh Connie, you're joking."

"No, I'm not," I said, easily defending myself. "I just talked to Maxwell about it on the phone this morning, isn't that right Maxwell?"

I turned to Maxwell, who didn't look me in the eye, but rather took up his fork again, and began eating vigorously even though he had already had his fill.

"Do tell us about this business, William," Maxwell said, avoiding my question altogether.

I just stared at Maxwell in the way I'd stare at someone if they just blatantly cheated in a game of chess, and because of his sheer ignorance to the acknowledgment of the move there really wasn't much at all to say, for that was twice now — the other being the nature of our fist meeting — and I had come to the discovery that Maxwell Price may indeed be a compulsive liar. I didn't like to think of him that way, for I had always liked Maxwell before, and deciding not to make more out of it than what it was, I sat back and let the conversation continue, allowing William — who's apparent modesty had finally been chiseled away by Gracie's insistence — tell his elaborate stories about the grandiose film sets and lavish, high-rise parties he had visited regularly over the last six weeks. I let my tired eyes drift down towards the pool, preferring the stimulation of the shimmering, sun-kissed bodies that lay hot and golden against the backdrop of the cool blue to the self-indulgence at hand. Further still I looked towards the horizon, where the large mansions in the hills caught up with the sky, and the deep, orange, evanescent sun that threatened to dip ever deeper beyond them with every passing moment of the day. Indeed, it was just as my consciousness was about to fade away that the rest of my party stood, and I was signaled promptly by the distinct scrape of chairs against concrete tile that roused me from my faded slumber.

Everybody was tired. The combination of sun, alcohol, and an excess of rich food had taken its toll, so we all retreated inside for a siesta to prepare for the coming evening — an event to which I couldn't have been more of an advocate — then, by five o'clock, everybody was rejuvenated, or at least enough to begin the day where we left off, so Gracie resumed mixing cocktails and we all headed down to the pool for the rest of the day.

In comparison to the other luxurious amenities at the elaborate hotel, the pool was no less monumental, with big, white day beds upon which golden bodies sprawled, and a view of southern Los Angeles that spread on indefinitely past the crystal gleam of the majestic pool that was filled with the perfectly shaped figures of the beautiful and bright, moving this way and that, up and down in the cool water. We found a spot near the corner and preceded to lay down our towels, save for Maxwell, who had finally found his opportunity to test his chair that he made such a compelling effort to bring. He took his time setting it up, circled around it a few times, admiring his work, then sat down and fell asleep almost instantaneously, his large mouth hanging open in the simplest of ways, and I unwillingly felt a great deal of affection for the man — pitying affection perhaps — but affection nonetheless. No sooner had Gracie set down her things than did she run towards the pool, splashing into the shallows like a child might if one could be so animated, and I wondered what it would be like to have everything one could possibly want in the world, and then I smiled, for I was completely content to watch her.

"Come on, Conrad!" She squealed in delight, beckoning me to join the experience of her simple ecstasy.

It was quite a sight — Gracie in her element — the way the small of her back arched inward, capturing the sunlight in such a way that made it flow perfectly into her slight hips, the tight, minimal muscles that tensed, stretched, and then tensed again as she waded, back and forth against the shallows, and then I admired her delicate, fixed chest as it rose and fell beneath panting breaths as the wind took up her curls, mixing them into a pristine hue of brown, gold, and white that shimmered effortlessly against the setting sun. Then she bravely ventured further from the safety of the shallows, and I held up my hand and gave a big smile, exaggerating it at the corners, believing that she could somehow sense my approval from fifty yards away, but I didn't think she cared, and I didn't think she needed to, for she was in her world — Gracie's world — and that was a world that nobody could touch, indeed, no one in all of existence, not even The Last True Artist, and somehow that gave me comfort. I closed my eyes, leaned back in my chair, and rested on what true art could be — she was true art, this creature from another world, alive and alone, dancing in the water, perfect and eternal, forever.

"It's a beautiful thing, isn't it?"

The voice came sudden and unwelcome. I looked to my left and saw William lounging on a reclined daybed a few feet away from me, peering through his black, square rimmed glasses that reflected the sun back towards the horizon. Admittedly, I hadn't even noticed him before, for the combination of sun, fading alcohol, and Gracie's intoxicating presence had done away with my surrounding environment, including all the other beautiful bodies and William's commanding presence.

"Yes, it is," I stated flatly, assuming he was referring to the many beautiful creatures that stretched out before us.

"The summer sun does strange things to a woman."

"I'm sure it does."

He looked over, and even from behind his black sunglasses I could feel his deep eyes studying me — studying me like a child that was full of desire — and he was more than aware of the girl that gleamed perfect in my mind, and what it was that I wanted from her. I felt completely undone, but not in a pleasant way, almost like I had been victimized somehow, and I suddenly wondered how women must feel when he looked at them like that, and I reasoned they didn't have a chance. The whole situation was making me very uncomfortable very quickly, and just when I couldn't stand it any more, he turned his face back towards the endless city, alleviating me just enough that I could remain intact a little while longer.

"How long have you known her?" He asked, gazing forward in self-appreciation.

"A few months, give or take." I lied, for I remembered the exact day I had met her, what time, where, and I figured he already knew this anyway, but I didn't care.

"I heard she auditioned for one of your films."

"That's right."

"Have you produced much?"

"No, no, just writing mostly. I'm looking to get into it further."

He smiled and turned his face back towards the sun — like Benjamin Trask might if he cared for nothing and no one in the world — and I despised and adored him at the same time, and wished to both be him and to also see him fail, and I somehow managed to love him for it, and I don't think I was the only person by the pool he had that effect on.

"Do you produce films?" I asked.

"Yes, I suppose that is what I do," he said coolly.

"Is that how you know Gracie?"

He paused as if he knew this question would eventually come, and even though he was aware of it, he wasn't fully prepared to address it, for it still found a way to sneak up on him.

"Gracie and I have…" He searched for the words. "An understanding relationship."   Silence followed, and I knew those words meant only one of a few possible things, and the thought of it hurt instantly like the sting of nettles on bare skin, and I wouldn't inquire further to save my own feelings, but as much as I tried to hide my reaction, I had such a dammed honest face it was of little use, and my mind was suddenly inundated with none other than Bobby Finch's squealing, boyish voice, going on in waves about the importance of guarding the feelings of my heart, and I wanted to shout out and scream, but I held my tongue, and my soul beat rapidly on the coat legs of my steady breath.

"My boy," he laughed. "You look like I just shot your dog."

"That so?" I said, stone cold. I didn't like being made fun of, and I was getting increasingly frustrated at my helplessness in the situation.

"Are you two?—"

"No," I answered shortly.

"Didn't think so," he said, calmly assessing the situation. "I see the way she looks at you, though. Maybe you should think about it."

I didn't want to think about it! I didn't want anything to do with it! I just wanted to be anywhere but there, for some sort of solid truth had risen to the surface at last, and the thought of them two together made me want to commit murder, and I felt like I would surely snap at any moment if the pain didn't subside. "All this time," I thought. "Surely I had been a fool. A boyish, naive, scrawny little fool."

"Oh, don't be like that," he continued. "There's nothing between us. It's purely beneficial you see. She provides something I need, and I, well, I provide something she needs."

"Uh-huh," I mumbled with growing darkness, not having any of it. "Why don't you elaborate?"

"Well, everybody needs money, Conrad. Everybody has a place. That's just the way it is."

I could only stare at him with contempt, and my damned honest face made sure of that.

"Like you didn't know," he said, laughing it off.

"No. I didn't."

"Please. The cars, the money, the fancy gifts, the cocktail parties, the champagne, where do you think it all comes from?" He adjusted himself and stretched his neck. Then he looked like he was going to get angry, but he managed to wave it off, as if a show of true, human emotion was an experience he wasn't accustomed to, and he didn't care to start. "Men, Conrad," he continued. "It comes from men. Men like me — men with money — Drive. Instinct. We make the world go round, understand?" He nodded at me, again in his assuming way. "I know you do. It's in you. I can tell. You'll see. In a couple of years, you'll be just like me."

"You're sick." I couldn't have stopped it from coming out if I wanted to, for I despised this man and everything he represented, and when and if I was fortunate enough to rise to power in the coming years, I would do away with his kind forever.

"Why are you here then?" He asked, loud and bold. "Why did you come from wherever the hell it was you came from to this city? And don't say it's to be an artist. I've heard that one way too many times now."

He was just a mouth to me, and a pair of eyes, and after today I wanted nothing more to do with him, but still I found myself listening attentively, and despite my greatest efforts I couldn't do otherwise.

"I'll tell you why," he said, his dark eyes locking onto mine like we were about to enter a business deal and our entire fortunes were at stake. "It's because you want to make something of your life, Conrad. You want respect. You want to be recognized — sure, you might want to be thought of as an artist, sure — but what you really want... is that." He pointed above us towards his penthouse. "And this." He spread his arms out wide, alluding to the whole environment we sat in. "And most of all, you want that." He pointed to Gracie, whose beautiful physique still shimmered golden blonde against the waters of the pool, the big, round sun setting behind her, bringing out her silhouette that held perfectly picturesque against the backdrop, and then, for the first time in my life, I knew he was right. I knew what I really wanted, and I hated myself completely for ever believing I could be any different.

"Let me tell you something right now," William continued. "We have no responsibility to make art. We have no responsibility to please people. We have no responsibility to do the right thing. Our only responsibility is to make as much money as we possibly can. That's it. That's why we're here. That is how we make our mark on the world. I hate to be the one to tell you that, but that is the reality — that is the way things are — and you'd be at your best to just accept it, align yourself with it, and buy every good and beautiful thing you ever see along the way."

I hated everything he said, but I knew it was in me, and, to some extent, some of it was true. I felt sick, like all the reality in the world turned to lead, and then fell like doom upon my shoulders — art, women, wealth — it was all nothing, and I became a reduced man, a burdened man, and it was with deep loathing that I continued drawing breath in the shadows of the drowning sun.

"What's the purpose then?" I asked, desperation now creeping in. "Is there anything left? Don't you want anything anymore?"

"For as long as I can remember, I wanted to be rich, Conrad," William stated in one blunt phrase. "Now I am. And I guess that's good enough for now."

He turned his chiseled, tanned face towards the city, and I saw a man, just shy of thirty, that had been broken by the six years that stood between him and me, and there was something simple about it, and incredibly sad, and I resolved that I would not be that man, no, I would never be that man, even if I had to die for it, I would never be that man, for I was and would always be Conrad Arlington, The Last True Artist, and my existence was far beyond any that he could possibly try and fathom, and I judged him completely for being a lesser being.

"Talk to her," he said lightly. "Tell her how you feel. Gracie's a big girl. She can handle it."

"She doesn't like words," I retorted strongly. "I'm afraid she hasn't the use for them."

He just stared at me, and I stared right back, and in that span of time a challenge had been issued over the life of a girl, a challenge for what was right and good, for Gracie Garrison was far beyond him in scope and capacity. Indeed, she was even beyond me, for he was truly nothing, nothing but a wealthy fool, and next to my existence he was made useless, and he knew it, so he turned his gaze, and any truth he ever had burned away, and I no longer had reason to respect him.

"You're a strong lad, Conrad." He stated with a chuckle. "A very strong lad. You'll go far in this business... I can see that already." He reached into his back pocket and pulled out a card, then held it out to me. "Take my card, if you're ever looking for industry work, you know who to call."

"I don't want it."

"I beg your pardon?"

"I said I don't want it," I repeated again. "I'm fine on my own, thanks, and I'm afraid you couldn't help me even if you wanted to. You haven't the ability."

For the first time since I met William he was truly beside himself, and he had no idea what to do, so he chuckled once again, and his weakness was completed at the edge of the pool. "What do you mean?"

"I mean you don't have any talent." I stated it strongly, and his whole front crumbled like the Berlin Wall. "Your money is useless to me, so I have no need for you. Now please be silent, I'm tired and it's been a long day."

"See here, you must be joking."

"I'm not," I snapped, and my eyes burned as my emotion brimmed over, and I could hardly control it. "You are a talentless fool, a taker, and a user. You know nothing about truth, or love, or anything that is good in the world! You have lied and cheated people for far too long, and now you have met your end!" I pointed to Gracie in this moment. "That girl," I stated. "Is more important to me than anything you will ever be able to comprehend, more important than anything you can possibly try and fathom, and you have disrespected her in my presence, and I think you'll find it was the worst thing you could have ever possibly done! For within that girl burns a truth like you can't possibly imagine! And death itself will be your lover in the end!" Then suddenly I laughed, I laughed like a madman would if he gave sanity too much credit. "Indeed, what am I saying? You can't even see it! You haven't the talent!" Then suddenly my voice became dark again, and the Great Arlington Pride that was my downfall became more deadly than the darkest weapon, and I would use it to destroy this man once and for all. "But you have tried to touch that truth — you, a talentless fool, have tried to touch it — even though you can't, and I despise you for it. Your very existence is despised by creation itself, and they laugh at you in unison, for compared to me you are nothing! Completely inconsequential in the presence of The Last True Artist and you know it! You've known it since you first laid eyes on me earlier today! And I laugh at your inabilities."

He stared at me like I was insane, like I was some dangerous madman that needed to be locked up, and I couldn't blame him, for perhaps I had gone insane. Perhaps that girl — who now sat all golden blonde at the end of the pool — had truly driven me to the edge of sanity and pushed me to the limits of my own self-involvement, but I didn't care, for I had hurt a great deal over the last year, and I would now give it back tenfold to those who did not appreciate the higher things of the world, and I would make them hate their own existences for being the wretched fools they were, and I would do it with all retribution, all wrath, and all magnificent fury.

"I think you'll find you are making a big mistake," William stated strongly.

"I think you'll find I'm not," I said, lazy from my seat, for he no longer existed to me. "But if you want to do something about it, you're welcome to try. I think you'll find that all your money is nothing without talent — of which you have none — so unless you wish to inflict upon me some kind of bodily harm, or have something useful to contribute, please remove your presence, for I'm tired and I haven't any use for nonsense."

With that, William stood up in a great haste, and judging by his demeanor it was probably the first time he had been bested in a great long while, and I couldn't stop smiling.

"I was trying to help you, that was all," he stated like death would if it were about to take a life. "I thought you showed promise, but turns out you're just a self-entitled, arrogant child. You'll never work in this town again. Never again."

"I highly doubt that," I said with disregard. "But if that happens to be the case I really don't care anymore, so I guess time will just tell, won't it?"

He looked at me and laughed bitterly, and I figured that was his way of dealing with things, so I didn't pay him any attention, for whether he knew it or not, he had done more damage to my soul that day than he could possibly imagine, and it wasn't his inconsequential life that would pay for it, but a being far more beautiful and bright than himself, and for that his soul would be required to make amends to eternity, and he would be required to experience fully everything and all that was coming to him — everything that was dark — and for that I pitied him a great deal.

With one last haughty breath he turned and headed back towards the lobby, leaving me alone on the edge of the pool with my thoughts, and with Maxwell snoring just a few paces down, and my mind felt like mush as all the goodness and firmness of faith was suddenly and violently yanked out of it, leaving nothing at all but dust, for the mystery that I so loved about the world seemed to unveil itself all at once, and all the glory and grandeur of pursuit dropped into my stomach and out my legs like it had never been there at all, leaving me frail and wasp-like in the fading sunlight. Then I looked out towards the gleaming pool and there was a shift. The wind died down and the water itself reflected my deepest yearnings, or, perhaps, it was just Gracie, who sat down at the far end of the pool, just beyond the shadows of the setting sun, staring out at the same horizon that I stared out at, taking up the same posture that I took, and it was as if we shared the same body, like she had been outfitted with my same form, and then she must have become suddenly aware of the blemishing discovery I had finally made about her existence, for her glowing silhouette was turned towards me now, and I felt her bright eyes shimmer with a knowing certainty from across the pool, and if I could see them, I would see crystal tears caught up within her fluttering lashes, her blue eyes, and her long, blonde hair… it was the most heartbreaking experience I had ever come to know in my life, and I knew this day sealed my fate of ever becoming a whole person.

***

We drove silently into the sunset, the Strip all bright and alive and swirling all around us with its horns, its traffic, and its colors of the coming night that dared us to be joyful, for a lot of discovery had happened that day, a lot of discovery that I wished I never came to know, and within me there was no desire to pry into these vague mysteries anymore, for there was only pain there — deep pain, and suffering, and strife that my frail body could not endure — things were indeed different now, things had changed, and between the sun, and the alcohol, and the fake smiles that passed back and forth between Gracie and Maxwell at the front of the car, I completely loathed the day I had ever met them, and the Great Arlington Pride that burned ever deeper within my soul demanded final answers, and it would get those final answers that night, for the last year had taken its effect on me, and the truth that flowed from the knowledge of Gracie's existence upon the world had completely made me, nurtured me, and then nearly destroyed me — nearly destroyed The Last True Artist — and through all the mystery, and magic, and endless time that I had pursued her, this would be the evening of our final vindication, for by day's end we would either entirely co-exist together — all young, and beautiful, and bright forevermore — or be destroyed by each other completely, and in that moment of that glorious conclusion, our bodies would finally find a way to encompass their distant freedoms, and together, we could at last pass gently into the night.

"Did you have fun, my boy?" Maxwell chimed as we turned off La Brea onto the backside of Franklin.

I didn't answer, nor did I react, I just continued to watch Los Angeles float past outside the window. Maxwell noticed my indifference and mumbled to himself as to relieve his own tension, for there was a tightness now for the unspoken things in the air, and the fact that Maxwell had blatantly lied about a trip to New York that apparently never happened at all had still not been brought up for clarification, but that didn't really matter now, and the fact that I was over it all gave me a kind of power — the power that comes from no longer caring — and soon I would know everything that was worth knowing anyways, and until that time I would stay my reason.

It was eight o'clock by the time we wove up through the hills of Studio City, and the summer sun hung low in the sky like a large gleaming orb covered by a blanket of violet blue, and I thought it could be the last sunset I'd ever see, and it was beautiful. Maxwell parked, and the three of us stepped out into the cool, balmy air, welcoming whatever calm it lent us, for tensions were high, higher than they had ever been, and it was then I realized that Maxwell had never even offered to take me home at all — there were other agendas at play.

We walked towards her mysterious apartment, and once again I felt small and estranged underneath its large glass window that stood looming over us with a silvery shine, reflecting the dying sun and the white rays of a growing moon that would soon be completely luminous in the fading dusk. It was a strange walk. Indeed, it was the strangest walk I had ever taken. It was as if we all knew something curious was upon us, and were content to accept that completely and without question. After all, Gracie didn't like questions, and I wouldn't be asking her any now, for as beautiful as she looked in the immediate present — all golden, and blonde, and glowing from the afternoon sun — I knew that all her loveliness could disappear with the night, and I would no longer sacrifice all truth to find her, for I couldn't. I simply would not live to see it.

We ascended the grand staircase, where Gracie unlocked the door and quickly burst inside, striding promptly to the liquor stand where she began fixing herself a drink. Maxwell and I followed suit shortly.

"Scotch and soda," Maxwell stated flatly as he moved to the liquor stand.

"That would be fine," I replied without any thanks, for we had reached the end of formalities, and I saw no reason to refrain from distaste.

Gracie took her cocktail and glided past me to the big window overlooking all of the valley, and she just stood like that for a while, all graceful and nimble with her back turned, and I wondered what she was thinking, for there was a connection between us that only the higher things could understand — I knew it, and she knew it too — so I took my seat nearest the door, the same seat I took on that one magical evening back in November, and I held my breath for the coming hour.

"Here you are, my good man," Maxwell stated as he placed a drink into my hand. "A nice scotch and soda." He then proceeded to his chair at the far end of the room — the chair nearest the window — and it suddenly felt like November again, except with Gracie all huddled near the corner instead of stretched out on her black velvet couch, and I remembered how I sat on that couch, and how she sat down next to me, and what I said to her, and I wondered again if I had done the right thing, or if I was wrong completely, but it didn't matter now, indeed nothing mattered, for together we were back to square one, and in this secretive place — a place filled with cocktails, and parties, and endless mystery — we would find our reason for greatness, and our young lives would become old stories in the summer moonlight.

No one spoke for a few moments, and the tension rose to higher and higher levels. We each had something very important to say, but no one knew how to go about saying it. I didn't care, for I had every right to be in that room, so I coolly sipped my drink and waited for one of the others to speak. Maxwell apparently felt the same way, for he mirrored my behavior at the other end of the space, and only Gracie showed any real signs of being physically bothered, for she was trembling near the window now, trembling like she was trembling from trembling itself, and without even seeing her face I knew which emotions were present, and it was the most beautiful tremble I had ever seen.

"It's all just pointless!" She exclaimed after a moment, throwing up her hands in a bout of released tension, and within moments her bright and glowing presence was gone from the room, gone completely down the hall, and with her she took all the light out of the space, leaving me alone with Maxwell in the dark.

"Don't mind her," Maxwell chuckled. "She's a woman, that's all... prone to these sorts of things."

"Prone," I stated, flat, and it hung thick in the air like the stench of cold soup.

"That's right — hot day, too much sun — she shouldn't drink so much," he continued. "I'm always telling her she shouldn't drink so much, but she never listens of course."

"Never listens," I stated, even flatter this time.

"You can't teach a woman, Conrad — you can't teach a woman at all. Don't ever try it."

"Try it, " I stated in finality, staring like evil at his large, round face that floated luminous upon his circular body in the vivid moonlight, for I wasn't interested in words anymore, just as I wasn't interested in excuses or flattery, I wanted answers, and that was all I would hear.

Maxwell took a drink of his scotch, and there was silence once again — vacant silence — and the silence continued for a great long while, and then words once again pierced the stillness.

"So," he began.

"So," I stated, staring back.

"So," he started again, breaking my stare with a light chuckle. "Here we are again, good boy."

"Again," I stated, toneless, and my blood boiled so hot that I thought I might explode, and then his demeanor changed, and all of a sudden he wasn't so friendly.

"Conrad, I have a feeling there's something you want to say to me."

My glare deepened, and in it he had his answer.

"Then you better ask it," he said, brushing it off. "It's better to have out with these kinds of things."

"Is it?" I asked, and I began to shake, for in front of me sat a man that told only lies, and I would get the truth I sought if it meant beating it out of him with my low-ball glass.

"I'd say so, yes," he stated. "It's best not to let things stagnate, so if you have something you feel like you ought to say, then say it."

I could hold back my anger no longer, and all held still below the starry night, awaiting a coming anger and a deep, deep wrath. "Stagnate?" I snapped, my voice rising with the question. "You think *I've* let these things stagnate?"

Maxwell pulled back his head and looked at me blankly, taking a pull off his scotch. "Let me tell you about stagnate, 'good boy,' for over six months I have been looking for the both of you! You told me we were going into business together — business, Max — there's a responsibility there!"

"You don't owe us any favors, Conrad," Maxwell interjected calmly.

"The hell I don't!" I screamed as I rose to my feet. "You pulled me into this mess and now I expect you to get me out!"

"What do you want to know?" He said softly, once again keeping his calm, and I despised the fact that he was able to do so.

"Who are you?" I demanded.

"What do you mean?"

"You know exactly what I mean!" I yelled. "You lied to me today! About your trip to New York! Why?"

Maxwell adjusted in his seat a little, and pulled his collar away from his thick neck to let some air in. "Why that's complicated, dear boy—"

"No, it's not complicated! It's not complicated at all! Why did you lie?!"

He just stared at me, and his face tensed a little, and I knew that behind all the smiles, and all the facades, and all the endless illusions, that there was guilt there, some kind of real guilt, and it was wearing at him. Despite my own convictions I would push him, I would push him until he broke, for I had felt too hard to show mercy, and the darkened souls would justify my behavior in the end.

"For God's sake, Maxwell, speak!" I demanded when he didn't do so.

"What do you want me to say?"

"The truth!"

"There is no truth, dear boy."

"There is truth!" I screamed. "There is truth right now! Right here! Why? Why am I here? Why did you call me today, and why did you bring me here? Answer me!"

He looked at me with his big, dark eyes, and then took a breath followed by a sip of scotch. "You're here," he began. "Because Gracie wanted you to be."

"Liar!" I screamed. "You made the call!"

"She wanted me to do it."

"What is it with you two anyway?" I snapped, bitter. "What the hell are you two about?"

"You wouldn't understand, dear boy," Maxwell said, somber.

"I understand plenty."

"Let it go, dear boy, let it go—"

"No!" I screamed again, and I realized I had my glass lifted above my head, as if ready to strike. "You will tell me what she is to you!"

"Conrad—"

"You will tell me what she is to you now, Maxwell!" I stated in absolution. "Or I will throw this glass into that window, do you understand me? I have come too far and felt too much to be lied to now, so you will tell me the exact truth and that will be the end of it!"

Silence took the room, and in the wake of my outburst it felt strange to hear nothing again, for my ears were still ringing with intense reverberation, and the dark shadows that stretched across the carpets in the moonlight seemed to bear witness against me, and all was once again quiet for the coming verdict.

Maxwell looked at me with those dark brown eyes that shone like saucers in the moonlight, and for the first time I saw that there was truth there — real truth — no masks, no facades, no anything, just Maxwell Price in his entirety.

"She loves me, Conrad," Maxwell said slowly, small tears hanging like droplets in the corners of his eyes, then he looked directly at me. "She loves me for who I am... it's something that you can't possibly try and understand.... it's not in you, thank God, it's not in you... you have none of my sickness in you... please, let that be enough now... I pose no threat... I pose no threat..."

He trailed off and it became so silent that I thought it might consume us, that the stars would somehow drift down from the sky and swallow us whole, but they didn't. Time continued and we were still alive, still alive among the living and the breathing of the earth, existing in some real darkness, somewhere, caught between the golden and the blue, and I would make no more attempts to judge him, for whatever choices the man had made in life that had made him into whatever he was now were on his own head, and without the clarity of an answer I had reached a point of exhaustion where I could resign to cut my losses and leave him up to his consequences. It was, Hollywood, after all, and sometimes relationships came down to nothing more than sheer bafflement and a lesson learned.

I rose to my feet, and as Maxwell's tears flowed freely, I let myself drift onwards towards the hall, leaving him in the middle of his conflict, a conflict that I perhaps would never understand, and I didn't want to, for I knew that Gracie saw in him something beautiful — something beautiful, and lovely, and bright — and as I reached the end of the room a tear rolled down my cheek, a selfless tear, the kind of tear that exists only for the brokenness of one human being to another. Then I brushed it away and plunged into the dark, knowing that deep down, past all the smiles, and all the formalities, and all the surfaces, and all the indifferent things that exist only in moments, that I wasn't any different, for we both loved the same girl dearly, and the rest we bear alone.

CHAPTER 14
— TRUE GRANDEUR —

I walked down the hall and stopped at her door, taken by feeling, stricken by timelessness. Then I took a breath, and let that breath sink deep into my body, further, even deeper than my bones, for once I passed that door there would be no coming back, no coming back amongst all the blue, and the gold, and the perfection created by something very real, and my life as it existed in the world of Gracie Garrison would be changed completely. Yes, there could be no turning back now, for there was but one choice that pressed in upon me in that hour — to knock — and then the choice would no longer be mine, but of someone far greater and more lovely than myself, so I trusted in the truth of it, lifted my hand to the door, and in two soft knocks I said goodbye to my earthly home, leaping boldly from my dreams into yet another endless pool.

I pushed the door open and was again taken by its splendor, for such a place is impossible to completely remember — then I saw her.

"Gracie?" I asked. "Are you all right?"

She didn't respond, just sniffled a little on the edge of her bed, her bright tears flowing freely down, and I was struck by how strange it was to be in there, indeed, my whole body tingled like it had found some sort of newborn awakening, a kind of brand new and unexplored imagining, for never in my life did I believe I would ever come to see her room again, and the sight of it was overwhelming, for it was sensual, marvelous — all of these things at the same time — and my dreams became alive, and real, and greater than all inspiration had ever been, and I experienced how good life could be, and I wondered how I ever felt any differently. Then my eyes opened, and they focused once again on the beauty at the center of the room, and I had my reason to believe.

"Gracie?" I tried again, and the soft tone was completely flush within the golden hum of the quiet space.

"Go away, Conrad," Gracie said in obligation, and I knew the subtext of it — she wanted me in that room, she needed me in that room even more than I needed to be there, so I chanced a step forward, and approached her bed.

I sat down next to her.

"Gracie."

I placed a courageous hand between her slight shoulder blades, and I felt her whole body tense against my palm, signaling a deep caution, but there was nothing to be cautious about now for The Last True Artist, for indeed I was nothing, nothing at all — dust and bone and skin and ash — and I would gladly trade it all for the relief death would bring.

The tension paused, then suddenly released, and breath returned to her tiny body, and in some inner fashion akin to the elegant queens of distant lands, she straightened up, and she gained some kind of real power, and The Last True Artist was helpless against her.

"I'm just tired, Conrad, that's all," she said in a high fashion, and she looked pristine in the golden light. "I'm feeling much better now, thank you."

" —Gracie—"

"Haven't you ever been tired, Conrad?"

"Yes."

"Then you realize what lack of sleep does to a person."

"I do, but, I don't think that's it," I countered, and I saw the discovery dance across her porcelain countenance, and then it was whisked away.

"Oh Connie, look at you" she stated, in flight once again, her big blue eyes darting back and forth across mine. "You're all worn out. Completely and utterly exhausted. All that sun and all that alcohol... you really must lie down."

"I don't need to lie down."

"Go on out to the living room and have a scotch and lie down," she asserted with a wave of her hand.

"I already had a scotch."

"Then go and lie down."

"I don't want to."

"But you really should."

"I disagree."

"Disagree all you want, but that's the way of things Conrad, and it won't do to think any differently."

" —Gracie— "

"Go on."

" —Gracie— "

"Go and lie down now."

"Gracie!" I shouted, grabbing her forcefully by her arms and turning her towards me so that I could see deep into her crystal eyes, for in that inevitability I knew that she was truly afraid, and I could feel her little body trembling beneath my grasp that held her vice-like beneath her shoulder blades, and I never felt weaker. "You have brought me here for a reason tonight! Now tell me why."

She stared at me without words, then the Great Arlington Pride rose up within me as quickly as light, and I felt my heart burn with a fire it had never burned with before, and I remembered my pain, and suffering, and I remembered how I connected with this girl, and how I held her tight, and how in the morning she was gone, and I thought about how easy it would be to do away with all those memories — those memories that haunted my dreams at night — how easy it would be to extract some deep vengeance, something dark and wretched, something I never knew was even there, and I wanted to do it, I wanted to take her right there, take her and make her mine and then squeeze the perfect life out of her, and by doing so remember what it was like to feel again, to be human in the most basic of ways, to execute some bodily order caused by some basic emotion, and then, in the waken quiet roused by her porcelain corpse, all broken and beautiful and golden upon the bedside, I might be granted my pardon to exist, and my body could go on drifting into the darkness.

Then, her eyes softened and I knew that I was wrong, and despite my greatest impulses I could not accomplish my internal vendetta against her, and amidst some truth beyond all that is primary in the spectrum of what is good and real, I softened my grip, and I accepted my fate to be tied to her forever.

"I-I'm sorry," I stammered. "I don't know what came over me."

"It's all right," Gracie replied softly.

"I-I didn't mean to hurt you."

"You didn't hurt me."

"I would never hurt you. You know I would never do anything to hurt you." I felt my eyes begin to glisten in the sparkling light.

"I know."

"Never in my life," I continued. "Never, never in my life."

"I know, Conrad, I know," she responded with a kind of real empathy, and that empathy felt like love, and that love shot out and burned my soul like fire, for she was the only girl I had ever met that had the ability to understand me, and until then I never knew what that was like, and it was everything.

"I'm sorry," I said in finality, clearing my throat.

"It's all right." She smiled again, and she touched my arm, and we breathed for a while in the sacred space, and it was wonderful to be with her.

"Conrad," she began after some time. "You're probably wondering quite a bit about things — you are a writer after all — always wondering…"

It was a quick deflection, but I held my eyes on her.

"And you have the right to wonder, you really do, if anybody in the world ever had the right to wonder I suppose it would be you — I do realize this — it's just… I-I just want to tell you it will do you no good — to wonder that is — and I'm sorry."

She said it with absolution as she chanced a glance at me, but the look on my face — which must have been terrifying in its dissatisfaction — for what she said was unacceptable, and I would not allow any more vague or flighty foolishness tonight, for if there were ever a time for specifics it was now, and I would settle for nothing less than the most precise of answers.

"I-I don't know what I want anymore," she continued, seeing that she must. "I... I don't know who I am anymore. Many men have tried to love me in my life, many good and honest men, Conrad, but I simply won't let them. I won't let them love me. It's just the nature of me. I am incapable of love, and if I hurt you I am truly sorry."

I looked at her, and amidst her bright eyes that glistened against her blonde hair, there could be no triumph for those living in the mortal world if it was in her mind not to allow it, so I said nothing, and only the Great Arlington Pride could avail me, but I could not find it, for it lay dormant.

"You are a good person, Conrad," she continued, nodding her determined head between syllables towards the passive ground. "You are a good person, and you deserve so much more than I could ever give you. I'm no good, Conrad, I'm no good for anybody, and if we ever became more involved than we are now, if you ever saw who I really was, surely you would resent me forever."

Then as quickly as her lovely words floated off her lips, her head fell, and little sobs more lithe and graceful than the moon fell perfect upon my ears, and I never felt more of an affection for creation than I did right then.

"Oh Conrad, what must you think of me?" Gracie asked through weeping sobs, and a kind of truth rose in my throat that can only be described as perfect, indeed, it was the most good and correct truth I had ever experienced, for in that moment I was simply a boy, admiring a girl, and creation made us perfect because of it.

"I think you're the most beautiful girl in the world," I stated. "I don't care who you are. I don't care what you've done. We are living here — now — and that's all that matters to me." I paused for a moment, and then I spoke the words I thought would fail me. "Gracie, I love you."

Her head snapped up, and a fear existed in her eyes that I had never seen before — some deep and awful fear — it was formidable, but I would defeat it.

"I loved you from the moment I saw you," I continued. "You were all bright and broken, and I thought you were the loveliest thing I'd ever seen, and I don't care about the bad. I only care about the good. Right now, you are dealing with someone who is capable of loving you with as much love as you are capable of giving to a person, and you've never met someone like that before, and I know that scares you, but at the end of the day that is why I am in this room — maybe it's why I am in this world — and I know you know that's true."

She looked at me with a certain fondness, and once again I was taken by those pools that shone deep and perfect in the lamplight, and then the fear rested, and a trust was born, a trust that wanted to believe, and I never saw such truth, indeed, there was more truth in her now than I had ever seen before, and I wondered if there ever had been such a moment in eternity that existed as perfectly as it did now — and I knew that there had never been — so I lifted a soft hand, and I touched her porcelain face, and I looked deep into her eyes, and I wondered who she was, and I knew that I would wonder who she was forever, and that was all I would ever need.

"You needn't fear," I began, and I was filled with something higher. "For within us burns a bright and beautiful truth, and that truth has given us everything."

She looked at me with so much vitality that I felt the whole house might collapse around us. If I did nothing else for the rest of my life my existence as The Last True Artist would be justified, for I had given this girl everything, all there was of me, and I loved her perhaps as much as any human being had ever loved another —

perhaps more, since it was not built on human standards — and if she did not join me in this moment then indeed I would be lost forever. The entire universe seemed to balance between us, waiting for the verdict in the shimmering lights, silent and alone beneath the stars of some specific place, warm, and cold, and distant, and quiet, yet here we sat, together in this moment, and I was completely ready to let it be my last. Then I moved my head towards the golden girl, and finally did what I had dreamt so long of doing.

I kissed Gracie Garrison on the mouth. She didn't react, but mirrored my kiss exactly, as if she had been expecting it. I held my face against hers and completely experienced what I had wanted to experience. Her lips were warm, soft, and thin, and the smell of her enveloped me totally like it only could, but something was different now, much, much different than I was hoping. We did not connect like I thought we would. The passion didn't flare up in me like I was expecting it to after all this time. No, there was a sadness that existed now, a barrier that had lodged itself between us, and in that moment when my hope faded and I had no more choice but to accept my reality for what it was, I knew exactly what had become of us, for we had both caused each other far too much pain in the last year to completely enjoy this simple, uncomplicated gesture, and when I opened my eyes and saw her big blue ones gazing back — unreactive — into mine, I knew she had already known this long before I did, and I felt like a child. Then I pulled away, and time began again.

We sat for a little while, content, in a way, with our dissatisfaction, for things were what they were now and that was it. If I could retrace my steps and implement the changes that would have given me the results that I thought I so deeply desired maybe I would have. Then again, perhaps I wouldn't, for maybe this was it, us both, here, now, experiencing this deeper kind of love, this complicated kind of love, and through it maybe one day we could look back and put a lens up to this strange phenomenon we called life, and maybe then one day I would see things clearly, and maybe all the pain and raw feeling would be worth it, maybe, but not yet. Right now it was all still foggy, just a bunch of fog around some murky glass, and the beauty of it all simply existing would have to be enough for now — Gracie, and her eyes, and her hair, and her room, and me there to witness it all — just pure existence, and when left at that, maybe it was nothing short of extraordinary.

I stopped thinking and once again I turned and looked at the golden girl, and for the first time since I could remember tonight her eyes were completely dry, and I knew that wherever she had gone it was someplace far, far away from here, someplace lost and distant, perfectly preserved by the grand walls of her beautiful dreams, and not even The Last True Artist could follow her there.

"It's been a long day, Conrad," Gracie said after a while. "I think I'll go to bed now."

"Yes, that sounds nice," I said, for I heard her speak, but I could see in her eyes that she still wasn't back. "Why don't you lie down?"

I pulled back her bed sheets as she motioned to lie down, and it was now somehow all very simple.

"Do you want to sleep in your dress?" I asked.

"It's all right," she said peacefully. "I'll take it off in the morning."

I moved a few strands of golden hair from her eyes and stroked her soft forehead. "All right, then," I said. "Sweet dreams."

With some real effort I rose and stood above her — my Gracie, she looked like an angel, all pristine and blonde against the linens, beautiful and timeless, perfect and eternal, just like she had always been to me, and just like she always would be. "Maybe this was truly the end of us," I thought. "Or perhaps somewhere, someplace, in some great heaven or some great world — maybe even now — maybe it was just the beginning."

I walked across the room and turned back at the door. "Gracie?"

"Yes, Conrad," she said softly.

"Do you remember that night — that night after the gallery, and the Boulevard, and the party — that night we came back here. You slept in my arms all night, do you remember?"

Suddenly, Gracie's big eyes shone a clear and crystal blue against the lamplight, and I knew she had come back, if only for this moment.

"I don't remember," she said truthfully, and then there was silence.

For the first time in a great long while I knew I had my answer, and I was thankful. "All right," I said. "Goodnight."

I flicked off the light and closed the door.

CAL R. BARNES

Cal R. Barnes was born in Salem, OR, in 1988. After briefly studying creative writing and drama at Portland State University in Portland, OR, Cal moved to Los Angeles in 2009 where he immediately began acting and writing screenplays. After a few years he also began producing films as well, enjoying all aspects of the creative process. Cal currently lives and writes in Los Angeles. He is a connoisseur of literature, film, yoga, fruits, vegetables, coffee, tea, and sunshine. True Grandeur is his first novel.